LAWS

OF

LOVE

AND

LOGIC

LAWS OF LOVE AND LOGIC

DEBRA CURTIS

BLOOMSBURY PUBLISHING

LONDON · OXFORD · NEW YORK · NEW DELHI · SYDNEY

BLOOMSBURY PUBLISHING
Bloomsbury Publishing Plc
50 Bedford Square, London, WC1B 3DP, UK
Bloomsbury Publishing Ireland Limited,
29 Earlsfort Terrace, Dublin 2, D02 AY28, Ireland

BLOOMSBURY, BLOOMSBURY PUBLISHING and the Diana logo
are trademarks of Bloomsbury Publishing Plc

First published in the United States in 2026 by Ballantine Books,
an imprint of Penguin Random House LLC
First published in Great Britain in 2026

A catalogue record for this book is available from the British Library

ISBN: HB: 978-1-5266-8350-2; TPB: 978-1-5266-8349-6;
eBook: 978-1-5266-8348-9

2 4 6 8 10 9 7 5 3 1

Typeset by Six Red Marbles India
Printed and bound in Great Britain by Clays Ltd, Elcograf S.p.A

To find out more about our authors and books visit www.bloomsbury.com
and sign up for our newsletters
For product-safety-related questions contact productsafety@bloomsbury.com

The novel is dedicated to my husband, Steve Butler,
and to our twins, Emma and Zoe Butler—together their love sustains me.
It is also dedicated to my incredible agent, Felicity Blunt,
without whom, dear reader,
we would not be having this moment together.

LAWS

OF

LOVE

AND

LOGIC

PROLOGUE

2005

Most autumns, the lavender skies and red dogwoods reminded Lily of the boy and all those years ago. Now in her forties, she pulled over to the side of the road to take in the autumn twilight. When they were young, she had believed that she and the boy would marry and spend the rest of their lives together. How could she have known anything about love's ruses or how life worked?

Pulling the memories through the years like a thread, she remembered a warm day in Escobar's cornfield. Dust on her shoes and ankles. She ran to the far end of an eight-acre field to make it harder for him to find her. It was a game, and it was her idea. "There will be a reward at the end, I promise," she told him. The cornstalks towered over them. She remembered waiting in her spot, giddy but quiet. Listening to the rustling and the sound of his heavy footsteps as he got closer.

When he saw her, he lowered himself to his knees. Sweat trickled down his right temple. Looking up at her, he wrested her jeans down around her calves. Smudges of dirt on the tops of her thighs where he had placed his hands. Dry leaves in the wind behind and over her. They stayed in the cornfield until the western sky was orange.

...

LILY HAD TAKEN TO walking around her house in just a long black cashmere sweater with no pants or underwear. She and her husband lived in upstate New York in a nineteenth-century house with floor-to-ceiling windows, but Lily didn't care: She wasn't an exhibitionist— she just didn't worry about what other people thought. What mattered most to her lately were forgiveness and the afternoon light. While her husband was making notes on the birds he had seen earlier in the day, Lily watched the white walls in her study. She followed the lines and patterns of light that shone through her curtainless windows as the sun set.

The way the sunlight hit the old cast-iron radiator reminded her of the double-slit experiment she had read about in college, where a light wave holds all the possibilities of the positions a wave particle might assume. Sitting there in her study, she recalled how she was drawn to the idea that subatomic particles could impact one another at great distances; it allowed for the possibility that she and the boy would one day find each other. She didn't want her life to be a bouquet of regrets, like the profound regrets some must feel in the slim moments before they take their own lives. Lily sensed something was about to change in her life the same day her husband could not identify a white-throated sparrow at the bird feeder.

PART
I

PORTSMOUTH, RHODE ISLAND

SEPTEMBER 1976

Early fall. Leaves of gold on the birch shimmered when the wind picked up. When no one answered the front door, Lily walked around the side of the house to the back deck. She could hear her boyfriend's father playing guitar and singing softly, a melancholy tune—familiar, but she couldn't quite make it out. The boy, like his dad, was musically inclined. Playing the guitar had a calming effect on Mr. Cooper, especially after his son's football games.

The back deck was unfinished, littered with tools and cans of paint with rusted lids—neglected since last spring—alongside a spare tire, two fishing rods, and a cooler. The boy's dad was on his seventh beer; by the time the day was over he would have finished off a case by himself. Lily didn't want to disturb Mr. Cooper and waited until he looked up from his guitar.

"There's my favorite girl," he said with a big smile, resting his forearm on the body of the instrument.

"Don't stop on account of me," Lily said. "I love hearing you play."

Mr. Cooper, still smiling, shook his head and leaned his guitar against a post on the deck.

"Some game, huh?" he said as he stood up.

He offered Lily his seat, the only one on the deck: a mustard-and-orange-webbed aluminum lawn chair. When she refused to sit, he remained standing.

It had been an exciting game that morning: Portsmouth against Barrington, rival teams. The boy, a senior at Portsmouth and the team's quarterback, had read the defenses instantly, successfully changing the play at the line of scrimmage three times when Barrington's defense had anticipated Portsmouth's plays and was prepared to stop them.

When the boy appeared at the screen door in a pair of jeans and a Creedence Clearwater Revival T-shirt, toweling off his long brown hair, his dad couldn't contain himself and gave the boy a hug, patting his back.

"Four hundred and ninety passing yards! That's a record. One game! That's my boy!" Mr. Cooper was smiling from ear to ear, so excited that he spat as he talked.

The boy watched Lily. She never seemed to mind that his father always drank and talked endlessly about the boy's football stats.

"Everybody knows he's the best the state has ever seen. When he was fourteen and there were sixty seconds left on the clock, he threw the ball fifty yards and that Portuguese kid caught it."

"Lil knows the story," the boy said, putting his arm around his dad. He was tall like his father but a whole lot bigger.

"I was there, Mr. Cooper—I saw the whole thing. Just like Roger Staubach!"

"Marry this girl!" the boy's father said. He took a long swig of his beer.

The boy knew that over the past five decades, the little state of Rhode Island had produced three professional quarterbacks; he was determined to be the fourth. He was ten years old when Joe Namath predicted that the Jets would beat the Colts in the 1969 Super Bowl. As a young kid, the boy had borrowed Namath's courage and boldness. Sometimes, standing in the locker room in front of his teammates, he would say, "We're going to win this one, I guarantee it."

The boy took Lily's hand, led her inside, and pulled the screen door shut behind him. He took two beers out of the refrigerator, and as he and Lily made their way downstairs to the basement, they heard his father: "Chuck at the hardware store said that the scouts will be coming around to have a look at you!"

When the boy was six, his mom took off and moved to Florida with the golf pro from Green Valley golf course. For Christmases and birthdays, she sent her son cards. The boy had learned that his mother was playing piano in a bar in Boca Raton. Back then no one had ever heard of Boca Raton but the boy found it on a map when he was in the second grade. Folks in town heard that the golf pro hit her occasionally and got one of the waitresses pregnant at the resort where he worked.

Every trophy the boy had ever won was displayed on the wooden shelves his father made for him. While football was his main sport, he also played basketball and baseball. The largest trophy was the one he'd received the prior year for football: MVP, a pewter sculpted figure—poised to throw a football—mounted on a wooden base. Free weights and a bench filled one side of the boy's basement room, with a bed, a TV, a set of drawers, and an old electric keyboard on the other side. In the corner was a brand-new Sony stereo, which his father had recently bought him for his eighteenth birthday. Albums were carefully lined up between two cinder blocks.

Lily placed her beer near a stack of library books on the chest of drawers and picked up the boy's sunglasses. Putting them on, she stretched out on his bed. The boy sat down at the keyboard.

"Did I ever tell you that my mom played the organ at Saint Barnabas and that's where she met my dad?"

Lily turned her head on the pillow to watch him. He had told her this, but she didn't mind hearing it again, not in the least. "Tell me" was all she said.

"He fell in love with her on a Sunday in between the Gloria and Communion."

"That's beautiful."

"After my mom left, he just couldn't go back there, so that's why we go to Saint Anthony's. I can remember our last Christmas together. Although, I didn't know it would be our last. She played 'O Holy Night' at Mass. I was real sad watching my dad cry."

Lily swung her legs over the side of the bed and sat up. Before she could say anything, he changed the subject and said, "Do you know this song?"

His hands moved tentatively across the black and white keys. Like birds pecking in the sand, his fingers bent lightly. He started and stopped a couple of times, but when he was able to pull it together, combining the chords with the right individual notes, Lily exclaimed, "How did you learn that?"

A little soft, but melodic, the boy sang: "*The screen door slams, Mary's dress sways / Like a vision she dances . . .*"

As the boy worked out the chords to "Thunder Road," Lily slipped her hand under his shirt and caressed his back. *Born to Run* was released the year before, and Lily and the boy both unknowingly bought the other the album for Christmas. The boy stopped playing and looked up at Lily. "That's as far as I've gotten."

"Call in sick tonight," Lily said.

"I can't. You know that."

"What's a party without the team quarterback?"

"Are you still planning on going?"

When Lily didn't answer, the boy rose from the keyboard bench and moved over to his bed. He worked Saturday and Sunday nights, but never Fridays, not the night before a game. He washed dishes at Reidy's diner on East Main Road. Late into the shift, when it was just the owner and the boy, the owner would fill Styrofoam containers with mashed potatoes, green beans, and meat loaf. The Saturday night special. He'd always add a couple of desserts, one for the boy and one for his father.

The boy sat on the edge of his bed. Lily followed him. She got down on her knees and wiggled herself in between his thighs.

"I promise you'll have a good time," Lily said.

She and the boy had been together since they were freshmen, and while they had yet to have sex, they delighted in each other's caresses with hands and mouths, here in the basement or in the field behind the school. With the tip of her finger, Lily moved a strand of her hair away from her face.

"I don't understand why you want to go to the party without me," the boy said.

"Am I supposed to sit home every Saturday night my senior year because you have to work?"

The boy looked away.

"I'm sorry," she added.

And she was. She knew the boy helped his father out with the basic bills: electricity, groceries, and sometimes the oil bill when the winters were at their worst. The boy had his first job when he was thirteen, a paper route. The factory in Fall River, where his father had worked for fifteen years and planned on working for the rest of his life, had closed down. Now his father earned a living working at one of the marinas on the island. Like many working-class kids, the boy was coming of age in a time of great economic anxiety.

"I'll go with Jane," Lily said.

"Yeah? And by ten o'clock either you'll be holding her hair back while she's puking or she'll be upstairs in one of the bedrooms with Jimmy Sullivan or some other guy she barely knows."

"That's my sister you're talking about. And what difference does it make who she's in a bedroom with?"

The boy knew that Lily would go to the party without him. He couldn't help but feel jealous, so much so that he decided not to tell her what he had been holding in all afternoon—something he hadn't even shared with his father: There had been scouts at the game today. He would tell her tomorrow. After the party.

PORTSMOUTH, RHODE ISLAND

1967–1972

After Lily's parents married, they settled in Portsmouth, where Martin Webb had been hired to teach. The Priory, as it was called then, was a monastery and an all-boys boarding school founded by a Benedictine community. Established on old farmland, the campus was built around a manor house and included dormitories, classroom buildings, sports fields, a chapel, and the monastery. The soft green slope of the grounds gave way to Narragansett Bay, bordered with two-hundred-year-old stone walls built from gray slate. Massive birches, Japanese maples, old oaks, and towering pine trees grew on well-manicured lawns lined with goldenrod from July to the earliest frost. In the fall, round bales of hay dotted the fields. There were solitary monks in long black robes on footpaths alongside boys in blazers with the school crest proudly displayed above the right breast pocket. The Webbs lived in a house on the grounds. Lily's dad taught science and coached sailing. There were a few day students from the town who attended the private boarding school, but the Priory was otherwise a world unto itself, tucked away near the bay and surrounded by acres of woods. Residents of the town of Portsmouth rarely, if ever, encountered or interacted with the monks and boarding school students, who were largely members of the upper class. Even though the public high school was less than two miles from the boarding school, the schools' respective sports teams played in different leagues.

Like many Catholics who had read Dostoevsky, Mr. Webb was compelled by the character Father Zosima, the mystic and monk in *The Brothers Karamazov*—so compelled that he thought he might find someone like the elder at the Priory. So he went in search of his own Father Zosima among the Benedictines. You could say Mr. Webb was a man haunted by a fictional character.

Carol Webb was a feminist and a Vatican II Catholic, which in part made her self-righteous. Her daughters inherited this trait, although to varying degrees; it would ebb and flow throughout their lives. In her more secular moods, Mrs. Webb looked for signs of civility in the most common places: in the checkout line at the grocery store, at four-way traffic stops, at entryways with heavy doors. In her more spiritual moods, she looked for signs of compassion in the same places, in the ordinary spaces where strangers encounter strangers. She wasn't one to give up on humanity. She was convinced that humans were essentially good, and if they weren't behaving as such, then she would intervene and provide the necessary instruction.

Despite her own strict Catholic upbringing, Mrs. Webb was intent on raising her daughters to be as open-minded and tolerant as she thought she was—exceedingly so, in her estimation, particularly compared to some of their Aquidneck Island neighbors whom she viewed as parochial. Once, at a dinner party, the spouse of another faculty member pointed out what the woman saw as a contradiction between Mrs. Webb's feminist ideas and Catholic doctrine, to which Mrs.

Webb responded, despite her husband's hand on her knee urging restraint, "Life is full of contradictions; just read the Bible."

One of the older monks would say in good humor, "Speak of the devil," whenever he saw Mrs. Webb coming. The first time she heard him say this, she threw her head back and laughed.

Mrs. Webb was the first woman to be invited to join the faculty reading group at the Priory. Members included male lay teachers and several monks. It was 1970. The girls were still in grade school when their mom came home one Sunday night after meeting with the group and discussing Leo Tolstoy's *Family Happiness.*

"It's like everyone else read a completely different book," she said. "Their insights into Tolstoy sounded like they all had doctorates in Russian literature. They must think I'm an idiot. Afterward, I turned to the monk leading the group and asked, 'How many hours do you read a day?' Guess what he said?"

Lily and Jane were sitting in the living room watching television, but they could hear everything their mom was saying. When Mr. Webb said, "I have no idea," his wife was quick to respond. "Eight! Eight hours a day. I'd give anything to read eight hours a day."

Mr. Webb knew his wife wasn't done.

"Do you remember the story? Masha wants to enter society life but her older husband doesn't. One night, an Italian man kisses Masha. After some discussion, the group leader turned to me and said, 'Let's hear from the lady in the room. Do you know women like that?' I had to do my best not to laugh. He was serious."

"Of course he was serious. Some of these men have never been around women."

Mrs. Webb looked at her husband approvingly.

...

MRS. WEBB WAS THE type of mother who would instruct her daughters on important lessons for life and then require the girls to recall them at the most random moments—for instance, while engaging in their monthly chore of matching lone socks.

"Now, girls," she announced as she scattered the socks over the bed. Her studious daughters always seemed to recognize the cue and say what was expected of them.

"We know, we know. Not everyone believes that Jesus Christ is the Son of God," the girls said in unison.

"And?" their mom added.

"We stand side by side with the poor," Jane answered.

"And why is that?" their mom asked.

Jane looked at her older sister.

"Because the needs of the poor are more important than anything else," Lily said.

"Good, now pass me that school sock."

...

THERE WAS A CERTAIN elegance with which the Webbs introduced Catholicism and scientific thought to their daughters. The Webbs shared a deep respect for scientific advancement in math, astronomy, and physics, matched by a profound awe for the mysteries of life. By the time Lily was six and Jane was four, Mrs. Webb had told them, "Don't ever let anyone tell you the Earth is four thousand years old. To the outside world, Catholics appear superstitious. We light candles, say the rosary, and pray to the dead. What they don't understand is that we embrace both faith and reason. Faith and reason—just like tea and milk, they go together."

At Mr. Webb's insistence, his daughters attended a small Catholic grade school on the property adjacent to the Priory. The plan was that the girls would then attend the local high school. When Lily was ten and Jane was eight, they were old enough to walk across the street and down a long driveway to get to Saint Philomena's, run by the Faithful Companions of Jesus. Most mornings before school, Lily would be outside on the front lawn waiting for her sister. Both girls dressed in gray shirts and blue-and-gray plaid skirts resting below their knees with two inches between their maroon-colored socks and their hemlines. On the mornings they had mandatory school Mass, Lily would pin her chapel cap neatly to her hair—and then wait. Jane was always late.

"You'd better be out here before I count to sixty," Lily would say at least three times.

On one of those mornings, carrying cinnamon toast in one hand and her book bag in the other, Jane pushed the screen door with her foot and body-checked the door to hold it open. Lily looked both ways and crossed the street with her younger sister in tow. It wasn't until they were a few feet from the main entrance to the school that Lily looked Jane over. Her gray shirt was untucked, her hair was unbrushed, and she had crumbs on the corners of her mouth.

"Where is your chapel cap?" Lily asked.

Jane reached up and touched the top of her head. She looked back to see if she had dropped it on the road. The glance back was just for show. She hardly ever packed it. Turning back to her sister, Jane made a face and shrugged.

"What are we gonna do?"

"I've got it," Jane said as she reached into her coat pocket and secured a tissue, a white unused Kleenex, which she placed on her head and then looked up at her sister. "Do you have any bobby pins?"

So at least once a month at the mandatory school Mass, while the other girls wore delicate lace chapel caps, Jane Webb sat with a white Kleenex on the crown of her head. Early on, it was clear: If only one of the two sisters was to remain grounded in her Catholic roots, it would definitely be Lily.

The girls' dad attended Mass daily at the campus chapel. Lily wondered if it counted, though, because most days Mass lasted only twenty-six minutes, depending on who gave the homily. On Sundays, the girls sat on wooden pews in the Priory chapel with both their parents. To those who noticed, including the dozen or so monks, the girls seemed incredibly devoted to the liturgy—sitting silently with their hands folded and eyes shut. But in reality the girls' minds were elsewhere: Lily worked on memorizing facts of various saints while Jane tested herself by multiplying two four-digit numbers.

As a child, Lily's favorite Mass—besides midnight Mass on Christmas Eve—was the traditional Easter vigil that began in complete darkness. Parishioners lined up outside the chapel to receive a white candle at the entrance, where a fire had been lit and blessed. Even when the girls were little, they were allowed to light their long white candles in the fire and then proceed into the chapel in total darkness. The Webb family liked being the first ones to enter through the massive copper doors; that way the girls could watch the chapel grow lighter, candle by candle. As the space gradually filled with light, Mrs. Webb would look down at her daughters to marvel at the wonderment displayed on their faces. The night's vigil was the holiest of all.

In the dining hall after one Easter vigil, Brother Mark, a young monk who had befriended the Webbs when they moved to the Priory, told Lily one of her favorite stories about saints. From the start, Lily was captivated. Jane, on the other hand, was a bit more skeptical.

"A long, long time ago," Brother Mark said, "there was a shepherd boy."

"How long ago?" Jane said, interrupting.

"It was 1445."

Without missing a beat, Jane said, "So five hundred and twenty-four years ago."

Pausing to do the math, Brother Mark said, "That's right. So, in 1445, there was a shepherd boy watching his sheep, and he heard a child crying in the fields. He found a toddler all alone. As he bent down, the small child vanished. A few days later, it happened again. This time, the child was silent but accompanied by two floating lights. The following summer, the shepherd saw the child again. This time a red cross appeared on the child's tunic and the child was surrounded by other children. These little ones became known as the fourteen holy helpers."

"Holy helpers," Lily said. "I like that. So they were little saints."

"Most definitely," Brother Mark said.

"What happened next?" Jane asked.

"Well, the shepherd and others in the village took it as a sign of healing and built a basilica," the monk explained.

Before Lily could ask for more details, they were interrupted by a faculty member. When the conversation with the teacher and Brother Mark went on longer than Lily would have liked, she got up and walked over to the dessert table. There, she unfolded a napkin, placed four chocolate chip cookies in its center, and carefully folded in the corners. When she returned to the table, Brother Mark was sitting alone. Lily placed the carefully wrapped cookies in front of him and winked. The monk smiled back impishly.

The sisters' exposure to cutting-edge science at a young age was due in part to the monks. On a cold night in December, when the girls were still in grade school, Mrs. Webb bundled up her daughters in winter coats, mittens, and wool hats that tied under their chins. Once outside, the trio linked arms and walked across campus to the monastery gardens, which were walled off from the rest of the grounds. Father Thomas had set up a telescope on the monastery lawn and positioned it toward the western sky over Narragansett Bay. Typically, females were not allowed in the monastery, nor in the gardens, but on this night, the monk made a special concession. Father Thomas, who had been a student at the Priory in the 1930s, had returned after working with Oppenheimer and other scientists as part of a research team at Los Alamos.

He joined the Benedictines after the atomic bombs were dropped over Hiroshima and Nagasaki. For all the years that Lily and Jane would know him, they never saw him in any other clothing than his black robes. He wore his hair in a crew cut, and his eyeglasses were browline frames, left over from the fifties.

The telescope was a powerful device. It gathered up the night.

"Wait," Lily said, looking through the eyepiece. "Stars die?"

Father Thomas nodded.

Lily stepped back from the telescope. "Well, that's the saddest thing ever."

"Stars don't really die," Jane said, putting her mittened hand on Lily's shoulder. "Stars are eternal."

"I read somewhere that the sky is haunted by the past lives of stars. What we see in the night sky existed millions of years ago," Mrs. Webb explained.

"What do you think makes the stars move?" Father Thomas asked the girls.

"God," Lily said.

"We can do better than that," he responded.

He did his best to explain what little was known about dark matter. He told the girls and their mother that a "lady scientist" had published a paper in an important journal regarding invisible matter, dark matter—an idea that astronomers had been reconsidering after its conception decades earlier.

"Do you mean black holes?" asked Mrs. Webb.

"No. Dark matter," said the monk.

Ten-year-old Jane asked, "How do we measure dark matter?"

"Measure?" Father Thomas asked.

"Yeah, measure. If we know its size, we might know what it does to the stars and planets," she said, wiping her runny nose with her mitten.

"Well, we can't measure it. We can't see it. Dark matter doesn't have light."

"That's what you think," Jane said. Then she giggled and added, "Maybe it's a different kind of light. Dark light."

The others might have thought that Jane was being poetic or just imaginative, but Father Thomas adjusted his glasses and looked down at the little girl, wondering if she understood the implications of what she was saying. It would be decades before astrophysicists understood dark matter as dark light and its dominance in cosmology.

Then, with no encouragement from her mom, Jane decided it was time to go. She turned and walked toward the garden gate. The small disk of light from her flashlight bounced on the ground for a few steps and then went black.

Out of the darkness, the others heard her voice: "Onward into the night."

During the winter months, when the ground was covered with snow, Mrs. Webb often saved stale bread and scraps of vegetables—dried-up carrots and wilted lettuce—to feed to the birds and deer. Mr. Webb discouraged this, telling his wife and daughters that feeding wildlife disrupted their natural behaviors. Mrs. Webb would nod earnestly as if she agreed with her husband, but then on the winter nights when he had dorm duty, she and her daughters would pile old bread and vegetables onto a tray. The girls would take turns carrying the tray as they walked through the fields near the train tracks, leaving bits of lettuce and carrots and pieces of bread in their wake. Some moonless nights when it was particularly dark they would hear coyotes howling in the distance. And while Mrs. Webb knew the chances of being attacked by a pack were extremely low, she would urge the girls to run as fast as they could back to the house. The excitement thrilled them.

...

ONE SPRING DAY, LILY stood in her backyard alone, thinking about Francis of Assisi, a gentle saint who used to give sermons to the birds. She looked up into the trees hoping to spot one. Jane was inside spying on her through the kitchen window.

When Mrs. Webb walked into the kitchen, Jane said, "What do you think she's doing?"

Their mother paused, looked out the window as Lily appeared to be gesturing and speaking to the bushes, and said, "Maybe she's preaching to the animals."

"Or maybe she's gone crazy," Jane said.

The two watched in silence through the window as Lily assumed a posture she had no doubt observed during Mass—her hands outstretched with her palms up. And then they watched as Lily squatted on the ground and cocked her head to peer under a bush.

"Many mystics talked to animals," Mrs. Webb explained.

"Were they crazy, too?" Jane asked.

Mrs. Webb turned to look at her younger daughter and said, "And many female mystics were radicals for their time. Don't speak so disparagingly about something you don't understand." Upon saying this, Mrs. Webb placed her hand on Jane's shoulder.

"Let me put it this way," she added, softening her tone. "Despite what the fathers of the church want us to believe, there's something powerful about a preaching woman."

"I like that people talk to animals," Jane said. "It's when people say the animals talk back . . . well, that's another story." Jane pointed her index finger toward her temple, making circular motions. Her mother chuckled and placed her arm around her daughter's back, squeezing her shoulder affectionately.

When Lily was twelve, she was fascinated by Catherine of Siena, the fourteenth-century mystic who ran away at the age of seven and stayed in a cave. So Lily thought she would have her own mystical experience, but first she would go back into the house to put on clean underwear. If there was a chance she was going to meet God, she wanted to be ready.

The only cave on the island that Lily knew about was an old coal mining cave, but it was cold out, and the cave was too far away and would require a long walk, and she was already kind of hungry, so instead she decided she would go into the woods surrounding the monastery near her house.

Again, Jane was spying on her sister from the window and watched Lily head toward the house. She heard the front door open and slam. She heard Lily run up the stairs and then back down and out the door. When Lily got to the edge of the woods, Jane went outside and quietly followed her. Jane managed to stay a good distance behind and avoided snapping twigs, then watched as Lily came to a clearing, a meadow.

From a distance and hidden behind trees, Jane watched Lily walk around the circumference of the meadow before sitting down on a fallen tree log, where she crossed herself and began to pray. Lily did this for two days in a row, and each time, Jane spied on her. It didn't take long for Jane to figure out what her older sister was doing. On the third day, while Lily was doing homework in the house, Jane ran out to the meadow and placed a blue feather she had found on the log where Lily would be sure not to miss it. Later that day, Lily found the feather and convinced herself she was well on her way to sainthood. Jane never told a soul.

...

ONE NIGHT WHEN JANE was in fifth grade, she announced at dinner that Sister Mary, the school principal at Saint Philomena's, whom Jane called "the Spanking Machine," wanted to see Mrs. and Mr. Webb in her office.

"What's this about?" Mr. Webb said, turning to Jane and wiping his mouth with a napkin.

Lily started to talk, mainly to defend her sister, but her father cut her off.

"She can tell us herself. And I want you to tell the truth, not like that confession incident last week," Mr. Webb said, gesturing to his youngest with his fork.

Jane had gone to obligatory confession. Halfway through her list of sins, the priest told her that he suspected she was making up her transgressions. Jane had explained her motive this way: "I was one of the last students in line. I thought he must be tired, and I just wanted to see if he was awake. It's not my fault my last name begins with a *W*."

Sitting at the dinner table, Jane told her parents that two days before, she had taken a 1967 issue of her father's journal *Science* to school. It featured an article on human evolution. In between lunch and recess, when the teacher slipped out of the room, Jane told twenty-five fifth-graders at her Catholic grade school that the story of Adam and Eve was a myth and that humans evolved from primates. Lenny

Boninelli's father called the school and complained that Lenny announced at dinner that we evolved from chimpanzees.

"Not chimps!" Mrs. Webb said, looking disgusted as she placed her knife beside her plate. "Wasn't he paying attention? Primates. We had a common ancestor."

The next day, sitting in red upholstered chairs donated by the diocese in Providence, Lily and Jane waited outside the principal's office while their parents met with Sister Mary, who opened the meeting by informing the Webbs that more parents had since called and complained.

Directing her comments to the older woman, Mrs. Webb said, "Now, I understand that not all Catholics are educated equally."

"Carol, please," Mr. Webb interjected, concerned that his wife was insulting the principal.

"I want to review with Sister Mary that Catholics have a long history of supporting the sciences."

"With all due respect, we don't need a history lesson on the Catholic church's position on scientific advancements," the principal said.

"Sister, I beg to differ."

Undeterred, Mrs. Webb began listing off famous Catholic scientists. "Jean-Baptiste Lamarck was a Catholic. His work on evolution predates Darwin. And, of course, Lemaître was a brilliant physicist who theorized the Big Bang. I need to stress that Catholics view evolution as a fact, not a hypothesis."

After Lily and Jane had waited for what seemed like hours, their parents emerged from the principal's office. With her back to Sister Mary, Mrs. Webb winked at Jane.

A few days later, Lily and her mom were sitting on the sofa looking at an archaeology digest the Webbs had borrowed from the monastery library. Inside were images of ancient frescoes in the San Gennaro catacombs of women preaching. Hands raised in the orans posture—outstretched with palms open. The afternoon light streamed across the wooden floor like a beam leading to mother and daughter, sitting side by side.

"Look at Bitalia's robes," Mrs. Webb said, pointing to the image. "These books flanking her are the four Gospels. This was painted about five hundred years after Jesus died. What might it mean?"

Lily studied the image on the page and then looked up at her mother. Eyes wide, she said, "Women were priests. They celebrated Mass."

Mrs. Webb nodded. "It certainly suggests that, doesn't it?"

"So who said women can't be priests?" Lily asked.

Before her mother could answer, Jane burst into the room. "Sounds like something Lenny Boninelli would say," she said in a loud voice.

"Or his dad," added Lily. Both girls laughed.

"Yes, indeed. And that, girls, is what Virginia Woolf called the patriarchy. A long line of church leaders decided that it was wrong for women to be priests."

"How long?" Lily asked.

"Long. Starting about one hundred years after the death of Jesus."

"Well, then that means not everyone thought it was wrong. I mean, if they had to keep telling people it was wrong, then women must have kept preaching," Lily said.

"You're absolutely right."

Satisfied with herself that she had raised such critical thinkers, Mrs. Webb smiled proudly. Jane sat down next to her mother, leaning in to get a better look at the images and text in the book.

"Frescoes like these make some Catholics, like the leaders in Rome, very nervous, because they challenge the norms of the church," Mrs. Webb said.

They were quiet for a moment, looking down at the images, and then Jane asked, "May I bring this magazine to school on Monday?"

Mrs. Webb looked over at Lily and said, "What do you think? Will we all get hauled into Sister Mary's office again?"

Lily and Jane giggled as their mother threw her arms around both girls, pulling them in to her and smothering their heads with kisses as she tickled their sides, causing them to squeal with delight.

...

LILY'S FONDEST MEMORIES FROM her childhood were of sitting on the shores of Narragansett Bay after school with her mother and sister while their father coached the sailing team. It had become their May and June routine. Snacks, books, and blankets. One day stood out among the rest.

Having removed her saddle shoes and knee socks, Jane waded knee-deep while Lily and her mother sat onshore nearby reading. About half a mile offshore, eight sailing dinghies cruised at a good speed up the bay. A wealthy alumnus had donated the Flying Juniors—or "the FJs," as Lily's father called them—so the school could have a competitive sailing team. A gull on the pier squawked. The wind had picked up. Whitecaps stirred the bay with small waves, one after the other, curling up onto the shoreline.

With her legs folded neatly beneath her, Mrs. Webb was engrossed in her book, which rested on her knee-length navy pleated skirt. Lily leaned up against her book bag reading *Valley of the Dolls,* which her mom permitted as long as Lily listened to her critique on the ubiquity of male domination and its impact on the daily lives of women. This Lily listened to willingly, but when Mrs. Webb inched toward talking about lesbian sex, a topic broached in the bestseller, Lily protested.

"We mustn't be closed-minded, Lily. Heterosexuality is not mandatory. Lesbians have existed since ancient times. Why, I knew two women when I was at Pembroke who were lovers at school, and no one seemed to mind. Everyone knew that Pam Jackson and Judith Simmons were together. Once, Pam's roommate walked in on them when they were—"

"Mom! Stop!"

Lily and her mom hadn't noticed that Jane had dragged a dinghy out to the water and rowed herself past the end of the pier until she started shouting. By then, Jane was standing up, rocking the wooden boat from side to side and shouting.

"What is she going on about?" Lily asked.

They both looked out toward the water at Jane, who was waving her arms.

"*I thank whatever gods may be / For my unquenchable soul,*" Jane hollered.

Their mom chuckled. "She's reciting Henley, at least she thinks she is. It's unconquerable, not unquenchable. Although, given our little Jane, the latter may be more fitting," said Mrs. Webb. This was only loud enough for Lily to hear. Then, raising her voice, she yelled, "Put your life jacket on!"

Mrs. Webb kept an eye on her young daughter, who was now bending over precariously, trying to position one of the oars in the oarlock while she slung the orange life jacket over her right shoulder. Lily stood up to watch her sister. She could have predicted that the dinghy would capsize given Jane's floundering about, and when it did, Jane disappeared beneath the water. Almost immediately, the orange vest popped to the surface. But there was no sign of Jane.

Moving fast, her mother stood, kicked off her loafers, unfastened her skirt, and ran into the water, leaving her discarded clothes on the shore. The wind picked up Mrs. Webb's scent of gardenia and jasmine.

Lily looked behind her. Sometimes the monks from the monastery stood up on the grassy ledge watching the student sailors. Lily didn't know whether she should be embarrassed by her mother's immodesty or worried about Jane drowning. Both girls could tread water—their mother had made sure of that.

Lily's mother swam expertly toward the boat and then disappeared, diving beneath the overturned dinghy. Lily was nervous. Several moments passed before her mother's head surfaced, her wet hair plastered flat against her scalp. Mrs. Webb turned back toward the shore, looking annoyed. Soon Lily spotted Jane peeking around the bow of the boat, holding onto its edge. Jane began kicking and pushing the dinghy to shore, until she emerged from the water as wet as a drowned cat.

Father Thomas's timing could not have been worse in terms of sparing him the embarrassment of seeing Mrs. Webb on the shore in her waist-high nylon underwear and white blouse, which clung to her skin. He probably would have walked away discreetly if Jane hadn't felt compelled to justify her actions.

"I'm practicing turtling. Tell my mom what an important skill that is," Jane shouted, looking up toward the cliff.

With his austere black robes blowing in the wind, Father Thomas bellowed in his baritone voice, "Yes, you're right, Jane, but from the looks of it, you probably should have warned the others!"

Looking down at Jane, Mrs. Webb said, "Knowing what to do when a boat capsizes builds confidence. You're absolutely right. Just let me know in advance the next time you decide to do it."

As they walked back through the fields to their house in single file, Mrs. Webb carried her shoes and held the canvas bag of snacks and books close to her, hiding her still-see-through blouse. Jane straggled behind. Before reaching the house, Lily turned to her sister and said, "You're such a troublemaker. And besides that, it's not unquenchable, it's unconquerable. There's a big difference."

"I knew that," Jane said.

"Then what does unquenchable mean?" Lily asked. When her sister didn't reply, Lily added, "Hungry, always hungry."

Jane thought for a moment and then called to her mother: "Mom, can a soul be hungry?"

Mrs. Webb stopped walking and looked off into the distance. Lily almost bumped into her.

"Absolutely," she said, without turning her head. "But I imagine it must be devastating."

That night when Jane and Lily were lying in their twin beds and their mother came in to listen to their prayers and say good night, Lily was anxiously trying to finish *Valley of the Dolls* before it was lights out.

"This is a sad book. All the female characters, Jennifer and the rest of them, are taking barbiturates and sleeping pills," Lily said.

"What's sad is that their lives are controlled by men. No one is ever really free—free will is an illusion—but the more options and opportunities we have, the more control we have over our lives. That's what the women's movement is all about," Mrs. Webb explained.

"What's a movement?" Jane asked.

"It's like the fight for civil rights or when women fought for the right to vote; it's when a group of people demand change."

Jane considered this and then said, "Maybe it should be called a revolution."

"The patriarchy has been conspiring to control women throughout time," Mrs. Webb said as she pulled Jane's quilt up and over her daughter. Lily wanted to know if there were any good guys. "There are a few good men," her mother replied. "Take Fred Rogers."

Mrs. Webb always called Mr. Rogers "Fred Rogers." When the girls were younger and his show was about to start, she would say, "Fred Rogers is on."

"Now, he uses his creative and leadership abilities to make a difference in the lives of children. Do you remember when he shared his wading pool with an African American policeman? He wasn't just showing children how to be kind, he was challenging racial prejudices."

"What about Daddy?" Lily asked. "Is he a good man?"

She smiled. "Ah, of course, that goes without saying."

Mrs. Webb had the same ritual every night. After she listened to her daughters' prayers, she would bend over each of their beds, kissing the girls on their foreheads, telling them, one by one, something they had done that day that pleased her or made her proud. "I noticed how you held the door at the grocery store for that elderly woman, that was kind of you." Or "Do you know how much I love your funny stories?"

The next day after school while they were preparing their snacks to take to the bay, Jane all of a sudden seemed to remember something that had occurred to her earlier in the day. Her face grew serious. "I know what happened to the witches at Salem." She looked at her mother and said, "The patriarchy." Mrs. Webb tried not to laugh. She nodded instead.

"Mom, this is all the more reason I need to learn how to turtle the boat by myself."

Mrs. Webb felt a surge of pride, but what she couldn't predict was just how dead-on her youngest was at registering imminent social change. A week after Jane turtled the boat in the bay, the Ohio National Guard fired on a crowd of Kent State college students protesting the Vietnam War, killing four. What happened at Kent State made a huge impression on Jane. She returned home from the fourth grade crying and asking, "Are the soldiers going to come to Saint Philomena's and shoot us, too?" For weeks after the Kent State shooting, Jane wouldn't go outside for recess and instead helped Sister Mary Agnes wash the blackboards and stuff envelopes.

There were other protests that same year that shaped the girls' lives. One August night when the sisters were upstairs getting ready for bed, little Jane surmised that her parents were discussing something that she and Lily were not meant to hear. Jane opened the door to the bathroom where Lily was brushing her teeth.

"Mom's going to strike," ten-year-old Jane whispered to her sister.

With toothpaste foaming around her mouth and down her chin, Lily said, "What are you talking about?"

Jane put her finger to her lips to hush Lily and then pulled on her pajamas. Both girls wore sleeveless cotton nightgowns with ruffles at the collars. The two sisters squatted at the top of the steps to get a better sense of what their parents were saying.

"You knew this about me when you married me, Martin," Mrs. Webb said.

"You can't be serious," the girls' father said.

"I'm surprised at you; you've always supported women's rights."

"But Carol, I could lose my job."

Mrs. Webb laughed.

"It's a pro-abortion rally, for God's sake."

"And your point?" Mrs. Webb said.

"What if the monks find out?"

"It's more than just a rally for reproductive rights—it's about equal pay and accessible childcare."

"Why are they calling it a strike?"

"It's a political strategy to remind people that it's about labor and equality. Think of it, Martin, it'll be one of the largest protests of women in fifty years: waitresses, secretaries, writers, and mothers. I hope somebody had enough sense to make sure it's not all white—" Before she could finish, her husband, who was clearly agitated, interrupted.

"And how will you explain this to the girls? And what about Jane and all of her nightmares since the Kent State shootings?"

"Well, let me put it this way: If we don't march and this society doesn't change, when she gets older, she'll be facing full-blown nightmares in the real world. I could take Lily with me. It would be a good experience for her," Mrs. Webb said matter-of-factly.

Hearing this, Lily pressed her hands together and mouthed, "Please let me go, God, please let me go."

"The bus leaves at five; we'll get to New York by nine."

"Who will get the girls up and make them breakfast?"

"It's a strike, Martin. That's the point!"

A week later, Mrs. Webb joined thousands of people, mostly women but some men, as they marched down Fifth Avenue to Bryant Park, where they heard Betty Friedan proclaim, "This is not a bedroom war, this is a political movement." That same night, back in Portsmouth after a dinner of grilled cheese sandwiches, Mr. Webb asked his daughters to help out with the dishes. Almost immediately, Lily got up from the table to help and started clearing the dishes and filling the sink with warm soapy water. Mr. Webb had moved into the living room to read the evening newspaper, while Jane stayed seated doing math problems.

"Jane, please get up from the table and help your sister."

Without looking up, Jane said, "I'm on strike, too."

PORTSMOUTH, RHODE ISLAND

1972

When Mr. Webb opened the front door, Lily put her finger to her lips as a signal for him to keep quiet.

"Mom's napping," she told Mr. Webb.

Lily, who was in the seventh grade now, went back into the kitchen to finish making dinner. She had taken it upon herself to make her sister and father tuna fish sandwiches with canned green beans. Mr. Webb went straight to the master bedroom, where he opened the door a bit and saw his wife sound asleep, her jaw slack, breathing deeply.

The girls had sat down at the kitchen table and started eating.

"Aren't these green beans supposed to be heated?" Jane asked, placing the palm of her hand over the vegetables on her plate.

Mr. Webb looked at Lily and then at Jane. "Just be thankful your sister made you supper."

Picking up a green bean from her plate to hold it up for inspection,

Jane said, "All I'm saying is that Mom usually puts the beans in a saucepan and heats them and then adds salt and butter. These are cold. Right out of the can."

"Enough," Mr. Webb said.

Mr. Webb's first thought was that his wife was pregnant. In the years they'd been together, he had known his wife to take naps only when she was pregnant with the girls. The next afternoon, when Mr. Webb returned home, the girls were busy doing their homework at the kitchen table, and Mrs. Webb was asleep again. He took his daughters to the dining hall where the students and monks ate. When they returned from their meal, Mrs. Webb was still asleep. She slept right through the night. The next morning a local doctor paid a visit. X-rays were ordered. Breast cancer. Had the cancer developed a few years later, perhaps doctors would have caught it with a routine mammogram, but in 1972, those were still a way off.

Father Thomas persuaded Mr. Webb to travel to Boston for a second opinion. Soon they learned what the local doctor had suspected: A small but aggressive primary tumor in her breast had spread to the lungs. Cytotoxic drugs were administered, but they only weakened Mrs. Webb's immune system.

She had some good days, but mostly bad. Her decline was rapid. She grew increasingly tired, lost her appetite, and had shortness of breath. On her good days, the girls stayed close by. Sometimes they sat with their mom on the couch looking through Mrs. Webb's books on art. She promised to take them to New York to visit the Met so they could see the famous paintings featured in her books. "I'll take you in the spring," she told her daughters. The sisters each made a list of the paintings they wanted to see in the museum.

Lily was drawn to Mary Cassatt's *Young Mother Sewing*. It was at the top of her list, because it reminded Lily of the closeness she shared with her mother. In the painting, a young girl, maybe three or four, leans on her mother's lap, gazing at the painter while her mother sews. Both girls put Picasso's painting of Gertrude Stein on their lists. At the top of Jane's list was *The Denial of Saint Peter* by Caravaggio. Mrs. Webb could have predicted that her younger daughter would be attracted to the dramatic contrast between light and dark.

Several months later, Mrs. Webb asked her husband to bring home a few art supplies. Nothing fancy, just a few large pieces of paper, some charcoal pencils, and erasers—things he could get from the art department at school. She thought it would be fun if she and the girls tried to draw one another. She wanted to do something with Lily and Jane, just to have them close to her.

The girls took the exercise seriously. They each taped their paper to one of their father's coffee-table books and strategically placed two chairs from the dining room table around their mother's bed. Mrs. Webb surprised the girls with a prop. Sitting up in bed, she placed a straw hat on her head and leaned against the headboard. The girls thought their mother looked beautiful. In the end, Lily showed the most potential with her drawing of Jane. When Mrs. Webb showed them her portrait of Lily, her daughters oohed and aahed, while Jane had her mother looking like a giraffe with a lampshade on its head. It wasn't intentional—that's just what it looked like—which naturally produced a lot of laughter.

Several weeks later, Lily found her mom and Jane in her parents' bed, both propped up and reading. It was a Saturday in October, and Mrs. Webb asked Lily to open her bedroom window so she could smell the autumn air. After doing so, Lily sat on the edge of the bed and placed her hand on her mom's bare ankle.

"Your feet are cold," she said.

"And dirty," Mrs. Webb said, waving her foot.

"I've got an idea," Lily told her.

When Lily returned to the bedroom, she was carrying a tray with a warm, moist washcloth, a towel, and baby oil. She stood at the end of the bed and gently wiped her mom's left foot. Jane looked up but then went right back to reading.

"You don't have to do that," Mrs. Webb said, smiling.

"But I want to."

After wiping both feet with the washcloth, Lily dried them and began gently rubbing in baby oil. She wanted her mom to relax but didn't want to hurt her or tickle her because that would defeat the purpose.

"Can you smell the pine?" Mrs. Webb asked, turning her head toward the open window.

Lily sniffed the air. "Yeah."

"Colder air holds fewer scents—it has something to do with the scent molecules and temperature." Mrs. Webb took a deep breath and sighed. "We'll ask Dad to explain it."

Lily knew that her mom, who was generally prone to offering long explanations and never missed an opportunity to provide instruction on all sorts of matters, was too tired to talk. By now, Jane had closed her book, turned on her side, and curled up with the arch of her back tucked in close to her mother. As Jane dozed off, Mrs. Webb stroked her hair, which was long and unkempt.

Both Mrs. Webb and Lily were lost in their own thoughts. Lily was trying her best to keep the pressure light and use just the right amount of oil—enough to soothe but not so much that her mother might slip upon rising. She made a mental note to pat the soles of her mother's feet dry when she was done.

Mrs. Webb had surrendered to her daughter's touch but couldn't help seeing the kind gesture from a deeper, more spiritually symbolic perspective. Foot washing, a ritual act, represented so many layers:

love, service, humility, and, of course, the sacrament of anointing the sick. Thinking about this caused Mrs. Webb's chin and lips to quiver. She closed her eyes and let her head sink into the pillow.

Looking up, Lily said, "It's okay, Mom."

...

ON THE MORNING OF Mrs. Webb's thirty-ninth birthday, while Lily was brushing her mother's hair in bed, Jane came into the room.

"I have something for you," Jane announced.

"Should I close my eyes?" her mother asked.

"You can keep them open." And then, standing next to her mother's bed, Jane proceeded to recite a poem she had memorized for the occasion.

"Look at the stars! look, look up at the skies! / O look at all the fire-folk sitting in the air! / The bright boroughs, the circle-citadels there! / Down in dim woods the diamond delves! the elves'-eyes!"

What Jane didn't know was that the poet had once sent it to his own mother as a birthday gift. Jane stood proudly while their tired mother looked on. Jane bowed when she was done.

"Where did you find that?" Mrs. Webb whispered, reaching out to hold her younger daughter's hand.

"In one of your books. Mr. Manley Hopkins wrote it. Isn't that a funny name for a man?"

"Sure is. And it's a beautiful poem," Mrs. Webb told her.

"I think it's a prayer," Jane said.

"You're absolutely right."

When Mrs. Webb slipped into a coma ten days later, their father let the girls sleep in their mother's bed. Jane slept beside her mom, her thin arm resting across Mrs. Webb's belly. Lily was at the foot of the bed. On the second night, after both girls had fallen asleep, Mr. Webb kept vigil in a chair looking on. Just after midnight, he noticed his wife's breathing pattern had changed. The death rattle, a harbinger of what was to come. Reaching over his wife's body to wake the girls, he said, "It's time, girls. It's time." Both girls raised their sleepy heads and looked up toward their father's face, watching as tears streamed down his cheeks and onto his chin. They quickly shifted their attention to their mother. Three breaths, and she was gone. Jane put one hand on her mother's chest, and with her other, she searched for her mother's breath, putting her fingers under Mrs. Webb's nose. When she realized she was dead, Jane wailed. Lily stood wide-eyed, in shock.

As the months passed, Lily suffered the loss of her mother quietly, while Jane's loss led her to a place where hungry souls devour themselves. It went on like this for years.

PORTSMOUTH, RHODE ISLAND

1973

While Lily was a dutiful daughter—studious and helpful around the house—Mr. Webb had his hands full with Jane. By the time Jane was twelve, she could do ninth-grade math with no problem, and Mr. Webb's fellow teachers knew the stories about her: How she would get out of her seat during math class, walk over to the board, use her sleeve to erase the teacher's mistakes, and write in the correct answers. Or, when the teacher introduced a new math concept, how Jane would repeatedly blurt out the answer before the teacher could finish. Or when classmates struggled with problems, how Jane would go from desk to desk, helping her fellow students.

This happened so many times, the principal decided that instead of attending math class, Jane should read to the few elderly nuns who were still living in the convent attached to the school. Because Saint Philomena's was a private school, the principal could get away with this. When Father Thomas, the former Manhattan Project physicist, learned of this arrangement, he volunteered to tutor Jane.

After Mrs. Webb died, the girls and their father took to eating all their meals in the dining hall at the boarding school. In the evenings, still in her plaid school uniform with paper and pen stuck under her arm, Jane would carry two desserts over to where Father Thomas was sitting in the dining hall. For the next five years, he tutored her in trigonometry, calculus, and physics.

If someone asked where Jane was in those grade-school years, there were two common responses: "She's looking for numbers" and "She's with Father Thomas." If Jane was "looking for numbers," it meant she was outside somewhere on the shore of the bay collecting shells, in the woods surrounding the monastery gathering pine cones, or in the gardens counting petals on daisies or coneflowers. Holding up a flower and pointing to its petals, Jane would say, "Math exists in the world; it's our job to find it."

Sometimes when Father Thomas gave Jane a problem that challenged her, she would pretend she was sick—too sick to go to school—and though she was supposed to be resting in bed, her father, who would come home to check on her in between his classes, would find her hunched over her notebook and scraps of paper, scribbling numbers and letters feverishly. Equation after equation. Sometimes she would rise at 5:20 A.M. and walk across the campus of the boarding school to wait for Father Thomas until he had finished morning prayers at the chapel to ask for a new problem.

One Tuesday night in winter, Mr. Webb knocked on Lily's bedroom door and asked, "Where is Jane?"

"Last I saw, she was in the dining hall with Father Thomas," Lily said, looking up from her notebook.

"Well, she's not home yet, and it's past eight."

A few minutes later, the front door opened. "Where have you been?" Mr. Webb asked his twelve-year-old.

"At Math Club." She was referring to the Priory's Math Club. By now, the name of the boarding school had changed to the Portsmouth Abbey, but most people continued to call it the Priory and old-timers simply referred to the school as Portsmouth.

"Did Father Thomas invite you?"

"He wasn't there."

Jane inherited her assertiveness and tenacity from her mother, but she was still heavily influenced by the traditional gender norms of the early seventies and, consequently, a little nervous about sneaking, uninvited, into the meeting of the all-boys Math Club at the Priory.

"So you went to the meeting alone?"

"Well, I didn't actually go alone. There were four students there."

"Jane, you can't go to the boys' Math Club."

"Why not?"

"First, you're not a student here."

"That's not a logical argument. Joey Simmons is ten, and he goes to varsity basketball practice. And Mikey Murphy is in my grade, and he goes to hockey practice with Coach Murphy."

"Yes, but they're boys. And this is an all-boys school."

Jane put her hand on her hip, cocked her head, and narrowed her eyes. "Well, then maybe it shouldn't be."

He knew instantly that his wife would have agreed with Jane.

Jane kept going to the Math Club meetings. First, she had sat with her notebook outside the classroom on the hallway floor, listening and peeking around the corner until, finally, they invited her in. In the beginning, she sat in the back. By the end of the academic year, she was in the front row every Tuesday night at seven.

Even though Lily was two years older, the girls were only one grade apart; Jane had skipped a grade. High school teachers would attribute both girls' academic success to their scholarly father. But, really, the girls inherited their mother's intellect and curiosity. The only thing the girls' high school teachers would come to know about Mrs. Webb was that she died of breast cancer when Lily was thirteen and Jane was eleven.

Jane discovered the promises of math to distract her from her sadness. Math allowed her to explore the world and her mind at the same time. Numbers saved Jane—until she discovered the promises of booze and pills. Lily dealt with her mother's death by transubstantiating one form of love into another, and by becoming a Catholic feminist, which would prove to have its own challenges and contradictions.

PORTSMOUTH, RHODE ISLAND

1973–1976

Lily didn't stand a chance against the darkness that took over after her mother's death. Then there was the season of blinding numbness when she felt little to nothing: The curious, smart, faithful, friendly girl faded. She felt emotionally vacant. Then she met the boy.

They were freshmen. Fourteen. Mr. Souza's honors English class. Lily was nervous on her first day. She knew that most of her classmates had known one another through middle school. But soon after the first-period bell rang at the public high school and she found Room E109, her nervousness morphed into a kind of calm. Lily took it all in—more than twenty-five students in one class, some shouting, some sitting on desks, two kids writing on the chalkboard, a few girls chewing gum and braiding each other's hair, and another kid eating his breakfast. On top of all this, the students kept talking when the teacher began taking attendance.

She settled into a seat in the second row. The boy took a seat next to her. Already six feet and still growing, he looked uncomfortable in his small desk chair. When the room finally quieted down, kids in the back row started giggling and then laughing hard. Someone tossed a bunch of marbles on the floor, and they went rolling down the aisles and under the chairs. Still standing in the front of the class, Mr. Souza bent over to see what the fuss was.

The poor teacher scrambled to collect the marbles, inciting more laughter. Lily wondered how they would ever learn anything. She looked over at the boy to see if he was laughing. He wasn't. In fact, she watched as he maneuvered his foot to stop one of the marbles from rolling away.

Mr. Souza asked if anyone wanted to read the poem they were working on aloud. No one volunteered. Lily recognized this type of teacher—the kind to inspire students, to make them want to learn. Had he been at Saint Phil's, the students would have been gathered around him, and all hands would have shot up. At her old school, reading poetry and literature was considered cool.

Lily was used to reading poems aloud. She was even used to recitations. The poem was Dylan Thomas's "Do Not Go Gentle into That Good Night." She had studied it in eighth grade. She felt bad for Mr. Souza, so she raised her hand. The room fell quiet. Lily read with ease and confidence. When the teacher asked what the poem was about, Lily knew enough not to raise her hand again. With a pencil behind his ear, the boy raised his.

"It's about courage."

"Say more," the teacher said.

The room was still quiet. The boy already had a reputation as someone to watch. As a freshman, he started on the varsity football team. So all eyes were on him.

"The courage to fight for your life—to defend it even against death."

Lily wrote down what he said.

When the bell rang, she stood up and caught him watching her. As they walked out of the room, they were side by side.

"What's with the marbles?" Lily asked.

"Everybody thinks that Mr. Souza sounds like he has marbles in his mouth when he talks."

"Wow! What a bunch of dicks," Lily said.

Caught off guard, the boy laughed. "I thought you came from Saint Philomena's."

"Well, even Catholic girls swear," Lily said, smiling. "How did you know I went to Saint Phil's?"

"Everybody knows it; you're the new girl."

When Lily made a face of disbelief, he added, "James Sheehan is a day student at the Priory. Lives in Lawrence Farm. He told everyone."

Before Lily could respond, another boy, whose nickname was "Head," came up from behind and pushed his way in between them, patting the boy on the back.

"This is Head," the boy said. "We've been friends since middle school."

"Best friends," Head said, smiling at Lily.

Head wasn't as tall as the boy and carried a little more weight. He had chubby cheeks, big brown eyes, and curly hair.

"Come on," Head said to the boy. "We have to get to the B wing."

Head pushed the boy from behind. The boy looked back at Lily, smiled, and said, "Where are you going next?"

"Geometry, B wing."

"You're gonna be in class with a bunch of sophomores. Come with us, we're headed that way. We'll find it together. You don't want to get lost on your first day."

Every morning, they had English together, and then she would look for him in the cafeteria and hallways. Early in October, at a social held at Saint Barnabas Hall, he asked her to dance. In late October, Mr. Webb took Lily, the boy, Head, and Jane bowling. That was the first time Mr. Webb met the boy, whom he described as "tall for his age and well-mannered." By November, they were meeting at the town library after dinner, sitting next to each other with their knees touching at the wooden tables. With the first big snowstorm in late December, Lily and the boy, with Jane in tow, spent the afternoon sledding at the Priory on the long sloping hills that ended at the tree line. Later that day, over hot chocolate, Lily asked Mr. Webb if she and Jane could meet the boy and Head at the movies. Head's sister was driving the boys to see *The Exorcist* and Lily wanted her dad to drop them off. "You'll see that movie over my dead body," he said, which he immediately regretted when he saw the look of terror on Jane's face. Trying to change the subject, he added, "We can watch *All in the Family* and make our own popcorn." To which Lily replied, "But Archie Bunker's a racist and calls men fags." For Christmas that year, the boy gave Lily a white stuffed kitty with a red ribbon around its neck, and she bought him a five-inch plastic statue of a little girl holding a heart from the local pharmacy's gift section.

...

IT WAS A COLD Tuesday afternoon in January and Lily had stayed after school to do her homework while the boy had basketball practice. She sat in the bleachers reading. There were two other girls, upperclassmen, watching their boyfriends, but Lily kept to herself. After practice when the gym cleared out, Lily and the boy sat in the bleachers together waiting for Mr. Cooper to pick them up. Lily pulled a hairbrush out of her bag and tried to undo a knot that had tangled her hair. Lily's hair was long—it fell to the middle of her back—and the knot was a pretty good size.

"Here," the boy said, as he reached for the brush. "Let me do it."

The boy stood, climbed up another step on the bleachers, and sat behind Lily with his legs apart. He separated her hair into sections and, starting at the bottom, gently brushed it.

"It seems like you've done this before," Lily said, tilting her head and looking up at him, smiling.

"I used to brush my mom's hair when I was little."

Lily raised her hand up and reached for the boy. When she felt his forearm, she squeezed it.

She closed her eyes, relaxing under his touch. A memory of her own mother emerged. Mrs. Webb used to brush and braid Lily's hair, and then, when she was finished, she would say, "Let me do that again, it didn't come out right." But Mrs. Webb was just pretending the braid wasn't right because she knew her daughter loved being tended to in this way.

"What else do you remember about your mother?" Lily asked.

Lily and the boy had been dating for three months. She had told him about her mother's death, but all she really knew about his parents was that they divorced when he was in kindergarten and his mom, whom he hadn't seen since she moved away, was living down south.

"Well, I remember brushing her hair, which was long and dark like yours. She loved it. Sometimes, she would give me a quarter just to do it."

Lily remained quiet.

"She used to spin me around the living room. I had forgotten about that until one day when I was in middle school and 'Be My Baby' came on the radio when I was in the car with my dad."

"The Ronettes," Lily said.

"Yeah. How did you know that?"

"My mom had their records, too."

"My dad said, 'Your mother loved this song,' and I had a flash, a memory of dancing in her arms. I must've been about four."

The boy had worked out the knot but kept brushing Lily's hair.

"She cheated on my dad. I don't know how she met the guy, but one night after supper, I heard them fighting in their bedroom. When my mom came out, she was crying and carrying a green suitcase. She grabbed me, hugged me real tight, and then walked out the door."

Lily let out a sigh. "I'm sure she loved you."

"Not enough," the boy said.

Lily worried she had said the worst thing possible. But as if reading her mind, the boy said, "It's all right . . . I'm okay."

He continued brushing her hair some more, smoothing it out with his other hand, and they sat in silence for a moment until he asked, "What do you miss the most about your mom?"

Without hesitating, Lily said, "Everything."

The boy put down the brush, and in a tender tone she had not yet heard him use, he said, "We'll be okay."

Lily bit down on her lip, trying to contain the sadness that washed over her.

Sitting on the edge of her bed that night in her flannel nightgown, Lily ran her fingers through her tangle-free hair and thought about what the boy had told her. The fact that he remembered the color of his mother's suitcase but had never seen her again made her cry. He was the only other kid Lily knew who didn't have a mom.

In spring, the dogwood trees in the boy's front yard were in bloom with pinkish-red starlike flowers. Lily and the boy sat on the front steps waiting for Mr. Webb to pick her up. She wore a blue-and-red argyle sweater-vest with a white turtleneck and blue denim skirt. The boy was dressed in a brown corduroy jacket and a new pair of bell-bottom jeans that Lily loved. She had her schoolbag between her legs.

"When my mom was a girl, she traveled to New Hampshire with her family for a vacation," the boy said. "She saw a house in the mountains surrounded by birch and dogwood trees. When my parents got married and bought this house, my dad drove all over New England in a truck he had borrowed to buy her those trees." The boy gestured with his chin to the ones that lined the Coopers' property.

"So is that one a dogwood?" Lily asked, pointing to the tree in bloom.

"Yeah," the boy said. "At first, it was just a couple, and then every year, he would plant more. It was my mother's idea of happily ever after."

The young teenagers sat in silence until the boy said, "I missed her like crazy when I was younger. You know the look on a little kid's face when he realizes he's lost in a crowd? That's what I used to feel like all the time."

Lily was familiar with this level of introspection from the boy, and she had come to expect it. "Do you ever still feel that way?" she asked, turning her head to look at him.

The boy looked back and held her gaze. The corners of his mouth lifted slightly. "Not anymore, Lil."

In their sophomore year, once he got his driver's license, they went parking at the grove, a place where the willows bent to the ground. At first, what Lily liked most was holding hands and kissing with their mouths closed. These early tender moments were painted by insecurities and the unknowing notions of bodies and pleasures. Awkward breaths. Moments when their teeth touched. They learned from each other mostly. By their senior year, when Lily discovered how to make herself come, she taught the boy.

They had approached having intercourse a few times when the

intensity of the moment demanded more from them. Yet he never pressured her. She never heard "You would if you loved me"—that worn-out refrain—from the boy. And while other girls at school drafted timelines—chronological projections of what would happen and when, like "lose my virginity by graduation" or "be married by twenty-two"—Lily never did. She thought about the first time they would make love—where they would be and how it might feel—but making a timeline seemed ridiculous. Still, she was caught up in the dominant idea that love and sex should go together. This was despite her sister's critique that physical desire can be separate from romantic love and thus acted upon. Whenever she and the boy talked about having intercourse, usually it was Lily who initiated the conversation. "Soon," she would tell him after a night of heavy petting and making out. The boy started carrying around condoms, just in case.

Love songs on the radio played differently. *Moons and Junes and Ferris wheels / The dizzy dancing way you feel.* Lily thought that Joni Mitchell knew her secrets and desires. She learned that, like death, first love was something no one was prepared for. What she was less aware of was how her mother's death had led her to him. Loss had been her compass.

NOVEMBER 1976

Ken Kenny, Portsmouth's football coach, had a young and attractive niece who worked the front desk of the Ramada Inn. On a Friday afternoon in November, two men checked in. The younger of the two scouts might have been trying to impress the girl—after a few drinks in the lounge, he told her he was in town to watch the game. The boy, his coach, and practically everyone in Portsmouth knew that scouts from local colleges had been attending games to observe and evaluate the boy's skills, but new rumors had been circulating that scouts from the big-name schools would be coming to watch him play. So as soon as Coach Kenny's niece got home that Friday night, she called her uncle. The next day, the boy tried not to think about the scouts, but on his way to the locker room to suit up, he wondered which schools the recruiters were from and whether Lily would transfer her sophomore year of college to whichever school offered him a scholarship so they could be together. He changed quickly into his pads and uniform.

The boy kept his gaze ahead of him as he jogged onto the field with his teammates. It was a crisp fall morning. The town had come out to see him play his final game, even those whose kids had long since graduated from high school. Bundled up in blankets in the stands and lined against the chain-link fence, the town's people showed up to watch the making of a hometown hero.

Portsmouth was playing Classical High, one of the best teams in the state. The home team won the coin toss and deferred; Classical had the ball. What surprised the boy the most from the sidelines was that Classical's offensive line seemed a whole lot bigger and faster than they had the previous year.

The second play from the scrimmage was particularly concerning for the boy. Classical's quarterback took the snap and faked a handoff.

Coach Kenny gestured from the sidelines, yelling, "Watch the play action! Cover him in the flat, dammit!"

Classical's tight end ran his route cleanly and caught the ball, resulting in a fifteen-yard gain. They were only one minute into the game. Three plays later, Classical's running back lined up in the backfield, successfully converting the handoff to a first down. He was tackled inches from the goal line. It had been only a few plays and Classical had marched down the field and dominated Portsmouth's defense.

The boy's coach looked ruefully at Portsmouth's stunned offense on the sidelines but then turned and looked at the boy and gave him two thumbs-up. Despite his usual confidence, the boy thought he was going to puke. Portsmouth's goal line formation prepared to defend against the run but to no avail. Classical's running back practically walked through, scoring the game's first touchdown. The opposing fans cheered.

The rest of the first half was much the same. Portsmouth seemed unable to convert third downs. Each time the boy left the huddle and surveyed the defense, it was as if they had studied Portsmouth's playbook: He found it almost impossible to execute a play successfully. With a minute and a half left in the half, Classical was up 14–0. Clearly outplayed, the boy wondered if they had been out-coached, too.

Right before halftime, he realized something—a weakness in Classical's offense. Classical's left tackle, No. 63, always got into a three-point stance when a running play was called, and for every pass play, the same kid took an upright stance. It was suddenly clear to the boy: Inadvertently, one kid on the opposing team was giving away Classical's offensive strategy. This was what Portsmouth needed to turn the game around.

Once in the locker room, he approached his coach and dropped what he considered to be gold dust.

"I've got something that's gonna help us," the boy started to explain to Coach Kenny.

"Listen, I know you're worried with the scouts here," the coach said.

Knowing his coach was going to try to talk him down, the boy said, "Just hear me out."

Back on the field, Portsmouth lost the ball to a fumble. Classical recovered on their own thirty-yard line. But now the boy's teammates could stop Classical because everybody on Portsmouth's defense knew what to look for: They were watching No. 63. Sure enough, when No. 63 went into a three-point stance, Classical's offense ran the ball, and every time Portsmouth managed to stop them short of the first down. Cheerleaders in the bleachers shouted, "Let's go, defense," followed by five fast claps.

Because Classical's offense couldn't convert, the boy was able to lead his team down the field. Before the end of the third quarter, Portsmouth scored two touchdowns. Whistles blew in their favor, and the marching band played the iconic "Victory March."

Everything had changed. With forty seconds left on the clock and a 14 to 14 tie, the boy knew this was his moment. He handed the ball off to Jimmy Sullivan and got as clear as he could. It was as if Jimmy read his mind. Jimmy passed it back to him; the boy caught it, juked two defensive backs, and ran it in for a touchdown.

Soon, letters from college coaches arrived—lots of letters. By the time his final season was over, the boy had led Portsmouth High School to three Class A state championships. By December, he had more than a dozen offers to play college football from some of the best schools in the country, including one from the coach who had met Ken Kenny's niece. He was from the University of Michigan.

Everybody in town was willing to bet that the boy, after being recruited by a powerhouse college team, had a real chance to go on to the NFL. Certainly, no one could say this for sure because they knew the chances of playing in the NFL after college were infinitesimally small. But his high school stats were written in the stars. A sportswriter for *The Providence Journal* called the boy a unicorn and said his potential was historic—the type of football legend who distracts fans from their own hardships, the kind of player who made people forget their own missed opportunities.

It was the best time of his life.

JANUARY 1977

Coach Kenny also taught history classes at the high school, and these were known to get sidetracked when his students got him talking about current events—like when former beauty queen and Florida orange juice spokeswoman Anita Bryant led a campaign to repeal a Florida county's gay-rights ordinance. But he also had a reputation for being one of the popular teachers for another reason. Portsmouth students looked forward to taking his class because he had a peculiar perspective about Christmas: He was the only parent they had met who intentionally told his kids there was no such thing as Santa Claus. Students had to wait until they were juniors when they took his U.S. history class to hear his explanation, the crux of which was: "Lying to children is wrong. Just plain wrong." In the instant the boy first heard Mr. Kenny say this, he disagreed and thought, *Lil and I will tell our kids about Santa.* He imagined himself assembling a train track for their son, just like his own dad must have done for him years ago, when he was young and it was just the two of them.

Lily had her share of ambivalence about the football coach, but it had nothing to do with Santa Claus. It stemmed from an interaction Mr. Kenny once had with Jane. Sitting in the back row in history class her junior year, Jane was admiring Betty Barboza's ring and had reached over to grab her hand and get a better look at it, their hands joined for some time. Perhaps because the coach couldn't hold her brilliant sister's attention, he resorted to bullying. Calling attention to Jane and Betty, Mr. Kenny said, "Maybe the lesbians in the back row could stop holding hands for a second and take notes on the Battle of Rhode Island." The class broke out in laughter. Betty's face turned beet red, while Jane quipped, "Aye, aye, Jerry Falwell."

More laughter.

But Betty suffered the most from that incident when Joe Hitchens followed up with, "Well, according to David, Betty is no lesbo."

David McCarren, a senior and class president, had taken Betty to the Homecoming dance that fall and spread rumors that he and Betty had gone all the way.

The weekend following the "lesbo" comment, Lily and Jane made T-shirts stenciled with the slogan "Anita Bryant sucks oranges." Despite their father's wishes, they showed up to school the following Monday wearing the T-shirts. It was a dig that everybody in school, including the coach, would recognize. The subtext was clear: "You suck, too, Coach Kenny."

Sometime after that, when rumors were running rampant about David and Betty, someone carved Betty's phone number into the wooden stands in the gymnasium with the word *SLUT*. With Jane standing guard at the glass doors that led to the gym, Lily managed to etch out the slur and phone number with her father's Swiss Army knife, which she had brought to school just for the occasion.

...

IT WAS A COLD January day, and it had snowed about six inches the night before. It would have been an ordinary Monday morning history class, but the final episode of *Roots* had aired the night before. The eight-night miniseries, which was watched by more than one hundred million people, followed a family during and after slavery in the United States.

"Why were all those Africans capturing other Africans?" asked Billy Dobbins.

Lily rolled her eyes and looked over at the boy, who just shrugged and looked down to doodle on his notes. The boy was more likely to cut Billy Dobbins some slack than Lily and the others were.

When David McCarren said, "I thought this was an honors class," everyone else laughed, including Lily.

David and Lily were the co-editors for the school yearbook. David's father was a wealthy lawyer, and they lived in Lawrence Farm, where all the doctors and lawyers in town lived. He never got over the fact that Lily wouldn't go out with him. In ninth grade at the Saint Barnabas fall social, he had asked her to dance and thought he had it made when the next song that played was Aerosmith's hit "Dream On," but after the second time he put his hand too close to her ass, she pushed him away and left him standing on the dance floor alone. He never had a chance once the boy asked Lily to dance that night.

"What about that scene when the slave master reads his Bible and just outside the plantation house are the sounds of a whip cracking? What sort of Christian sanctions that?" Lily said.

"Here we go again," said Pam Grey snarkily. The comment was said low and only meant for the few kids sitting in the back of the room, but others heard it, including Lily.

"I heard that," Lily said.

"I'm glad. You're such a conceited bitch."

"Hey, watch your mouth, Ms. Grey. We can discuss this without resorting to profanity," Mr. Kenny said. Before he could finish, Lily turned around and glared at Pam, who was sitting a few seats behind her. "Conceited? You call me conceited because I believe that the teachings of Christianity are incompatible with slavery."

"Oh right, as if that's an original idea. You weren't the only one in honors U.S. history," Pam fired back.

Lily turned around to face the front of the room and held up her middle finger.

"Well, Ephesians 6:5 says, 'Slaves, obey your earthly masters,' " Kevin Walsh said.

"Shut the fuck up, Walsh," said David.

"Don't get so worked up, man. It's just history," another boy added.

"What, do you have memory problems?" Lily replied, turning to face her classmate. "Just last year, the Boston PD used tear gas on protesters who didn't want their kids going to school with Black students."

And then the classroom got quiet, and some students turned to the back of the room where the only Black kid in class was sitting, a new boy named Tim Jones whose father was in the navy. Tim had moved to Portsmouth right before the Christmas break, so no one really knew what to make of him yet. For most kids in town, he was the first Black kid they had ever met. In the nearby town of Newport, half the kids at Rogers High School were Black, but in Portsmouth, which used to be potato-farming land, most families were white.

Coming to Lily's defense, David added, "Lily's right. Don't you people read the newspapers? In Southie, they're killing each other over desegregation. Staties have to patrol the schools. Hell, they even had to cancel a football season."

Lily glanced over at the boy, who was still drawing something in his notebook, and wondered how he could remain so calm. Didn't he care? The bell rang, and as they were moving through the crowded halls, Lily said, "You didn't seem to have much to say in class."

"What's the point?"

"How could you sit there and let those idiots go on like that? Fucking Kevin Walsh quoting the Bible, and Billy—"

The boy interrupted her. "Billy Dobbins's dad has hit him in the head so many times, Billy barely remembers his own name. Walsh is only in honors class because his racist dad is on the school committee."

He stopped at his locker and leaned against it.

"Okay, but still, why didn't you say something?" Lily asked. "Everybody in that room thinks you walk on water."

"Not McCarren." The boy took the stack of books and notebooks that Lily was carrying and put them on the top shelf of his locker.

"Who cares what he thinks? He's an entitled prick," Lily said.

Lily definitely thought that David McCarren was an asshole in terms of the way he treated Betty Barboza, but when it came to matters of race, he was one of the more outspoken liberal students in the school. She knew that it bothered the boy that David had come to Lily's defense.

Later that week, after the last bell rang, Lily and the boy were making their way down a newly shoveled sidewalk to Lily's car when they heard kids shouting near the tennis courts. It had snowed the night before, and the parking lot was clear minus the huge piles of snow created by the plows.

"I want to hear you say your name," shouted one of the students.

Three senior boys, all football players, had the new kid, Tim Jones, up against the fence; he was clutching his books to his chest. Tim was tall and lanky, and Lily assumed, not knowing anything about Tim's family other than his father was an officer at the War College, that Tim wore his hair cropped short to please his dad.

"What's your name? Say it!"

The boys had co-opted a line from a devastating scene in *Roots* in which a young slave boy hangs by his wrists as the overseer whips him, trying to get the boy to say his new slave name and reject his African past. Lily could see Tim looking for help or a way out. One of the boys started pushing Tim. "Who do you think you are, Kunta Kinte?"

"Aren't you going to do anything?" Lily asked the boy.

He reached over and pulled Lily's hat down over her ears; he then pulled his own leather jacket—lined with faux shearling—tight around his chest, holding it there without taking the time to zip it up. He studied her face carefully.

"They're not going to hurt him. They're just giving him a hard time."

"So you're just going to stand here and watch," Lily said. "What kind of person are you?"

"Those guys are my offensive linemen; we wouldn't have been state champions without those guys."

"What about all your talk about being a leader? Vince Lombardi this, Vince Lombardi that—*A man who belittles another is not a leader*," Lily quoted back to the boy.

The boy did his best to emulate qualities that Lombardi subscribed to—competitiveness, perfectionism, and discipline. In the face of victory, the boy showed humility. Even at eighteen, he knew enough not to gloat, and he always congratulated the other teams' captains after games. Yet Lily often wondered what it was that made him not take advantage of the influence he wielded given his status at school. She admired his unassuming nature, but today, something else motivated his unwillingness to help the new kid, some sort of code—like the kind that dictates an old boys' club, the kind her mother warned her about years ago.

Please go help him, she thought. *Show me you're one of the good men.*

"They're my teammates, Lil."

Lily yelled up to the boys, "Hey, what's going on?" In that instant, Tim made a break for it and ran toward Fort Butts, into the woods behind the school. The other boys chased him, slipping on the icy path. Leaving the boy behind in the parking lot, Lily ran toward the fort. By the time she got up the hill, the boy's teammates emerged from the woods, laughing. Tim was nowhere in sight.

PORTSMOUTH, RHODE ISLAND

FEBRUARY 1977

Mr. Webb never remarried. He managed Lily and Jane's teenage years alone. It was easier when they were younger and he could take them clam digging or owling or simply read one of Madeleine L'Engle's latest stories to them. He tolerated, although never understood, his daughters' generation's music, but he had to admit, given the number of times Jane played and replayed "What Is and What Should Never Be," it grew on him. On Sundays, when he didn't have to teach, he would play air guitar and dance around the kitchen just to hear them laugh while they ate pancakes together—probably the only meal they shared the entire week due to his teaching schedule and dorm responsibilities.

Jane had a life-size Robert Plant poster hanging in her bedroom, with his bare chest, tight hip-hugger jeans, wavy shoulder-length hair, and iconic bead necklace.

It wasn't any easier for him to listen to Lily's albums—"the girls," as he liked to call them: Carly Simon, Joni Mitchell, and Carole King—because the music reminded him of his wife. That river song, the one with the sad Christmas tune, got to him every time.

Jane, more so than Lily, reminded Mr. Webb of the hippies he used to see on the news protesting the war. He didn't begrudge the protesters, especially the students in Ohio; it was their America just as much as it was anyone's. But Mr. Webb believed with all his heart that his wife would have been better suited for the girls' adolescence.

When Jane was a junior, Mr. Webb got a call one afternoon from the school principal. Sitting in the administrator's office, both men were wearing dark suit coats and ties while Jane had on a burnt-orange suede coat lined with faux cream-colored fur. She wore the coat and a pair of oversize translucent orange sunglasses all the time. Jane dressed like a cross between a Led Zeppelin groupie and Gloria Steinem.

"Jane, please take off your sunglasses," Mr. Webb said before the meeting started. Then, turning to the principal, he added, "What's this all about?"

"It seems that Jane has been skipping classes and hanging out with the motorheads and mondos."

Mr. Webb made a face and asked, "Who?"

Before the principal could say anything, Jane said, "Motorhead is slang for predominantly working-class kids who aren't academically inclined. They have a proclivity toward auto mechanics—"

Mr. Webb interrupted his daughter. "I know what a motorhead is. I wasn't born yesterday. What's a mondo?"

"Mondos smoke a lot of weed," Jane said.

"A derelict?" Mr. Webb asked.

"Well, that largely depends on your perspective," she said.

"Yes," the principal interjected, "most definitely. Kids who aren't going anywhere. Burnouts. Potheads. Whatever you want to call them. My point is that Jane has huge potential. She could go to any school in the country. Extraordinarily gifted, but she may be messing up her opportunity by hanging out with the wrong crowd."

The principal and Mr. Webb both looked over at Jane.

"You both seem to be missing something. Just because a person is gifted, doesn't mean they want to be," Jane said.

...

VALENTINE'S DAY, 1977. MR. WEBB was at Saint Benet's dorm about two hundred yards from his house making sure the boarding students were studying and not sneaking out to the railroad tracks to get high or playing poker in one of the older boys' rooms. It was a school night and Jane was at the public library. Lily was a little taken aback when she heard a knock at the front door and, upon opening it, saw the boy standing there under the porch light with snowflakes in his hair and a dozen red roses in his arms. Instantly, she knew they were going to make love.

They had two hours before Jane would return from the library and Mr. Webb from dorm duty. The boy followed Lily upstairs to her room, admiring the way her jeans hugged her ass, and watched as she carefully set the flowers in a vase on her nightstand. Her hips and the shape of her breasts mesmerized him. The boy locked the bedroom door even though no one was home. He didn't want to take any chances. Once, Jane walked in when Lily was going down on him and Lily never heard the end of it. "Well, good morning, Linda Lovelace" and "Look who's been reading a little Henry Miller on the side," Jane teased. She wasn't policing Lily's sexuality; she was just having fun. Besides, by the time Jane graduated from high school a year later, you couldn't swing a dead cat in town without hitting one of her old boyfriends. When other girls called Jane a slut, her retort was, "I've never given a blow job to someone who didn't want one." She was rail thin, beautiful, and reckless with her long summer-blond hair and green eyes. Lily had inherited her mother's dark hair and curves.

The boy turned his attention to the books that lined one of the walls in Lily's bedroom—mainly books from her mother's collection—and leafed through a slender book of poems.

"Do you think she read all these?" he asked, looking up from the book.

He wasn't the kind of person who thought it was best to ignore the dead; Lily liked that about him.

"Absolutely. I never saw her without a book, even when she was cooking."

"She must have been really smart," the boy said. "What did she study in college?"

"English lit," Lily said. "She used to love to attend lectures at Pembroke by famous writers. When it closed in '71 and Brown went co-ed, she thought it was a great step toward gender equality."

The boy looked at her long and hard. He was checking in. Often, when the two spoke of their respective mothers, the boy or Lily might pause, just to make sure the other was okay.

Lily pulled an album out of its cover and put it on the record player. After the first five notes, the boy grabbed Lily from behind, spun her around, and said, "No, not again! How many times do we have to listen to this? Every time I come over, you put this on." Lily laughed and looked up at his face. She reached under his shirt, the tips of her fingers gliding over his rib cage. By the time Harry Nilsson got to the chorus, the boy had pulled his shirt off and crooned along, *"I can't live, if living is without you."*

He unbuckled his belt. To Lily, his muscles and lower abs looked and felt as though they were carved in stone. Against his collarbone sat a green-and-white beaded necklace that Lily had made for him. Outside, the wind blew, spinning the snow around. It was supposed to be a light dusting, but about two inches had accumulated on the ground.

"Let's—" The phone rang, interrupting the boy. They both looked over at it beside the bed. It was turquoise blue and marketed as a "princess phone." It rang again and then stopped. He glanced past the phone to two photos, framed, on Lily's nightstand. One was of Lily, Jane, and their mother all dressed up for Easter Sunday, and the other was of him; a newspaper photographer had taken it last fall, and Lily had gotten a copy. It was a shot of him standing on the field after a big game holding a football over his head. If someone didn't know him, they would have thought he was a typical athlete consumed by victory, but in the instant the photo was taken, he was thinking, *Where's my girl? I gotta find my girl.* And, of course, when he scanned the football fans, there she was, up against the fence with her arm around his father, both of them waving and waving.

The boy took Lily's face in both his hands. He kissed her lips and moved down to her neck. He was a generous lover. When Lily's head hit the pillow, she caught the scent of the roses; moments later, she grabbed the sheets and the monastery's chapel bell tolled while his face was between her legs. When Lily was good and wet, the boy sat on the edge of the bed hunched over. Lily, who was still laying down, reached over and ran the tip of her finger down his back. She knew he was putting on a condom, but it was taking longer than she expected. "Do you need help?" she asked. The boy chuckled. "I got it."

As he moved inside her for the first time, Lily took a deep breath and held onto his shoulders. He only managed to last a minute, and after he came, he choked back his tears.

Once fully dressed, Lily pulled her hair back. Using an elastic band she picked up from her nightstand, she put her hair in a ponytail while the boy sat on the edge of the bed, tying his boots. She thought it would be best to open her bedroom door just in case her father returned home earlier than expected. But the young lovers had never heard the front door open. Mr. Webb was already home.

"Lily, are you up there?" he said from the foot of the stairs.

Lily shot a look at the boy, smoothed out her hair, and said, "I'll be right down."

Neither of them moved, their wide eyes locked on each other. Time seemed suspended. They were both still a little elated from the adrenaline—from the intimacy and now this. Lily moved first. She took a deep breath and walked out of the bedroom and down the stairs. The boy followed her.

Mr. Webb was standing in the kitchen. He looked the boy up and down, homing in on his pants, just below his waist. The boy instantly put his hand over his lower abdomen, checking his zipper. It was undone. The boy was mortified. Just as his eyes met Mr. Webb's, the phone rang. It was Jane calling from the library; she needed a ride home. Lily seemed not to have noticed the exchange between her father and boyfriend. She handed the boy his coat and ran back upstairs to retrieve her winter boots. Typically, the boy would have tried to make small talk with Lily's dad—they had a cordial relationship, the boy was respectful, and Mr. Webb was friendly and had come to a few of the boy's games—but Mr. Webb had turned his back on him.

Once his daughter was upstairs and out of earshot, Mr. Webb turned back to the boy and said through his teeth, "I swear, you'd better be using rubbers, or your ass is grass and I'm a lawn mower."

The comment was laughable given that the boy towered over Mr. Webb, but nobody was laughing. Lily's father opened a cabinet and grabbed a bottle of scotch from the highest shelf. He poured himself a shot and sat down on his recliner in the living room in the dark.

When Lily came back downstairs, she headed right out the side door. The boy was still standing in the kitchen, dumbfounded. But before he left the house, he walked over to the entrance to the living room and said, "Mr. Webb." Lily's dad remained silent. "I just want you to know, I plan on marrying your daughter."

...

THAT WINTER THERE WERE snowball fights on the football field, a senior ski trip to Mount Snow, the pervasiveness of Fleetwood Mac's *Rumours*, and—at least for Lily and the boy—spontaneous sex in the music room. They were so full of love and energy and felt so distant from life's inevitable inheritances of pain and loss. At least until late spring.

PORTSMOUTH, RHODE ISLAND

APRIL 1977

Lily waited on the side of the road to take the 60 bus from Portsmouth to Providence, a forty-five-minute ride. She had left school that afternoon as soon as the bell rang without telling Jane or the boy where she was going. She paid the fare and caught a whiff of an older man in one of the front seats—in his sixties, unshaven, and wearing dirty pants. He glanced at the seat next to him and then became animated, talking and gesturing and saying things that didn't make sense. Lily looked across the aisle at an older Black woman, who looked back at Lily and shrugged. *Poor guy,* Lily thought. *My problem pales compared to this guy's.*

She was a month late for her period and couldn't wait any longer to find out. The woman on the phone at Planned Parenthood had given her directions from the bus station to 46 Aborn Street. Lily looked out the window as the bus drove over the Mount Hope Bridge; it was a warm spring day and there were plenty of sailboats and powerboats in the bay. Lily was nervous, but she took in the coastal towns, the shimmering water, and the small harbors on the way into the city.

She knew the building. She and her mother had driven by it when she was younger. Mrs. Webb had told her that good people had been dispensing birth control out of that building for a long time. The memory comforted Lily. Were her mother's lessons on local feminist history her way of imparting knowledge Lily might one day need— one day when she wouldn't be there to help her? Did her mother know she wouldn't live long enough to see Lily through something like this? It was the kind of forward thinking she wouldn't have put past her, and Lily felt a bit of consolation with this realization. But she would rather have had her mother sitting there with her, holding her hand.

The older man up front disrupted her thoughts when he blurted out a delusional claim that his dick had painted the clouds in the sky. "That's enough," the bus driver said. "Nobody wants to hear that kind of talk today."

...

SHE TOLD THE BOY she was pregnant a few nights later when they were sitting in his car in the high school parking lot after baseball practice. The boy was silent; he took a few deep breaths but couldn't say anything. Lily knew he was trying not to say the wrong thing. Recently, one of his teammates had gotten a girl pregnant and insisted she have an abortion, saying it was the only option. But the girl refused, and instead her mother sent her away to a convent in Florida where she had the baby and gave it up for adoption.

The boy reached for Lily's hand, and the only thing he managed to say was "How are you feeling?"

"I don't want you to worry; I'm having an abortion. I've already thought it through—it's not an issue. I'm not ready to be a mother, and there's no way that you can play football and go to college and raise a baby."

They sat in silence for a while watching others on the field mill around.

"I want to go with you," the boy said. "I want to drive you, and I'm paying for it," he insisted.

He had turned so his back was against the car door, while Lily looked straight ahead.

"My mom and I used to watch *Maude* together. We used to curl up on the couch under the same blanket and eat popcorn, just the two of us. Do you remember the abortion episode?"

The boy was listening and watching Lily carefully. "I didn't see it when it originally aired," the boy said. "But I remember watching it at Head's house with his sisters the summer before we started high school. It was a rerun."

Mrs. Webb had used every opportunity to impart lessons to her daughters that fall of 1972. In the episode, Bea Arthur's character gets pregnant at forty-seven and decides to have an abortion, which was legal in New York, where the show took place. Lily watched every minute of the two-part episode with her mom beside her. They had aired the same month she died.

"My mom told me that legalizing abortion would change every-thing. It would mean true independence for women."

"I get it. You're lucky, Lil. You really knew your mom. I couldn't tell you one thing my mom believed in." The boy reached over and stroked Lily's head, then he played with her hair.

Lily turned to look at him. He had a way of allowing for moments when memories of her mother became his own. With him, Lily felt her mom's presence honored.

"Do you think I'll be allowed in the room with you? I want to be there."

She gave the boy a faint smile. "I doubt it," she said.

Lily was incredibly aware of the rapidly changing gender roles—what it meant to be a woman—exploding around her. She was the product of revolutionary discourse, and her mother had highlighted the struggle at home when she told Lily that pregnancy was not a biological inevitability.

…

LILY SAT IN THE waiting room with a Black girl and the girl's mother and a younger white girl who couldn't have been more than fifteen. The girl and her mother sat close together looking over a magazine. The mother looked up and smiled at Lily when their eyes met, but all three girls avoided making eye contact. Lily thought, *It shouldn't have to be this way.* Lily knew that if the girls were waiting for a dentist, they would have at least acknowledged one another. Maybe even engaged in some chitchat. *What school do you go to? Do you know so-and-so?* That sort of talk. Lily was nervous, but she felt some sense of responsibility toward the girls. So when the Black girl's name was called and the mother and daughter got up to follow the nurse, Lily tried talking to the younger girl.

"Are you doing okay?" Lily asked.

Without looking up from the magazine she was thumbing through, the girl said, "Yeah."

Lily didn't give up; she felt she owed it to all those women who had worked to make abortion legal to help make this girl comfortable.

"Do you have someone picking you up?"

"No, I'm taking the bus."

"Well, if you don't mind my boyfriend's old car, we'll drive you."

"You don't even know where I live," the girl said, looking up.

"It's a small state."

The girl finally smiled.

"Don't be scared," Lily told the girl. "And don't be ashamed."

Hours later—after being seen and treated by several people in white coats, doing their best to forget the sounds of suctions and the sensations of speculums, and still a bit groggy—Lily and the young girl walked out of Planned Parenthood together, into the parking lot and a bright spring sun. She asked the girl to wait on the sidewalk for a minute and then knocked on the boy's car window. Lily saw that he had been crying. She motioned for him to roll down the window.

"Everything is okay, but you can't be crying about this," she said as she leaned in to kiss his head.

The boy wiped his eyes and looked over at the young girl standing on the sidewalk waiting for them.

"Who is that?"

"We're going to give her a ride home. She came here all by her-self."

Normally, the boy would've introduced himself and asked the girl her name, but under the circumstances, he thought he should respect her privacy.

"I think a trip to McDonald's is in order," the boy said.

The girl was sitting behind Lily, and every once in a while, she glanced at the boy, trying to figure out how she knew him.

"What's your favorite kind of milkshake?" he asked the girl. "Chocolate or vanilla?"

When he came back to the car, he had two vanilla shakes and two large fries for Lily and the girl, who offered to pay for her share, but the boy wouldn't take it. When they pulled into her driveway in Bar-rington, there were no cars. It looked as if no one was home. Before the girl got out, Lily repeated some of the instructions the nurse had given them.

"Take it easy, remember, don't exert yourself, and it's okay to take something for the cramps. If you get a fever, which I don't think you will, you have to call the doctor, okay?"

Lily had turned around in her seat to look at the girl. The girl had her hand on the car door handle, but before she got out, she looked at the boy and said, "You're that football player from Portsmouth, right?"

The boy smiled. "Yeah."

"Is this your boyfriend?" the girl asked, looking at Lily.

"Yeah."

"You're really lucky," she said to Lily, and as she got out of the car, she turned to the boy and said, "My dad says that you're gonna go on to play professional."

Lily leaned on the boy's shoulder as he drove down Route 114 back to Portsmouth. They listened to WBRU on the radio and didn't talk much. When Lily reached down to undo her jeans and zipper, he asked if she was okay. The cramps were constant and she felt a bit nauseated, but there was no need to tell him; he was already an emotional wreck.

"My jeans are too tight, that's all."

As they were driving through Bristol, a small coastal town, Bob Seger's "Night Moves" came on the radio, and the boy reached over to turn it up.

"You don't even like this song," Lily said.

"I know, but you do, baby."

And as they climbed the Mount Hope Bridge over the Narragansett Bay, they belted out Lily's favorite lines together. She believed the boy might really be one of the good men. She needn't have worried.

...

Never one to be inspired by domestic chores, Jane didn't know how to cook, so that even at sixteen, she could barely boil an egg; she would have been fine living on bread and butter as long as she had math problems to solve. Still, she insisted on making dinner for Lily and the boy when they returned that night from Providence. Mr. Webb was required to attend the weekly sit-down dinner with all the students at the boarding school, so it would be just the three of them. Lily and the boy returned an hour earlier than expected.

Standing in the kitchen, Jane asked, "How long should I cook a six-dollar chicken?"

"How much does it weigh?" the boy asked.

"I don't know. How much does a six-dollar chicken usually weigh?"

"Oh my God, Jane! What am I gonna do with you?" Lily said from the couch. "The outside of the package should tell you how much the fucking chicken weighs."

"All I know is that it's pretty big, and its wings—at least I think it's the wings—are hanging over the side of the pan."

"You didn't put a whole chicken in one of the small square brownie pans, did you?" Lily asked her sister.

"I might have."

Jane picked up the pan with the chicken and walked past Lily and the boy—who was applying a heating pad to Lily's belly—to head upstairs.

"Where are you going with the chicken?" the boy asked.

"I have to weigh it," Jane said matter-of-factly.

"But where?"

"The bathroom scale."

It was the first time Lily had laughed aloud in several days.

Weeks later, Lily returned to Providence to get on birth control, and when she and the boy had sex again, Lily started to cry right after the boy came; he was still breathing heavy in her ear and had come to rest on top of her with his elbows bent. He felt her tears on the side of his face.

PORTSMOUTH, RHODE ISLAND

MAY 1977

It was a clear day in late May and the water was calm. Lily and the boy had taken one of the old wooden dinghies from the boarding school over to Prudence Island, one in a series of islands in Narragansett Bay that also included Patience and Hope. Over the years, it was always a big deal when the older boys from the boarding school, accompanied by a rowboat, swam from island to island.

The boy brought up the oars when they were halfway to the island, resting them in the oarlocks. As they faced each other, Lily read aloud from *Moby-Dick;* she was close to finishing chapter 1. The boy listened attentively but also took in the view: To the north was the Mount Hope Bridge, the suspension bridge that connected Portsmouth to the mainland, and to the south was the mouth of the bay and Newport.

A slight wind picked up out of the southwest so that when the boy stopped rowing, the boat rocked and moved with the current. A large gray gull circled above them. Lily stopped reading and rested the book in her lap. As they drifted in the bay, Lily admired her boyfriend's legs, long and all muscle. Even his thighs were cut. She tucked her own legs under the bow seat to make room for his. He was wearing a fitted gray T-shirt—tight around his arms, accentuating his biceps. Relaxed and in his element, he leaned over the boat and dropped his hand into the water.

"Why did you stop? You're coming to one of my favorite lines," the boy said.

Lily looked down at the book. There were only two paragraphs left of the first chapter, and before she could figure out which line was one of his favorites, he said, "*I love to sail forbidden seas, and land on barbarous coasts.*"

"Did you memorize the whole book?" Lily asked, laughing.

The boy simply looked back at her and smiled.

"Did you ever hear the story about the Anthony family, who tried to take a little boat like this one to the island?"

"No, but keep reading," the boy said.

"Why don't you want to hear the story?"

"Because what you're reading is a much better story."

"Oh my God, how do you know?"

The boy had been trying to get Lily to read *Moby-Dick* since the fall when he took an elective on nineteenth-century literature and she took one on astronomy.

"My story happened close to one hundred years ago and it's true. Not like your whale story."

"My whale story, as you call it, is one of the greatest books ever written."

Lily made a face indicating she was not convinced, prompting the boy to give a little speech. "The story opens in New Bedford, right down the street. It's about a search for an enigmatic white whale, a voyage around the world that takes years."

Lily didn't pout but she surely didn't appreciate the boy's patronizing tone. When she looked down to find her place in the book, the boy said, "I'm sorry, Lil, tell me the story."

Lily looked up at him. And while it wasn't her intention, her gaze was both charming and seductive.

"Come on, tell me," he said once more.

"At the turn of the century—" she began, but the boy interrupted her.

"Is this a long story?"

"Stop it," she said, as she swung her foot out to playfully kick the side of his leg. "A local man had taken his wife and two children out in a small boat headed to Prudence Island to pick blueberries. The boat capsized, and one of the parents managed to put the smallest child, an infant, in a baby carriage and support it with the oars. The baby, the only one to survive, washed ashore."

"No way," the boy said. "That's wild. And it's fucking sad. Thinking that you have it all, and then *bang*! Everything's gone."

"There's a tombstone in Saint Paul's cemetery marking where the family was buried. The baby went to live with an old wealthy aunt in the estate across from Reidy's."

"No shit," the boy said. "The mansion?"

Lily seemed impressed with herself—that her story was better than the boy had anticipated.

"Now it's your turn to read, and I'll row," she said.

Carefully, they changed positions, and Lily took up the oars. She had learned to row at an early age. With her hands parallel to the boat, gripping the oars, she allowed her legs to do most of the work. She got herself into a nice rhythm. Around the time the boy was halfway through reading chapter 3 and just at the part in *Moby-Dick* where the landlord of the Spouter-Inn tries to explain to Ishmael that the harpooner is out selling shrunken heads, Lily stopped rowing.

"Look over there," Lily told the boy. "What do you think that is?"

Something was moving along the surface of the water.

"It's a seal," the boy said.

As Lily got closer, they could see brown-and-white fur bobbing in the water.

"Oh no, it's a deer, and I think it's drowning," Lily said.

The boy took over rowing—reaching and pulling hard—and when they were a few feet from the small animal, without telling Lily what his plans were, the boy jumped into the water. He wrapped one of his arms around the backside of the deer, and with his other arm, he managed to lift the fawn's head out of the water. Turning over, he floated on his back and kicked gently. The young deer was too tired to struggle.

"Should we try to get it in the boat?" Lily shouted.

The boy turned his head to see how much farther it was to the shore. "I can make it," he told Lily.

He swam toward the shore like this, and when he could touch bottom, he stood and carried the fawn the rest of the way. The poor thing struggled to stand, its front legs buckling.

Lily dragged the dinghy to shore a good twenty feet from where the boy and the small animal were resting. Not wanting to scare it, she watched as the boy crouched down next to the fawn and stroked its sides in silence. It was in shock, its ears were twitching, and it started bleating like a baby goat or lamb. After a few minutes, the fawn stood and took off into the dune grass.

"The poor thing lost its mother," Lily said.

"It's a good thing you spotted it."

"Do you think a coyote will get her?" Lily asked.

"Let's try not to think about it."

But she couldn't help it. The irony of the scene struck her: the drowning motherless fawn, its panic, the way the boy jumped in—it could have been them. But they had rescued each other.

They retrieved their belongings from the rowboat and headed toward the lighthouse. Lily had packed lunch in her mother's old picnic basket—peanut butter and jelly sandwiches and homemade chocolate chip cookies.

The lighthouse was about thirty feet tall—an octagonal tower built from granite blocks painted white and topped with a black birdcage lantern. It was up from the sandy beach, surrounded by brown dune grass and beach shrubs. After lunch, Lily and the boy lay on their stomachs on towels.

"My father asked me if I wanted to invite my mother to graduation," the boy said.

"What did you tell him?"

"I told him no."

"You don't want to see her."

The boy took a deep breath and sighed. "When I was little, I'd lay in bed at night before big events like my birthday and Christmas hoping she would surprise me, just once. I spent my childhood wishing she would come visit. She never did. If she was to show up now, it would just mess things up." He paused and looked at Lily. "Even though we both grew up without moms, I bet your mom held on to her life with both hands. Mine just let go. What kind of mother leaves a six-year-old boy behind?"

"A desperate one," Lily said.

"What the fuck does that mean?"

"I mean a sad one . . . a selfish one," Lily said.

But by then she didn't know what she meant; competing ideas circulated in Lily's mind. There were so few options for people like Mrs. Cooper in the late fifties. No birth control. Few opportunities. A woman was either a mother or a spinster. Can you blame some of these women? But then when she looked into the brown eyes of the boy next to her, his loss was palpable. Imagine coming home when you're in kindergarten and being told that Mommy's gone—or worse, watching her practically run out the door, suitcase in hand, and jumping into another man's car while your dad begs her not to leave.

Lily watched the boy as he reached for the copy of *Moby-Dick* and flipped through the opening chapters. His hair—made wavy from the water and the wind whipping around the lighthouse—hung in front of his face. She looked at the muscles of his wrists and forearms. Every part of him toned, well-conditioned. Trained for agility and strength. He was beautiful.

"Where were we?" he asked absentmindedly, continuing to turn the pages of the book.

"I need you to explain something," Lily said. Part of her wanted to distract him from the sadness that had pulled him away from her. But she was also genuinely curious about what was happening in the scene in the novel where they had left off.

"What did the landlord mean when he said that the harpooner is out peddling his head?" As she asked this, Lily looked as if she was uncertain she wanted the boy to explain it to her.

The boy laughed. "Not his own head or blow jobs; he's talking about shrunken heads."

She had him now; he seemed to have recovered from the thoughts of his mother.

"I can't believe you've never read *Moby-Dick*. This summer we're going to finish it together. The harpooner is a good guy named Queequeg. He's from the South Seas and he sells shrunken heads on the streets of New Bedford."

The boy laughed again at the face Lily was making. She had lowered her eyebrows, and her eyes were completely shut, as if to shut out the image.

"That's messed up," Lily said.

"No, it's actually a really cool part of the book," the boy said.

"Shrunken heads?" Lily said in disbelief.

"No, wait. You see, Ishmael and Queequeg couldn't be more different: Queequeg has black geometric tattoos on his face and body and worships a dark wooden figure—"

"Okay, but I need to know about the heads."

"That's not important."

"Just tell me."

"Maybe Melville needed an example of something that was totally different—and what could be more different from Christianity than headhunting? I mean, there's that whole thing about the Eucharist as a form of cannibalism, but for Melville, Queequeg's character on the ship, along with others, is about democracy, a society based on plurality . . . and the coolest thing is he wrote this in 1851."

"Can we go back to the shrunken heads? Why do they hunt heads and how do they shrink them?"

"I don't know why they hunt them, and I guess they boil the heads in hot water."

"Do you think there are people who still do that?"

"Maybe, but that's not the point. The point is, we need to focus on our common humanity, not our differences."

PORTSMOUTH, RHODE ISLAND

JUNE 1977

When Jimmy Sullivan ran through the cafeteria—in one door, around the tables, and out the other, wearing only a ski mask to hide his easily recognizable dark curly hair—the upperclassmen went nuts, cheering, clapping, and standing on the chairs to get a better look. No one could figure out who it was. "Is it Tom Mandis?" someone shouted. "It's Bobby Rogers!" said another. Jane, who was standing on one of the lunchroom chairs, yelled, "No, it's Jimmy Sullivan. I'd recognize that dick anywhere."

A few days later, at the senior talent show, the boy performed "American Pie." The audience was still as he began to play, but by the time he got to the chorus for the second time, everyone in the auditorium was singing along.

It was the last month of school, which meant graduation was imminent and their daily lives together would soon change forever. The boy had accepted a scholarship to attend the University of Michigan.

Lily was accepted to Smith, an all-women's college in Massachusetts. They would be twelve hours apart by car. The thought of not seeing the boy every day was unbearable for Lily. Unbeknownst to her father, she intended on transferring to the large Midwestern school after her first year.

...

IT WAS THE SEASON of high school pranks, and Lily and her friends were intent on wringing life dry. It had been a senior tradition to paint the class year on the slanted roof of an old barn near the school. There were just a few problems: It had to be done at night; Mrs. Pacheco, a nosy old woman, lived in a yellow Cape close to the barn; and somebody needed to bring a ladder from home without getting caught. On top of that, a guy named Richie from the class of 1976 had fallen off the barn and broken an arm the year before, and his parents threatened to sue the school. So this year, the dean of discipline, Vice Principal Carr, made it clear that any student caught vandalizing the barn would be suspended and not be allowed to attend the senior prom or graduation ceremony. (Lily and Jane thought the threat had more to do with the fact that a member of the covert group had also painted "Carr Sucks" on the upper-right corner of the roof.)

The group was made up of senior boys—Jimmy Sullivan, Head, the boy, and Tim Jones, whom the boy had invited—plus Lily and Jane, who was going out with Jimmy at the time. Ever since that day in winter when Tim was being harassed near the tennis courts, the boy had gone out of his way to make friends with him.

The night concealed them. Nothing truly bad would ever happen to any of them. They were living out the age-old story of thrill-seeking teenagers who believe social rewards outweigh risk. They couldn't put a name to it, but they felt immortal; at least they thought they were when they started the clandestine operation on a Saturday night in June.

They parked Jimmy's truck about a quarter of a mile away, and the guys took turns carrying the ladder through the fields abutting the campus. It was Lily's idea to wear dark clothing, except that Head had showed up wearing white painter's pants. With only one or two streetlights on—the others were burnt or smashed out—the school grounds were particularly dark. There were no cars. No evening student events. There was no one around. A few porch lights were on, scattered around the periphery of the high school property. Jimmy Sullivan steadied the twelve-foot wooden ladder against the side of the barn. The girls stood watch—on the lookout for local police patrolling the school or anyone else who wouldn't approve of their prank. The boy held the ladder while Jimmy, Tim, and Head climbed up to the roof of the barn. Before climbing the ladder himself, the boy adjusted it to ensure it was on level ground. The boy and Jimmy carried cans of paint; Tim and Head had paintbrushes and a few old putty knives in their back pockets to open the cans. Once the boys made it to the roof, they got to work. The words "class of" had already been painted in ten-foot letters by past students. This year, they could've just painted over the old ten-foot numeral 6, but it was Jane's idea to use a different color than the previous class, and she talked Jimmy into buying "patriot red." Now they had to first paint over the '76 and then paint '77. The boy couldn't believe that Jimmy had conceded to this plan, which would take longer and therefore be riskier. *Jimmy is definitely hoping to get laid tonight,* the boy thought.

Jane and Lily were about fifty yards away from each other lying on their bellies in the grass.

After about ten minutes, Jane abandoned her post and walked over to her sister. "I gotta go to the bathroom," Jane told Lily.

"Jesus, Jane. You should've thought about that before you left the house."

"Well, I didn't have to go before I left the house. I have to go now."

Jane squatted near the edge of Mrs. Pacheco's garden and Lily stood watch. Nobody thought that old lady Pacheco's dog would have to take a piss before they finished painting. Once the dog started barking, the old lady yelled, "Who's out there?" She aimed her flashlight on the girls and caught Jane's ass in the beam of light.

"I'm calling the cops," Mrs. Pacheco shouted.

The girls ran toward the barn to warn the others.

"We have to get out of here," the boy said.

"Almost done," Tim said in a voice barely audible. He was busy painting something else near the apex of the roof.

When Tim was finished, the boys scooted along the slanted roof to get to the ladder.

As Tim and Jimmy climbed down, the girls noticed that the backs of their pants were covered in wet paint. The boy was on the top rung of the ladder when he saw that Head hadn't moved.

"I'm stuck," Head said.

"Come on!" Lily yelled from down below.

"What do you mean you're stuck?" the boy said.

"It's my pants." Head tried to shift from side to side.

"The cops will be here any second," Jimmy said.

"You can't leave me here," said Head.

"I'm not gonna leave you. Just take off your goddamn pants."

"Can't. I can't move my ass. I'm caught on a nail."

Everyone heard panic in Head's voice. Tim climbed back up the ladder, and it took both boys to get Head out of his pants.

"Car!" Jane shouted.

A pair of headlights appeared from the access road closest to the football field, and Mrs. Pacheco was now out in her garden shining a flashlight in the direction of the barn. Jimmy held the ladder.

"Hurry," Lily pleaded.

Tim and the boy each grabbed an end of the ladder, and they all started running up past the tennis courts and down a windy footpath to the old fort, Head wearing only his underwear. Through the trees, in the distance, they saw a second pair of headlights. Lily led them to an embankment where they crouched and hid. After a few minutes, their legs grew tired from squatting, and they sat down on the leaves and brush. Lily leaned into the boy.

Nobody spoke. They were trying to catch their breath. Crickets and cicadas chirped. Twigs snapped under the steps of a deer or coyote. There was very little growth—some bitternut and large poplars and a cluster of birch trees. Just enough for cover in the dark. Jane was the first one to speak, whispering to Tim.

"This is where the British fought the Continental Army. Right here."

"No way," said Tim quietly.

Jimmy added, "One of my ancestors was General Sullivan; he led the Battle of Rhode Island right here in this very spot."

"Would you guys shut the fuck up," Head said. "We're gonna get arrested."

"Nobody's going to get arrested," said the boy.

Rustling sounds, then an evening love song of a bachelor mockingbird followed by the constant call of a whippoorwill.

Jane lit a cigarette, cupping the flame under her hand, and whispered, "Mrs. White is psychic, and she told us she hears soldiers at night and once saw a wounded man carrying a musket in her kitchen."

"Don't listen to her, Tim. Mrs. White is crazy," Lily said. "Like Newport-Hospital-eighth-floor crazy."

"You just don't like her because she said that you two wouldn't last, that you aren't meant to be," Jane said, gesturing to her sister and the boy.

"I'm really allergic to poison ivy," Head announced, scratching his ass.

The boy looked at Lily. "Why didn't you tell me you saw Mrs. White?"

"Shhh," Lily said.

The boy was right; Lily hadn't told him that she went to see the fortune-teller. Mrs. White knew things that the girl had never told anyone, but when the fortune-teller told Lily that she would never marry the boy, Lily freaked out and then convinced herself that Mrs. White was a scam artist.

"Why didn't you tell me about Mrs. White?" the boy asked again.

Lily lied. "Jane got it wrong."

But really, the thought of what the old woman had said about her future made her shiver.

"We need to split up the group," the boy told the others. "We'll leave the ladder here for a couple of nights. Jimmy and Jane, you head toward Dyer Street. Lily and Head, wait here for twenty minutes and then head down Education Lane."

"But why do we have to wait? I'm the one in my underwear."

Ignoring Head, the boy said, "I just think it'll be less suspicious if a cop sees two people walking together than a group of us. Jimmy, gimme your keys."

"But I'm in my underwear."

Jimmy reached into his pocket and tossed the boy his keys.

"Tim and I will make a run for the truck and pick you guys up."

The boy and Tim stood slowly. No headlights in sight. They took an access road that circled the fort. When they got to Sprague Street, David McCarren drove by, and the boy flagged him down. McCarren's

1975 Pontiac Grand Ville stopped in the middle of the road and then backed up.

"Hey, man, you two playing cowboys and Indians? You got paint on your face," said a kid in the passenger side to Tim.

Tim tried to wipe the paint off.

"Can you give us a lift?" the boy asked.

"No fucking way, you guys are covered in paint," David said.

"Come on, man, we need a lift."

"Did you just paint the barn?" asked the kid in the front seat.

McCarren laughed. "Sorry, man, not this time."

"Suck my dick," Tim yelled as the car sped away and he and the boy were left standing in the dark on the side of the road.

That Monday, when Lily and the boy were driving to school, they approached the campus from the north so they could admire their handiwork. There on the barn, painted in ten-foot letters, read, "Class of '77." It was only then that they both noticed that "Carr Sucks" had been painted over.

"It must've been Tim," the boy said.

"Fucking brilliant," Lily said. "A contingency plan in the event that we were caught. He painted over 'Carr Sucks' to mitigate the retribution."

The boy chuckled and said, " 'To mitigate the retribution'? You're the one who's brilliant." He put his arm around the girl and pulled her in for a long kiss. "I love you, Lily Webb."

Later in the morning, between second and third periods to be exact, Tim and the boy were walking down the hallway together. When they turned the corner, Mr. Carr was approaching them with a smirk on his face that made them nervous. *There's no way he can prove it was us,* the boy thought. He and Tim slowed down a bit as Carr got closer.

"Nice job, boys," Carr said as he walked past them.

"How did he know it was us?" Tim asked.

"Fucking McCarren," the boy said.

...

IN THE AFTERNOON A few days later, when the school was empty except for the janitors and a few kids from the theater club, Lily and David were working in one of the classrooms trying to organize the yearbook orders. David kept making salacious comments, and Lily was growing increasingly uncomfortable. First, he tried flirting. Complimenting her ideas, her organizational skills. When that didn't work, he resorted to being crude. A tactic of entitled boys.

"Are you sucking his cock?" David said, closing his eyes, pushing his cheek out with his tongue so it bulged, and pumping his closed fist back and forth near his mouth.

"You really look like you know what you're doing there," Lily said.

Apparently, that was the wrong thing to say.

When Lily tried to leave the room, he came up from behind her and held the door shut with one hand. Lily turned around to confront him, and he pushed her against the door, shoving his meaty tongue down her throat. He grabbed one of her breasts so hard that it ached for days after. When she told the boy what had happened the next day, he walked across the cafeteria at lunch and punched David in the face. Some of the guys from the football team had to pull the boy off David. Lily had conflicting feelings about the boy's reaction. She liked that he was protective of her. It was reassuring. But she worried that he would get in trouble. And she wasn't entirely sure how she felt about how quick he was to fight.

The next morning, both boys and their fathers met with the principal. This was the first time the boy had ever gotten into trouble, and he was ashamed of his father, who was disheveled and mildly drunk, while David's father wore a suit with cuff links. He was a well-respected lawyer—a really good one and not the type you wanted working against you. Each and every time David got into trouble at school—talking back to a teacher, repeated tardiness, smoking in the bathroom—father defended son. In the meeting that morning, the lawyer's glare gave off a warning. Nothing was said about what David had done to Lily, about her aching breast.

PORTSMOUTH, RHODE ISLAND

JULY 1977

One night, a month after graduation, the boy pulled up to the old campgrounds near the beach. In the car next to his, he saw a couple going at it in the back seat; somewhat visible through the foggy windows, the girl was on top, her shoulders bare. The boy tried not to look. He wore a pair of low-cut Levi's that Lily liked best, his crewneck varsity sweater, and a brown leather belt she had given him for Christmas. Lily had been offered a babysitting job that night but turned it down. She didn't know he was going to show up at the party; he planned on surprising her. Plus, he thought she had been getting a little too hammered at the past couple of keg parties post-graduation. He was concerned and had told her so, but she had replied, "I can take care of myself." He knew Lily was anxious about the fall and what lay after, her plan of transferring to Michigan and moving even farther away from her sister and father. But it was a sacrifice he hoped she was still willing to make.

While the boy worried about Lily's partying, Lily worried about

Jane. Going off to college wasn't as exciting as it should have been for Lily because part of her felt like she was abandoning her sister. It made her nervous to think that her closest friends would be moving away, heading off to college, and Jane would be left alone. Who would make sure she got home safe on Saturday nights? Lily couldn't share her concerns with her dad because she thought she would be betraying her sister. After all, she partied, too.

Their friends smoked weed and drank, but they avoided the harder stuff. Jane, however, was drawn to anything that would bring her to oblivion. Weeks before, on graduation night, Wavy Davey, a local dealer, had offered her PCP. "It's angel dust," he said, as he passed her a pin-thin joint. To which Jane responded, "Sounds divine." But before she could reach for it, the boy jumped in and said, "Stay away from that shit! It's horse tranquilizer." She hadn't. But Lily never blamed Jane. When it came to other people's questionable choices, Lily was able to look beyond—at the social and emotional conditions structuring their lives—though it would take years for her to do the same for herself.

The boy smelled weed coming from the beach as soon as he opened his car door. He surveyed the scene, looking for Lily. A crowd had gathered near a bonfire and burning ash fluttered upward in the dark. Cars were parked haphazardly with headlights shining on two drunken girls walking arm in arm. Kids were sitting on the hoods of cars, draped over each other, with a sophomore in bell-bottom jeans so stoned she had to close her eyes. A red Camaro pulled up next to him. Latecomers, like the boy. Five kids crawled out of the back of the car; one after the other, they kept coming.

One of his defensive linemen, Big Ted, leaned up against his car with a gorgeous girl from Jane's class who wore a daisy flower crown in her hair. The boy had to pass by them to get to the bonfire.

Ted yelled, "Hey, everybody, look who's here!" This announcement was followed by cheers from the crowd.

"Hey, man," Ted said, raising his hand for a high five.

The boy returned the gesture. "Have you seen Lily?"

"Yeah, but it was a while ago," Ted said. "But look, there's Jane."

Sure enough, the boy spotted Jane, her head thrown back and with it a fifth of Jack. She was wearing a suede halter and high-waisted white cords. From some other car's eight track, Lou Reed's "Sweet Jane" played. The good version—the one from *Rock n Roll Animal*. Jane danced alone, swaying to the music. Like every other guy in the school, the boy thought Jane was attractive, but he also sensed that there was something exceptionally vulnerable about her that concerned him the way a big brother might be concerned for a younger sister. But in that moment, he was focused on finding Lily.

"Hey, Head, seen Lily?" the boy asked.

"I saw her on the beach."

The boy spotted David McCarren, who was coming from the direction of the dunes. David stopped in his tracks and for a second appeared taken aback, caught off guard. He collected himself rather quickly and said, "Are you looking for Lily? She's up in the dunes. I just washed the stink of her pussy off my hands."

The boy heard a girl groan and whimper. About thirty feet off the path, in the dunes, he found Lily with her dress up and on all fours, and she wasn't wearing underwear. She started dry heaving and rocking back and forth on her knees until she threw up.

"Did he hurt you?" the boy asked.

"Is that you?" Lily was blind drunk and started sobbing. "Don't be mad."

"Did he hurt you?"

"Where's my underwear?"

There was vomit on her chin; she wiped it across her face along with a lot of sand.

The boy sat her down, wiped her face with the back of his hand, took off his sweater, and put it over Lily's head, gently moving her arms into the sleeves. She looked like a doll in an oversize dress.

He yelled to a group of girls near the lifeguard stand and asked one of them to keep an eye on her.

David didn't know what hit him from behind. The boy tackled him; the two rolled on the ground, the boy clobbering him with his fists. When a few of the guys from the football team tried to pull their team's captain off David, things took a turn for the worse. The boy wasn't ready for the fight to be over. He lunged at David's shoulders, shoving him back down, and the side of David's head hit a massive rock. Tim Jones appeared out of nowhere, wrapped his arms around the boy's waist, and pulled him back.

"What the fuck is going on?" Tim yelled. But before the boy could say anything, Tim shouted, "Why would you do that?"

The boy looked shaken and said, "He raped Lily."

Tim grabbed the boy by his shoulders like he wanted to knock some sense into his friend. "What the fuck are you talking about?" Tim shouted.

Then someone from the crowd said, "He's not moving."

One of the guys from the team got into his car and told everyone he was going to the gas station to call an ambulance; he warned the underage kids to leave. By the time the ambulance and police arrived, there were only a few kids left besides the boy, Head, Tim, Jimmy Sullivan—and a still unconscious David. They had carried Lily to Jimmy's car, where she was passed out in the back seat with Jane, who had sobered up awfully quick for someone who had been drinking Jack Daniel's straight out of the bottle.

None of them would forget the sight of the flashing lights and the sound of the siren as the ambulance drove away.

PORTSMOUTH, RHODE ISLAND

FEBRUARY 1978

The trial began in February and was held in Newport. The Webb sisters had been to the courthouse once before with their mother to see Gilbert Stuart's eighteenth-century painting of George Washington, which hung on the second floor.

While getting dressed for the trial, seventeen-year-old Jane had said, "Don't wear mascara or rouge. They'll think you're a whore." Together the sisters decided that Lily should wear a navy-blue turtleneck under a navy plaid jumper with blue tights. Jane tied Lily's hair up with a matching ribbon.

The whole town had heard what had happened—that Lily had been found in the dunes half dressed, that David had boasted about having sex with her, and that the boy had lost control. Lily was caught somewhere between what the boy and Jane and the rest of the town believed had happened and what she couldn't remember. The memory loss around that night haunted her. How could something so significant, so life-changing, disappear? This triggered an immense amount of anxiety for Lily.

At first, David had been taken to Newport Hospital, twenty minutes away. The next day, the town learned he had been transferred to Boston Children's. He had sustained a depressed skull fracture, and some speculated that his disability would be permanent.

The boy had been charged with aggravated assault and battery.

That summer and beyond, the townsfolk had debated whether it was a crime of passion. Blind rage. People talked about it at the grocery and hardware stores. They gossiped about it after church and with their neighbors. They all had heard that Lily was found on all fours wearing no underwear, drunk. Students who knew David said he had it coming. They remembered the story of David grabbing Lily after school. Said he was an entitled prick. Everyone in the town, including Mr. Webb, believed that Lily had been raped. And while he never told anyone, Mr. Webb felt a new affinity for the boy for being so protective of his daughter.

The boy didn't party the rest of that summer; he had been afraid of any little thing that might jeopardize his record. A speeding ticket. Drunken driving. He worked around the clock at the diner, and when he did have a night off, he and Lily hung out in his basement, listening to music. He had fought to remain optimistic, hoping that the judge would be sympathetic. Lily had wanted to postpone her first year of college, but her father and the boy insisted that she start as planned. When fall came and the other guys went off to college, the boy never took up the invitations to visit them. Lily saw him when she came home for Thanksgiving and Christmas. She wrote him long letters and called weekly from the one telephone in her dorm.

During the seven months leading up to the trial, they had all learned a bit of law. The boy learned that third-party defense of another could not be invoked. One can't defend someone after an attack; the attack must be imminent. Otherwise, it was called revenge.

The courthouse was a massive brick and granite building on Washington Square. The floors, stairs, and wainscoting were white marble, and the walls were matte gray with elaborately stacked crown molding. Iron chandeliers hung from the ceiling, and the American flag and Rhode Island state flag were on display. Inside the courtroom, a curved, molded oak rail formed a semicircle like a crescent moon, separating the judge's bench and well of the court from the gallery. Any other day, the Webb family would have appreciated the building's grand architectural style.

It had snowed the night before, so there were puddles on the wooden floor and frost on the paneled windows, darkening the courtroom with a winter gloom. The place smelled like wet wool. The windows were not quite floor-to-ceiling, just about eight feet high, but nevertheless, Lily felt the room pressing down on her.

In the first row, Lily sat between Mr. Cooper, who was stone-sober but shaking, and Mr. Webb. Jane sat to her father's right. Behind them, wearing suits and ties, sat Jimmy Sullivan, Head, Tim Jones and his father, Coach Kenny, Mr. Carr, and the boy's honors English teacher. The boy sat up front on the left side at the counsel's table. The rest of the courtroom was packed with people from the school and town, including the high school principal, two guidance counselors, a handful of teachers, and reporters from *The Providence Journal, The Newport Daily News,* and the *Sakonnet Times.* About a dozen football players who had graduated with the boy and gone on to college returned for the trial. They all wore suit coats, and many wore ties, however haphazardly.

Behind her, Lily could hear people talking in hushed tones. Latecomers arriving and settling into their seats. The only voice she could discern was Coach Kenny's, which she wished she could drown out. She was certain he was the type of man who would blame her for what had happened. This, of course, only fueled her own belief that she was to blame.

Heads turned as the McCarrens entered the courtroom. Lily gasped when she saw David, and her father reached for her hand. Others whispered and stared. David walked with a limp and a cane. His injury had left him with an ocular palsy, which prevented him from looking to his side. He had to pivot on his good leg and grab hold of the back of a wooden bench to sit down. As he sat, one leg remained straight. Only the end of the scar that ran along the back and top of his head was visible; the rest of it was covered by his hair, which had grown back after the surgery. His affect appeared limited, as if he didn't know why he was there. Lily felt nauseated looking at him.

The McCarrens sat on the other side of the room. For at least five months following the altercation, the parents had spent all of their time in Boston, an hour north, where their son was in a rehabilitation facility for patients with severe brain injuries. No one in town had seen much of them leading up to the trial—not even at the grocery store or at church. In court, Mrs. McCarren wore a cranberry wool suit with a cream-colored silk blouse and pussy bow. She was rail thin. Shoulders hunched. She appeared broken and barely looked up. Her husband, on the other hand, was dressed in a three-piece black suit, looking like he was ready to kill.

Lily had been worried sick since the night in July. Worried about the boy alone in Portsmouth without his friends, worried about Jane, who cried when they dropped Lily off at college that past fall. And now this. She didn't sleep well most nights, and when she did, she had bad dreams. One night, she dreamt the boy was drowning.

The prosecution presented its case, calling witnesses who testified about what they had seen—namely that the boy had attacked David from behind. Big Ted was called to testify. When asked, he described the sound of David's head hitting the rock. Said it was the second shove that "did him in." The classmate whom the boy had asked to watch over Lily in the dunes testified that she had never heard cries for help or any other sounds of commotion coming from where Lily had been found. No one had witnessed David and Lily together. No, the boy had not been drinking. And no one actually heard David speak to the boy.

Then Lily was called up. Her legs felt wobbly. Walking to the front of the courtroom required every ounce of courage she possessed. She felt as though she were walking into a trap and the boy's fate was in her hands. As the prosecuting attorney approached the witness stand, Lily looked over at the boy. If he could have, he would have said, *I'm sorry you have to do this.* Instead, he gave Lily a sad smile. Most people in attendance believed that Lily's testimony would mitigate the sentencing. Except for Mr. Jones, who told his son, Tim, to expect the worst.

The prosecuting attorney had blow-dried hair and a mustache, and he wore a brown suit with a wide, striped tie. After the trial, Jane would call him "Mr. Fuck-Face." Before testifying, Lily took an oath.

And then the lawyer asked his first question: "Had you been drinking that night?"

"Yes."

"What were you drinking?"

"Jack Daniel's and beer."

"How much?" the lawyer asked.

"Maybe six beers and four shots."

"Did you take any drugs?" he asked.

"No . . . well, maybe a little pot."

She knew this was his strategy. The boy's lawyer had warned her that the prosecution would try to assail her character.

"How long have you been dating the defendant?"

"Four years."

"Did you go to other parties without your boyfriend?"

"Not always."

"Please answer the question, yes or no."

"Yes."

"And did you drink at these parties?"

"Yes."

"Were you a virgin before the night of the incident?"

"No."

"Is it true you had an abortion this past year?"

Before answering, she glanced at her father, with whom she had never talked about the pregnancy. He offered her a look of reassurance.

"Yes," Lily said.

At this point, a woman who was sitting in the gallery huffed. The judge looked up and cocked his head in the woman's direction to signal his disapproval at her outburst. Lily thought of her mother and fought the sense of embarrassment. She drew strength from the memory of her mom and borrowed her courage.

Jane was right, she thought, *they are trying to make me out to be a drunk slut.*

Lily kept her gaze focused on the prosecuting attorney and felt a sense of rage stirring. Mr. Webb did his best to keep his eyes on his daughter, but every once in a while, he closed them and breathed deeply. The boy's body tensed up and his fists clenched at the line of questioning. His lawyer leaned over and whispered in his ear, reminding him that the jury was watching.

The attorney continued. "Do you remember seeing the victim that night?"

"No."

"Do you remember having sex with the victim?"

"No."

"Did the victim rape you?"

"I don't know. I don't remember."

"One last time, do you remember having sex with the victim?"

"No."

"I have no further questions, Your Honor."

Lily knew she had failed the boy. Before leaving the stand, she wanted to stand up and shout, "He's a good man! He wouldn't hurt anyone!"

But he had.

The trial was over in three days, and the jury deliberated for six hours. Once the jury had reached its verdict and the court was notified, the gallery quickly filled back up with spectators. The judge reentered the courtroom, climbed the stairs to his bench, pushed his sleeves back, and adjusted his black robes. When the judge took his seat, the boy closed his eyes. Tim and his father sat straight up, not moving. Lily put her arm around Mr. Cooper, who still had the shakes. Despite her seeming composure, Lily's head was spinning.

I could have lied. I could have said I remembered everything.

The jury found the boy guilty of aggravated assault and battery. When the judge sentenced the boy to three years in prison, the courtroom erupted. The people closest to Mr. McCarren heard him say "Yes," with much aggression. Mr. Webb turned to David and shouted, "You son of a bitch, you raped my daughter!" In an instant, the judge said, "Maintain order," as he banged his gavel. Mrs. McCarren put her arm around her son to shelter him from the crowd. Jane could be heard saying "Jesus Christ," and Head, who couldn't hide his sadness, kept his lips tight, but there was anguish all over his face. The coach had his head in his hands. Lily and Mr. Cooper fell into each other's arms. The judge was still speaking when Lily began to sob. David seemed to have no clue what was happening. Some thought he was acting. Others understood that the old David was gone.

The prosecutor had proved that the boy intentionally inflicted bodily harm. It didn't appear to matter that he had an outstanding academic record, that he was a state legend, and that he had had a full scholarship to play college ball.

The University of Michigan stepped away.

Lily and the boy were too young to know about love's uncertainties, the unexpected turns, and the false promises of the future. When it came to romance, their innocence had protected them—until it could not. Decades later, when Lily recalled this time in her youth, she would be reminded of an old Longfellow poem: *The tide rises, the tide falls.* Her failure to understand, in the moment, the inevitability of change would bring her great sorrow.

PART II

NORTHAMPTON, MASSACHUSETTS

1980

Lily didn't know what to expect from the evening's event at Smith. She sat in the back of the auditorium filled with female undergraduates and faculty. She was here because her biology professor, a young woman in her thirties, had encouraged her. "He's extraordinary—knows more than a thousand bird songs. Spent years in the Amazon." Lily was curious but even more eager to impress her professor. Final exams were coming up, and she had planned to leave after the lecture—before the Q&A—but the speaker hooked her early on and then reeled her in. Did he have any idea of the effect he had on his audience?

He touched upon his research in Manaus, Brazil, on a vulnerable bird species in deforested landscapes, and he charmed the audience with stories about hummingbirds the size of bees and how male bowerbirds build love nests and decorate them with colorful objects like berries and shells—all to attract females. Lily soon concluded that his talk was really a summons: a call of sorts to nonspecialists, to the average citizen. Bird species in decline reflect who we are and what we value and the moral outcomes of our lifestyles. This was his real message. Someone from the audience asked him how he had become interested in birds.

"This isn't the first time I've been asked the question, but it will be the first time I share this story," the speaker said. "I've not disclosed it in public before because I wasn't sure how my colleagues would receive it. It might be a little too anthropomorphic. But I'm a bit further along in my career now."

The audience laughed lightly.

No one moved; even the tech guy sitting on the steps in the aisle listened as if he were a child at story time. As a boy growing up in Southport, Connecticut, the speaker had learned from his father how to erect mist nets—invisible nets for trapping small birds. On foggy mornings, he and his father would set out to lure birds to the net, band them for observation, then release them soon after.

"Here's the part I've never shared: My grandmother was something of a poet and naturalist. Like Teddy Roosevelt, my grandmother set out on foot to find her own America, and she found it not far from her backyard in the estuaries and marshes of the Mill River. Her journal suggests that she was obsessed with the nesting patterns of black rails and ospreys. In an entry dated July 3, 1911, when she would've been sixteen years old, she described wandering through short grass salt marshes and cattail reeds. Eventually she came upon a pond, its borders covered with pretty blue pickerelweed. There she saw two mute swans: One was an adult, and the other—not quite as bright white—was a younger bird. A mother and a cygnet. The cygnet swam around its mother, who lay lifeless on the pond's surface, dead. The young swan swam and squawked. Distressed. Flapping its wings. My grandmother observed this, and what happened next shocked her. The young bird drowned itself."

A few gasps. Everyone was taking it in on their own terms. And then silence.

In that moment, Lily thought of her own mom and Jane, whose drinking and drugging had intensified. *Is Jane slowly drowning herself?* Before she knew it, she had stood up and raised her hand and was called upon by the speaker.

"So are you saying that birds grieve?"

She was wearing a red wool coat that had belonged to her mother and a black turtleneck. Later, Marshall Middleton, the renowned ornithologist, would tell her that when he first saw her she reminded him of an exquisite vermilion flycatcher.

"To posit that birds grieve," he said, then paused, took a sip of water, and cleared his throat, "is to open the door to a host of questions about animals and consciousness, about animals and emotions."

And so, for the spring semester of her senior year of college, Lily signed up for an elective scheduled right after her optics course: Professor Middleton's "bird course," as it was affectionately known. Lily spent hours sketching birds and memorizing facial markings and plumage patterns. In early April, the class took a field trip to an open wooded area a few miles from campus. White pine. Hemlock. Red maple. The forest canopy was uneven, with gaps allowing for spots of blue sky. While the others worked in pairs, Lily, with a set of binoculars hanging around her neck, attuned herself to the stories of the woods. She knew that the old stone walls, once boundaries for an eighteenth-century farm, were the artifacts of a colonial family's history. She imagined that perhaps they belonged to a young couple starting out: a father stacking the stones, a mother teaching her children their evening prayers, siblings growing into friends.

Pine scent reminded Lily of the woods that surrounded the monastery at home.

Bittersweet choked the trees but not the songbirds. Lily stopped and listened. "What do you hear?" Professor Middleton had come up from behind her.

Lily leaned into the sound of the songbird that seemed to be coming from the south, several yards away, off the narrow footpath. A sweet whistle rose and fell.

"A rose-breasted grosbeak," Lily said.

"Well, then, let's find it."

Lily and Professor Middleton stepped off the path, with Lily in the lead pushing branches back with her forearms. Through the green veil of leaves, perched on a thin branch, was a black-and-white bird with a blood-red marking on its throat and chest.

"Nice work; they're not easy to find."

They were standing next to each other with their faces tilted up, using their binoculars.

"They are returning from Central and South America—a long migration."

"What about this one?" Lily asked.

"What do you mean?" Professor Middleton let the binoculars rest on his chest.

"What about this one particular bird? What's his story? Where has he been?"

Professor Middleton sighed. "It'll take us another twenty years to be able to answer that question."

The professor kept his eyes on Lily, studying her. He had remembered her from the lecture he gave in the fall and the urgency in her voice when she asked whether birds grieve. And sometime early in the semester, after she'd visited him during his office hours and they'd talked into the early evening about the recovery of the American robin population after widespread use of DDT and pesticides, he knew he needed to be careful. She was luminous.

Lily displayed a level of curiosity that was unmatched by her peers. In his classes, Lily peppered him with questions. On counting breeding pairs, Lily asked: How do we know the sample size is statistically significant? Are there data from last year and the previous years—in other words, long-term monitoring? On male territorial songs, do they imitate, or can they improvise?

Now, in the distance, high in the trees, they heard another soloist. They smiled at each other.

"Let's go track him down," Lily said.

...

TWO WEEKS LATER, LILY received a call from Jane's college roommate.

"Jane is missing," the roommate said.

"What do you mean missing?"

"She hasn't slept in her room or been to class in a week."

"Have you called campus police?"

"No, she would kill me if I did that."

"I don't care. I'll call the police."

"I think I know where she is. She met this guy a few weeks ago. The thing is, he's not a student here."

Lily decided not to call her father. It would only worry him. Jane had done this once before, over Easter break during her senior year of high school, when she took a bus to New York City alone. Mr. Webb was worried sick; the entire student body searched for her in the woods and along the bay. The local police got involved. Jane called about two days later. At first, Lily thought whatever conscience she had had forced her to call home. Lily later learned Jane was bored and had run out of money.

About a half a mile from the Peter Pan bus terminal in Northampton, on her way to find Jane, a black Audi pulled up alongside Lily.

"Would you like a ride?" It was Professor Middleton.

"I'm just going to the bus station."

"To count pigeons?" the professor asked, smiling.

At that moment, Lily remembered she had a data report due based on a spot mapping exercise she had performed the prior weekend.

Lily said, "No, no. I have to take a bus to New Haven to find my sister."

"Is she missing?"

"Her roommate called; she hasn't gone to classes in a week."

"And no one has seen her in a week? Did you call the school?" Professor Middleton looked in his rearview mirror and turned back to Lily. "Let me park."

Lily waited for him on the sidewalk. His manner of dress was similar to the boys' uniforms at the Priory: He was wearing a sports jacket, an oxford button-down, khakis, and penny loafers without socks.

As he walked up to her, his face was serious but not grave. "Listen," he said, "if you take a bus, it'll be dark by the time you pull into the station in New Haven. That's not a good place to be late at night. Trust me. Let me give you a ride and we'll be there in a little over an hour."

He opened the door to his car and waited for her to get in, then shut it. By the time they got to I-91 South, he had managed to get her to tell him about her background—her mother's death, how she was raised by her father at an all-boys prep school, and her rebellious sister. She said nothing about the boy.

"A few weeks after my mom died, one of the cooks from the monastery came to visit my father and brought him dinner. My father had started smoking—he's quit since, but he smoked the first year after my mother's death. I heard the cook tell my father that children are resilient, something like that—that Jane and I would bounce back, recover from my mom's death. Of course, I'd heard that expression, 'children are resilient,' but it's bullshit. We appear resilient as children because the stakes are so low—a missed homework assignment, a poor grade in history. But we grow up.

"*Grief is a Mouse*, just like Emily Dickinson said. *And chooses Wainscot in the Breast / For His Shy House.*"

Hidden out of sight. And while hidden in the walls, it chews on electrical wires, and by the time the fire spreads, it can't be put out.

She stared out the passenger-side window and wondered if she had said too much.

"And what about you?" Professor Middleton asked. "Are you re-silient?"

Lily laughed. "That's a good question."

She knew he was single—all the girls at Smith knew, and they had guessed he was in his thirties. Looking at his profile in the car, this close up, Lily thought he looked closer to forty, but he wasn't; it was just all those years working in the Amazon.

At first she couldn't tell if she was nervous about Jane or nervous that they would spend the next hour alone together. She had not thought about another man like this. For the past three years, she had fixed herself on her studies, struggled to put the past behind her. Now, sitting next to Professor Middleton, she looked at his hands on the steering wheel and remembered how gentle he could be. She recalled the first time she watched as he untangled a swallow from the mist net. She craved that tenderness.

Lily had an address where Jane's roommate thought Jane might be—not the exact address but a description of the apartment building and the name of Jane's new boyfriend. Dixwell Avenue and Webster

Street. Sirens, high-rises, public housing, concrete steps, boarded-up windows, flashing blues, neon-green graffiti.

So this is where Jane wants to be, Lily thought. Another siren, this one closer. As they parked the car, Lily looked up and saw a woman leaning out a window three stories up, resting on her elbows on the window ledge. As Lily got out of the car, she felt a few drops of rain.

"Excuse me, I'm looking for a man named Howie?" she shouted up to the woman.

"Ain't we all," the woman in the window said.

"Actually, I'm looking for my sister: blond, thin, about my height."

"Yep, I was wondering when someone was going to come looking for her."

"Can you tell me where Howie lives?"

"First floor. Third door on the left."

A young kid about fifteen years old was sitting on the concrete steps.

"You looking to score?"

"No. Thank you," Lily said.

The kid laughed. "The only time people like you come to the projects is to buy something."

Professor Middleton held the door for her. Inside the apartment building, more spray-painted graffiti was on the walls: *Adele is a fucking cunt.* Jane came to the door when she heard her sister's voice. She was braless, wearing a long T-shirt. Lily's first thought was, *She better be wearing underwear.* Jane was drunk. Lily had seen her drunker, blind drunk. As the door opened, a rank smell drifted out of the apartment.

"Yo, sis. How'd you find the tribe?"

"Let's go," Lily said.

The professor craned his neck to see inside.

"She ain't going nowhere."

The door was wide open now, and Jane, leaning against the door-jamb, shrugged and closed her eyes. The guy Lily assumed was Howie was now standing behind Jane with his hand on her shoulder. Professor Middleton could see empty containers of take-out food, a bag of cocaine, a spoon, and a box of baking soda on the coffee table.

"She owes me money."

Professor Middleton didn't hesitate and took out two hundred-dollar bills from his wallet and asked, "Will this do?"

Howie looked at the money, took it, and disappeared into the apartment.

"Wait here," Jane said and then shut the door, leaving the couple in the hallway.

"My sister's in trouble," Lily said.

"What was your first clue?"

Lily looked like she was going to cry.

"I'm sorry, I was just trying for some levity given the situation," Professor Middleton said, reaching over and touching her arm.

"Do you always carry around so much money?" Lily asked.

"Yes, just in case one of my favorite students' sisters ends up in the projects in New Haven and needs a way out."

Lily smiled weakly.

By the time they got back outside, it was raining lightly. Lily looked Jane up and down. She barely had her pants on, and she looked like she had lost ten pounds since Christmas. She had a worn-out leather bag slung over her shoulder. Not only was she speaking like she was raised on the streets, but she moved differently, like her spine was loose.

"Why are you talking like you're from the Bronx?" Lily asked.

"Don't criticize me; you're so bourgeois," Jane said, searching her bag for a cigarette.

"What are you talking about?"

"You're so invested in the trappings of the middle class," Jane mumbled.

"You're a theoretical math student at Yale."

"Not anymore. I dropped out."

"Jesus Christ, Jane! This is going to kill Dad."

Jane threw her head back and said, "*Courage to be is the key to the revelatory power of the feminist revolution.*"

Lily scoffed. "I'm not convinced that your courage to give blow jobs in exchange for cocaine is what Mary Daly had in mind when she wrote that."

Professor Middleton had never met young women like the Webb sisters. They were from a whole other world compared to the girls in his social circle, the debutantes of New York's high society who attended invitation-only balls at the Waldorf Astoria, wearing Chanel and Dior. Sure, he had met different types of women through his years in academia. But the sisters were unconventional, irreverent, beautiful, and smart. He was drawn to them immediately.

Unable to find her cigarettes, Jane buckled her jeans on the street, and Professor Middleton opened the back door of his car for her. She slid in and rested her head on the backrest.

"Where did you find this Brahmin?"

"This is my professor," Lily said.

"How cliché; I love it."

"Professor Middleton, Jane Webb. Jane Webb, Professor Middleton," Lily said as she buckled her seatbelt.

"Middleton? Any relationship to Middleton Hall on campus?" Jane asked.

"Yes, that's my grandfather."

"Well, la-di-da. What's your first name?"

"Marshall."

"Well, I owe you, Marshall. That dude was startin' to bug out on me. Real paranoid, like, bringing me down," Jane said as she reached forward and patted him on the shoulder.

It was hard for Lily to be angry at Jane; at first, she was embarrassed that they had found her in that apartment under those conditions, but she had been so young when their mother died, and it had crushed her. What Lily wasn't capable of seeing clearly was how her mother's death had shaped her, as well—her sense of self, the ways she loved, and how much she feared abandoning others.

The plan was for Jane to stay with Lily for a few days in Northampton. Professor Middleton would make a few phone calls to try to save Jane's scholarship.

As they rode in silence, Lily wanted to be sitting in the back seat close to Jane, telling her, *I'll never leave you. There's nothing you can do to keep me away. Nothing.* About thirty minutes into the trip north, Lily turned around to look at her. Jane traced a raindrop with the tip of her finger on the windowpane. When their eyes met, Lily reached back for her sister's hand.

NORTHAMPTON, MASSACHUSETTS

MAY 1984–1985

Three years after Lily graduated, the biology professor who had encouraged her to attend Marshall Middleton's lecture received tenure, and she invited Lily to a party in Northampton. Lily had been working as an assistant to an assistant editor at a science journal outside of Boston.

By the time Lily arrived at the party, there was a good size crowd on the outdoor deck, and she recognized a couple of the younger faculty members tossing a Frisbee in the backyard. Lily got a beer from a keg and mingled with a few former classmates. *Repo Man* with Emilio Estevez was all the buzz, and Casey, a girl she had met in one of her physics classes, cornered her and started talking about the movie, despite the fact that Lily had never seen it. The girl described it scene by scene. It was so awkward. Lily only got away when another student walked up to them.

More faculty and students were gathered inside the house in twos and threes talking about research and politics. The host had recently purchased the new Macintosh computer, so naturally a small group gathered around it talking about whether Apple stole its GUI from another company. Most agreed that it was Apple's technology. Jane had already told Lily the ins and outs of the computer and why it was so revolutionary.

Lily had not seen Marshall Middleton since graduation. At the party, she was standing in the kitchen, talking to a former classmate, when he walked in, and within an hour, they were making plans to meet the next day.

The following morning, they drove to an old railway bridge that crossed the Connecticut River; it had been part of a rail line for passenger trains in the twenties. They took a trail to a beaver pond. Light breeze. Crisp. Clean. It carried the scent of spring. The sunlight on the canopy of leaves offered a variation on the color green. Every few feet, one or the other would pause to listen. Marshall knew all the bird songs by heart.

"How's Jane?"

"She graduated and had lots of job offers, but she decided to go to California to wait tables."

Marshall nodded. Lily took note of the fact that he didn't seem to pass judgment on her sister. A cool breeze passed. He bent down and pulled up a plant, roots and all. "Bishop's goutweed," he said and noted how invasive plants were destroying the landscape. Lily thought about her sister, about how drugs and booze were destroying her beautiful mind.

They came to a clearing in the woods, and her gaze swept over the field. Spring wildflowers bloomed: small purple violets, yellow daffodils, white starflowers. Cattails in the distance, a red-tailed hawk in flight, soaring and dipping. *Could Jane ever find peace in a place like this?* Lily wondered. Her sister's heart and soul wanted more than life could give. *What about me? Maybe there's something here for me. Maybe I can find peace.*

Since that night at the beach, guilt had consumed her. If she hadn't gone to the party, their lives would have progressed as planned. She blamed herself because her presence was the catalyst for the events that unfolded. For all her feminist education, it would take years for Lily to have real clarity. As she saw it now, she had destroyed two lives, not counting her own. Every time she thought of the boy and David, she felt like she had been involved in a hit-and-run: Sure that she had hit something, she had looked into the rearview mirror but kept driving.

In a conversation with her sister right before Jane moved to Santa Cruz, Lily had said, "It was my fault. . . . If only—" Her sister had interrupted, grabbed her by the arm, and said, "Listen, David should have served time for raping you. And as far as your 'if only'—the first time I watched someone shoot up and a look of bliss appeared on his face, it scared me. I thought to myself, *This is something that I've got to stay clear of.* That's like you. Stay clear of your if-onlys."

Lily would have waited for the boy. Letting him go, extricating herself from their emotional bond, never seeing him—these were the hardest things she had ever done. And none of it had been her choice.

She watched a painted lady butterfly, with its winged elegance, flutter through the tall grass. Scalloped orange wings with black-and-white spots.

"Where have you been, distant traveler?" she whispered.

Then to Lily's surprise, the butterfly landed on her forearm. Delighting her. With her face tilted down, she could observe the insect. Its wings closed. Prayer hands. She held her breath, barely moving, merging with the stillness.

God's utterance, she thought, recalling a Manley Hopkins sentiment.

And with that thought came another: the image of young Jane reciting one of his poems to their mother on her last birthday. Lily had returned to the Jesuit's poetry in college and had come to understand his desire to see God in all of nature. She understood why her mother loved Hopkins.

A moment later, Lily recognized a smooth melodic song. She so wanted to get it right, to impress him. She remained still; Marshall watched her standing in the meadow with her long dark hair and intense dark eyes. Lily smiled, raised her hands, and said joyfully, "Who doesn't love a purple finch?"

Marshall laughed.

...

THEIR COURTSHIP RITUALS WERE traditional and gendered, and Lily loved it all. It took her by surprise, but she didn't fight it. Marshall opened and held doors for her, brought her flowers, took her dancing, big-band style. He used her middle name, calling her "Lily Remington," after her paternal grandmother. She liked it. It was a new identity. They had been dating for nearly a year when Marshall asked Lily to join him on a trip to Louisiana to look for an Attwater's prairie chicken. Lily was hoping to see an elegant whooping crane or white ibis. When she told Jane she was going to Louisiana with Marshall to look for a chicken, her sister said, "Why? Is there a shortage in Massachusetts?" And then Jane added, "Make sure you don't get eaten alive by a fucking alligator!"

In early spring, they traveled to the Bayou Teche region, a coastal prairie. They left their hotel in the early morning hours. Surrounded by tall grass, Marshall wore high boots, a birding vest, binoculars around his neck, and cargo pants with deep pockets to carry a knife, compass, and small notebook. He wasn't one to buy new clothes; in fact, the birding vest was from his days in Brazil, and he had a Barbour waxed cotton jacket from his years as a graduate student. Lily marveled that he still owned a pair of burgundy corduroys from his senior year at Yale. Later, when Jane got to know him, she would say he dressed like an English aristocrat. But sometimes Marshall's pants were a bit short; Lily found it charming and attributed it to his absent-minded-professorliness. It was how her father's pants used to fit.

Marshall understood marshes, rivers, and ponds like he had been born outside, like he had never slept on monogrammed sheets or known the convenience of having one's breakfast prepared, one's shirts pressed—as had actually been the case.

Being in the fields reminded Lily of the days she had spent exploring the wooded landscape around the monastery and the times she had spent playing make-believe, pretending to be a saint—one of nature's mystics.

Now, in the tall grass, Lily watched Marshall. They stopped speaking and stood in silence. He scanned the landscape, first without his binoculars, looking for movement. They both heard the whirring sound at the same time and turned their heads to smile at each other. Marshall's lips parted, his eyes widened, and then, there it was, stamping its little feet like it was dancing, one of the most endangered birds in North America. Quick repetitive movements. Its head bowed with a bright orange air sac in the neck, blown up. After several minutes, Marshall took his handkerchief from his pocket and wiped his eyes. When he looked down at her, Lily raised her chin and kissed him on the lips.

"He's looking for a mate," Marshall whispered.

They hadn't yet talked of marriage, but Lily knew he was falling in love. She could see it in the way he held her gaze and feel it in the way he touched her. They had resisted talking about their pasts—their loves, their pains. She got the sense that Marshall was self-conscious about his wealth and blue blood. Lily, meanwhile, needed not to think about the boy. She avoided talking about him even with Jane. She went out of her way to keep her distance from the old high school gang. And she resolved never to tell Marshall about the night on the beach. To him, she wanted to appear whole. Unbroken.

Marshall kept his eye on the waterfowl. Lily looked up at the morning sky, and soaring above was a massive hawk. Speaking softly, Lily said, "Look, a red-shouldered hawk."

Marshall looked up and then reached over to Lily, putting his arm around her waist and pulling her toward him. In preparation for the trip, Lily had memorized the features of several birds, including this particular hawk. She took satisfaction and pleasure in committing to memory its red chest, long tail, and white bars.

"Where have you been all my life?" he asked, looking down and kissing the top of her head.

"Is that a line from a movie?"

"Probably," he said and then added, "You have my heart, Lily Remington."

She didn't say anything. With her finger, she reached up and wiped a droplet of sweat from the side of his face. Lily wanted to say something in return, something heartfelt and tender. She believed she could love Marshall solidly. But what she didn't know was if she would ever be able to love him only. Lily was confident, however, that he was one of the few good men her mother had suggested were out there.

They would spend hours in fields, in wetlands, on rocky paths, among tall firs and pines. He would teach her the names of trees, wild-flowers, insects, shrubs—like teaching a child a new language. When Lily would drive from Boston to Northampton for the weekend, they would set up nets—hidden among the dense shrubbery—and wait for the birds. They worked quickly, banding them, then releasing them.

The first time he taught her how to hold a bird, she was reminded of Saint Francis of Assisi. She held the bird's neck ever so gently between her index finger and middle finger, and with her thumb, she secured the bird's wings. What was it the saint had said? *My brother bird* . . . She marveled at the softness of its feathers, its pulsing heart, and the fragility of life. Each time after that, she spoke to the birds. One day while cradling a songbird in the palm of her hand, she recited a line from Shelley: "*Teach us, Sprite or Bird / What sweet thoughts are thine?*"

Marshall could not get enough of her—in the fields, in bed, everywhere. Wherever she was, he wanted her.

NEW YORK, NEW YORK

JUNE 1985

Months after their trip down south, Marshall arranged for Lily to meet his mother on a summer day in New York City. An afternoon tea. Three o'clock. Lily wanted to make a good impression, but what she didn't know was that this wouldn't be possible. For her to make a good impression she would have had to be meeting an open-minded, or at the very least tolerant, person, and that was not Mrs. Middleton. When Marshall told his mother about Lily, she asked if Lily was a New England Catholic, as if they were a separate species.

Marshall bought her a Lilly Pulitzer dress for the occasion. "Lilly for Lily. You could wear it with your single strand of pearls."

When they arrived at Marshall's mother's Upper East Side apartment, the concierge greeted Marshall as if he were royalty. Lily was unable to manage her facial expressions when the elevator operator stepped aside and the doors slid open to the apartment's entrance. Her jaw dropped. The apartment was massive, with views of Cen-

tral Park. Opulent Gilded Age architecture. Dramatically high ceilings.

The first thing Lily noticed about Phoebe Middleton, besides her
subdued smile and thinness, was her well-coiffed hair. She wore it
short in a low bouffant, not a strand out of place. Her skirted suit, in a
neutral-colored tweed, seemed to be made just for her. She was flaw-
less.

In one room, Baker sofas covered in silver fabric sat before hand-
painted metallic wallpaper. When describing the apartment's multiple
renovations and "past aesthetic influences," as she called them, Mrs.
Middleton dropped names like Lady Elsie de Wolfe, an interior designer of whom Lily had never heard. The woman was someone Marshall's grandmother had hired—despite or perhaps because of her
"Boston marriage" to the famed literary agent Elisabeth "Bessie"
Marbury. When Mrs. Middleton didn't get the reaction from Lily she
thought she would, she explained that "Boston marriage" meant a
lesbian relationship. Lily had not responded because she was a little
unnerved by Mrs. Middleton's conservativism. She thought about the
way her own mother had spoken about lesbians.

Lily was reminded of her mother again when she noticed that
there were no books around. Carol Webb used to tell her girls when
they were young that books and arrogance were linked: The fewer
books someone has in their house, the more they think they know. It
was so unlike Marshall's house with its wall-to-wall bookshelves and
stacks of periodicals.

Her mother would have been impressed, however, with an oil
painting of Marshall's great-grandmother completed by John Singer
Sargent, at his studio in the Chelsea neighborhood of London in 1903.

Lily walked over to a table where Mrs. Middleton had a number
of photographs on display, family photos and others of the Middletons
with celebrities and politicians. There was one photo of Mrs. Middle-

ton with Alexander Haig and another of her standing in between the Reagans at President Ronald Reagan's first inauguration. Mrs. Middleton picked up the framed photo of herself and Haig and said, "He was right about Kennedy. . . . That Khrushchev quailed before Kennedy is just a myth, a public relations story that his men spun." Lily tilted her head, not knowing what to say. She wasn't even sure what "quailed" meant in this context.

"Do you read the *National Review*?" she asked Lily.

When Lily shook her head, Marshall's mother said, "You should. Bill Buckley is a genius."

Lily was still trying to make a good impression but knew instantly that she and Mrs. Middleton had little in common and no matter how hard she tried that afternoon, this woman might never warm to her.

Savories, scones, delicate sandwiches, and sweets were served on a three-tier curate stand. Silver sugar tongs. An array of sterling silver knives, forks, and spoons. Jam and clotted cream. Wedgwood bone china.

"This is delicious," Lily said. "What is it?"

Mrs. Middleton looked at her son and then at Lily. "It's a simple spring radish sandwich: butter, salt, and young radishes."

Dear God, Lily thought, *she must think I was born in a barn.*

Lily watched Marshall and his mother carefully. Mrs. Middleton didn't stir her tea; rather, she carefully moved the spoon back and forth. Before Marshall ate a pastry, Lily watched to see which petite knife and fork he used.

Lily wasn't completely without a sense of decorum. She had the manners of a middle-class girl, she was the daughter of a schoolteacher. She knew how to shake someone's hand upon introduction and make eye contact; saying "please" and "thank you" came naturally to her. But she still used the side of her index finger to scratch her nose, and she slouched a bit, like a girl who had gone to public schools all her life.

Lily's mother had never been one to insist that her daughters keep their legs tightly closed and crossed at the ankles.

A petite woman wearing a knee-length black dress and white apron appeared in the entrance to the room and left just as quickly.

"I'm having difficulty finding new dailies," Mrs. Middleton said.

Lily looked on sympathetically but had no idea what Mrs. Middleton was talking about. Later, Marshall explained that "dailies" were domestic help who arrived daily, as opposed to live-in maids. This included her cook, an Irish woman she'd had for years and to whom she would give the weekly menu. Marshall referred to it all as old-world Waspy.

This is a whole other world with its own customs and rules, Lily thought.

When his mother reached for the tongs, Marshall glanced at Lily and rolled his eyes.

"Do you know the Drexels?" Mrs. Middleton asked, sitting back in her chair.

Lily wiped her mouth with her napkin and said, "No."

"I spent the summer of '39 in Newport at Mimi Hamilton's house."

"Lily is from Portsmouth, Mother. Not Newport. Her father teaches at the Portsmouth Priory."

"It's called the Portsmouth Abbey now," Lily said.

"Yes, dear, I remember. It's where Bill sent his son, Christopher. I believe Robert Kennedy attended the Portsmouth Priory, too. Isn't that right, Lillian?"

"Mother, it's Lily."

"Yes, Mrs. Middleton, you're right. But I don't think he graduated from the Priory. I think he transferred—"

Before Lily could finish, Mrs. Middleton appeared distracted and turned her attention to her son.

"When is your book coming out?" Then, turning back to Lily, she said, "We were all so surprised when Marshall told us he wanted to be a professor." Then, "They'll want you to speak at the club, I'm sure." This remark was directed at Marshall. "The club" was code for the Knickerbocker Club in New York City, on East Sixty-second Street, a prestigious, private all-male social club. Turning once more to Lily, she asked, "Are you Catholic?"

"Yes."

"Bill Buckley's a Catholic, too," Mrs. Middleton said.

Lily realized that it was her way of telling Lily that her Catholicism would be tolerated. When Marshall left them alone for a few minutes, both women seemed at a loss for words until Lily commented on the architecture of the apartment. "It's gorgeous," she said. "I've never seen anything like it." Mrs. Middleton told Lily that her bedroom had been designed by Parish–Hadley. Lily smiled, not knowing what to say.

"I didn't really have a choice at the time. Hadley had worked for the Kennedys, but I hired him nonetheless." Mrs. Middleton's disregard for the Kennedys had been trumped only by her need to be seen as two or three steps ahead of New York's high society.

Lily had never met anyone who didn't like the Kennedys. Brother Francis, a monk at the Priory, had been in school with Robert Kennedy when he attended. He used to tell Lily's father that Bobby was kind and had a strong dislike for bullies. After Robert Kennedy was assassinated, Brother Francis would say, "They didn't like him because he wanted to help the poor, Black and white alike." Lily always wondered to whom Brother Francis referred when he said "they." When she asked her mother, Mrs. Webb had said, "You would be surprised who wages wars against the poor."

Later that night, when the sun had set and they were walking around the city, Lily asked, "How did I do?"

"You were terrific! I'm sorry if my mother was a little haughty."

"Haughty?" Lily laughed.

"Overbearing? Is that a better word?" he asked, looking over at her. "I should've warned you. My mother is the type of woman whose priorities are to attend as many social events as possible, with as many photographers as possible. I'd return from boarding school, and it was more important for her to attend a ball or a charity event at Lincoln Center than to have dinner with me."

Trying to be positive, Lily said, "She loves you."

"I guess you could call it love. Look, I see her only a couple times a year or if I have to come to New York for a meeting."

Lily's first thought was how she'd have wanted to see her mother all the time if she were alive. And then she thought about how proud she'd have been introducing her mom to Marshall.

They walked down Fifth Avenue holding hands, moving through layers of city sounds: police sirens, car horns, people chattering, the screech of the bus brakes. And then the sound of birds: the trilling, chirping, and tweeting. She thought she heard an osprey but became distracted by the sound of a car horn reverberating. Marshall looked up at the artificial brightness emanating from buildings, streetlights, and billboards and lamented the impact of scattering lights on migratory birds.

"Birds navigate by the stars," Marshall said.

"It couldn't get any more mystical."

"It's science," he said, stopping on the sidewalk to look down at her.

"It's both," she said, tipping her head back to give him a peck on the lips.

Marshall had her on the bed before she could take off her sandals. After they made love, lying naked in the sheets, he said to her, "I've thought about you every day since our first hike along the river, and I'll think about you every day until I die." She squeezed his hand and smiled. Lily drew strength from the certainty of his love, the kind of strength that would sustain her in the future. His love had an undeniable pull. And maybe even the capacity to extract her from her past.

Later that same night, while Marshall was taking a shower, Lily called Jane at her home in Santa Cruz to fill her in on how the visit went with Mrs. Middleton.

"Being anti-Kennedy is like being anti-American," Jane said.

"Not according to Marshall's mother."

"Are they anti-baseball, too?" Jane asked.

Lily laughed. "I think they're the kind of people who play tennis."

"Well, then how do they feel about hot dogs and hamburgers?" Jane asked seriously.

Lily laughed again. "What are you talking about?"

"Well, if they're anti-Kennedy and anti-baseball, then I just assume they are anti-hot-dog and hamburger."

"I don't think anyone is anti-hot-dog or hamburger," Lily said. "But she is definitely pro-Reagan and pro-life, and at one point she told me that she has dinner regularly with Phyllis Schlafly."

Jane shot back, "You can't marry into this family. She sounds dangerous!"

"We haven't even talked about marriage."

"Well, how does he feel about football?"

"I don't know, we've never talked about it," Lily said. And then she added, "It's been a long time since I've watched a game."

"You know I'm happy for you. I just want you to be sure," Jane said.

"About what?" Lily asked. She was a little taken aback.

"About marrying him," Jane said.

"He hasn't even asked me yet."

"He will. And if he does, I want you to be sure that he's the one you want to spend the rest of your life with. You know, the man of your dreams, your knight, the love of your life, all that shit."

"He's the one. He's everything I want in a husband: He's kind, patient, doesn't drink too much, rock solid."

"Don't forget filthy rich," Jane said.

"Mom would have loved that he's a scientist. She would've loved his knowledge of natural history. And how his mind works. So analytical, yet so humble. He's like a cross between Mr. Rogers and Richard Feynman."

Her sister laughed. "That's saying something."

What Lily didn't say was that she did have her doubts, but they were fading. At least she thought they were fading.

The line went silent until Lily said, "I would have liked to have met his grandmother. He talked about her the first time I heard him lecture. She was a naturalist herself. I think that's where he gets it."

"Am I going to be an auntie someday?" Jane asked.

"I hope so," Lily said. Then she added, "What about me?"

"Maybe," Jane said. "You never know what life's going to throw at you."

NORTHAMPTON, MASSACHUSETTS

MAY 1986

They were looking for warblers in the spring and were joined by eight senior citizens, members of the public who had signed up weeks in advance for a three-hour bird walk. Since joining the Smith faculty, Marshall had organized a half dozen hikes like these, so he recognized about six of the names on the list. Regulars. Retirees. Bird enthusiasts who had participated in the annual Christmas Bird Count. They were told to bring binoculars, field journals, and bug spray. Marshall supplied the snacks—apples and cheese that he and Lily packed the night before.

Marshall took this aspect of his job seriously. He believed he had a responsibility to educate the public—he was carrying on a tradition in ornithology, a field of study that had depended upon amateur birders for close to a century.

The plan was to meet at the college and then carpool to West Whately, Massachusetts, about ten miles from campus. It was a motley crew of men and women in their sixties and seventies, dressed in brightly colored windbreakers and hats of all sizes. One man walked with a stick, some carried backpacks, everyone had binoculars around their necks. Lily thought the hats might be just as interesting as the birds.

Birders, Lily thought. *What an interesting group of people. And now I'm one of them.*

In her estimation, birders tended to be well educated. Birding required a certain mindset. Patience and focus and a curiosity about nature. Identifying birds by sight came relatively easy to Lily, but identifying birds simply based on their songs and calls took more time.

She had to admit, she was keen on the fact that Marshall was an ornithologist. It was an honorable profession with its focus on conservation and the protection of nature. She sometimes fantasized about the social capital she would acquire in the future if she said, "My husband is an ornithologist." Her little fantasy could be viewed as snobbery, but it meant something to her to be associated with someone others viewed as doing something good in the world. Playing professional football was certainly nothing to be embarrassed about, but saving the environment was more admirable. Lily believed all of this—she needed to.

In a small parking lot near the trailhead, Marshall talked a bit about taking notes.

"Write everything down. Nothing is inconsequential. When you see a bird you don't recognize, try to compare its size to something you're familiar with. A turkey, a crow, an American robin, or a sparrow. Does it have a short beak or a long one? Record all its colors. Notice the markings on the neck or wings, for instance. Where was the bird? On the ground or perching? How did it move? Did it hop or run? Where was it foraging or looking for food?"

The group had formed a semicircle around Marshall. They were nodding and looking around, already peering off into the trees. Eager to contribute to science.

"One more thing," Marshall said, reaching into his bag and pulling out whistles.

"Ah, the whistles," one of the regulars said.

"Is this in case we see a bear?" a newcomer named Erin asked.

"No. It's in case we get lost," the man with the stick said.

"I thought we were supposed to stay together," said a second newcomer.

"That's the goal," Marshall said. "But I like to take precautions."

The women smiled at him. Lily wondered if one or two of the older women in their sixties were just there to spend the day with Marshall.

Two years ago, when they first started dating, Marshall had told Lily about the time he'd lost an undergraduate in this area. He'd searched for the student for more than an hour before finding her nearby in a deep wooded valley with low visibility. He had been worried sick over the lost girl. Ever since then, he'd been using whistles. When he told Lily this story, she had been impressed with the level of conscientiousness he had displayed—the same way he had taken care of Jane that night in New Haven.

Standing there, watching him hold up the whistles, Lily thought of the nylon mist nets they used to capture birds for banding. *I have been caught, netted by this man, and I don't want to be released.*

Among the hemlocks, oaks, birches, and white pines, the group set out to look for warblers and other migratory birds. They stayed together in the beginning, following narrow trails through the forest. Stopping every few feet to listen, watch, and take notes. They spotted thrushes, starlings, wrens, nuthatches, and swallows. They studied in silence. A few fell behind. The group waited.

In a clearing near a pond, Marshall stopped the group to talk about the high mortality rate of juveniles and how it might be linked to a lack of proficiency in foraging.

"I suppose it would vary from species to species, but what determines a juvenile's ability to acquire foraging skills?" Lily asked.

Marshall tried not to smile at his girlfriend's question, which was spot-on.

"A number of factors: weather conditions, the abundance of prey, maturation, and social conditions."

"Social conditions?" Erin asked. "Like parties," she added, smiling.

Marshall smiled back at her and then explained: "Sibling osprey, for example, have greater success when they forage together. It also appears that they have similar techniques."

"Which they've learned from each other," Lily interjected, directing her comments at the older woman.

"Osprey siblings influence each other's behavior, increasing each other's chances of a successful catch and, thus, survival," Marshall added.

Lily thought of her sister: She and Jane were like osprey siblings. The birds reminded Lily of who they were and who they became after their mother died. Surely, they had helped each other survive. Now Jane was like a raptor, plunging feetfirst into life and soaring with the kind of freedom that birds of prey claim—a quality of freedom that Lily recognized she might never know. Lily would like to think that she and her sister were as resilient as raptors, but *were they really?* she wondered.

As the group ventured into a wooded area again, Lily took the lead, and Marshall fell behind with several older women. They meandered on the long trail, stopping to peer into the woods and grasslands with their binoculars.

"What's that? Can you hear it?" one of the birders asked Lily. She waited and then heard it. It was a complex song. Intricate. It took Lily a second, and then she said, "It's a bobolink." She knew she had gotten it right, and she was tickled and couldn't wait to tell Marshall.

In that moment, she thought, *If someone had told me ten years ago that I would be birding by ear, I never would have believed them.*

Of course, she never would have believed a lot of things that had transpired.

From back down the trail, Lily heard Marshall blow his whistle once. Somewhere in the distance, they heard two tweets. Marshall blew his whistle again, hoping that the lost birder would follow the sound. When the third and fourth tweets sounded as if the person was moving farther away, Marshall blew his whistle three times, signifying that the whistler was going the wrong direction.

About forty-five minutes later, Marshall and the others appeared on the trail. Erin looked a little teary-eyed but managed to fake a smile.

"Sorry to hold you up," the older woman said.

She explained that she had spotted an orange bird she wanted to follow. Stepping off the trail, she became disoriented.

Still a little emotional, she said, "All I could think about were the bears."

Marshall put his arm around the woman's shoulders, trying to distract her.

"Tell us about the bird. What did it look like?"

Erin looked up at Marshall. "It was bright orange and black, with white marks on its wings."

"That's an oriole," the man with the stick said.

Marshall pulled out his field guide from his backpack. "Was it this?"

Erin leaned in to look at the image. "That's it," she squealed.

"What did it sound like?" Marshall asked, looking at Erin and knowing full well the whistling tone of these birds—their songs and calls.

Humility at its finest, Lily thought.

Lily wasn't so naïve as to think that Marshall was perfect. He probably wouldn't have made it this far in academia without a little self-promotion, but it never came at the expense of others. Marshall could have easily told the group what sort of bird it was right off the bat, without even consulting his field guide, but he didn't need to show off.

"Like a flute," Erin said.

"Excellent," Marshall said. "You're a natural."

Later that afternoon, after they said goodbye to the group back on the campus and were driving home, Lily reached over and touched Marshall's shoulder. "My mother would've adored you."

...

A MONTH LATER, WHILE they were visiting Lily's father in Portsmouth, Marshall proposed. The ring was spectacular. A family heirloom. It had an eighteen-karat white gold band with a five-carat Asscher cut diamond. As Lily undressed for bed that night, she felt her first pang of anxiety. She shuddered at the idea of a lavish wedding. Who would she invite? The few girlfriends from college? The guys? She hadn't seen her high school friends in years. And what of the expense? Her father would feel obligated to contribute funds when his own savings were limited. And Mrs. Middleton at a Catholic ceremony? It all seemed overwhelming. Dreadful even.

In bed alone, with her hands resting on her belly under the covers, Lily fingered the ring and thought about the boy. The ring was heavy, and she was not yet used to wearing it. She removed it and placed it on the nightstand before rolling over and closing her eyes.

NEW YORK, NEW YORK

OCTOBER 1986

It was a late afternoon in autumn on a Wednesday. A civil wedding was planned at the Office of the City Clerk in Lower Manhattan. It wasn't what Lily had imagined as a Catholic girl from Rhode Island, but neither was marrying a man fifteen years her senior, her former college professor, and a member of one of New York's elite families. It certainly wasn't what the socialite Mrs. Middleton had in mind for her only son's wedding. She had tried to persuade the couple to have the ceremony at St. James' followed by a reception for at least two hundred guests at the Rainbow Room. Marshall vetoed his mother's plans. It wasn't his cup of tea, and it certainly wasn't Lily's.

In the months leading up to the wedding, Lily missed her mother tremendously. It was another milestone her mother would not be there to witness. Lily longed for her presence. But in that space of longing, she felt a deepening sense of gratitude for her mother's boundless love.

Marshall had wanted to hire a car for Mr. Webb, but Lily's father insisted on taking the three-hour train ride to New York. Reservations were made at the St. Regis for Mr. Webb and Jane, who flew in from Santa Cruz; Marshall thought his father-in-law-to-be would appreciate the Newport/Astor connection. They chose Marshall's college roommate, George Mellon, and Jane to be their witnesses. George, whose family wealth came first from tobacco and then from oil, worked on Wall Street and lived in the city.

The Webbs dressed at the hotel, and a car was sent to collect and ferry them to the Manhattan Municipal Building. As the driver rounded the final corner, Jane said, "There they are." Marshall, his mother, and his college roommate were waiting outside on the curb. When the car pulled up, Lily leaned over and kissed her father on the cheek. Marshall opened the door and extended his hand to Lily. When she stepped out of the car, Marshall closed his eyes and lowered his head. When he finally met her gaze, they both blushed. It felt like such an intimate exchange in front of her family. Lily would later tell Marshall that she felt pulled out of time as the city rushed around them. Taxis and cars whizzed by. Fast-talkers. Walkers. Shouting construction workers. Not-so-distant sirens. Lily noticed none of it.

But what she had recognized, months before this day, was that in marrying Marshall she was moving into a world of certainty and logic, a world that valued science and academic rigor, a world not so different as it might appear from that of her childhood.

The night Marshall had proposed, her dream of marrying her high school sweetheart had been folded like an old dress and put away. She had slipped into a new fairy tale, one that would last a lifetime, one that wouldn't break her heart, one with a certain future.

She wore a full-length white crepe wedding dress with long sleeves and a boatneck and carried a bouquet of orange French peonies, burgundy roses, and pale-yellow dahlias with ferns. Marshall wore an

Italian-made black single-breasted tuxedo with a notched lapel. Others were dressed less formally. Marshall's mother wore a light-gray Chanel suit with a modest hemline and pearls. Jane, on the other hand, wore a tight-fitting turtleneck maxi sweater dress in dark amber, which Lily thought was a perfect color for the occasion. The men wore suit coats and slacks.

Inside, it was a delightful atmosphere. How could it not be? It was a place filled with people who trusted love. And there were signs of it as couples exchanged whispers and tender kisses. The municipal building was as grand and important as New York City itself, with its soaring ceilings, Tennessee marble, and Roman architecture. Other couples in line to wed included a big, bearded man in a suit and tie with a Japanese woman wearing a red bridal kimono; a biker couple in leather; and an older Hispanic couple in their sixties, the woman wearing an orchid in her hair. While Marshall and Lily waited in line at the registration desk to verify their IDs and marriage license, the others got acquainted. George Mellon and Mr. Webb talked about the 1983 America's Cup race in Newport and the legality of the keel design. That left Jane standing alone with Mrs. Middleton, who was in a generous mood and, like the others, caught up in the excitement of the occasion.

"I had ten bridesmaids," she told Jane.

"Ten?" Jane said, a little surprised.

"Yes. I couldn't leave anyone out. They were my girlfriends from childhood and then my girlfriends from college. We were all in each other's weddings."

"They all married men? All ten of them?" Jane asked.

Mrs. Middleton nodded.

"And none of them were gay?"

"I beg your pardon?"

Mrs. Middleton wasn't being snooty; Jane's question was so beyond her scope that she didn't quite know if she heard Jane correctly, so Jane repeated herself.

"None of them were gay? They were straight?" Jane was genuinely curious. Her tone was dispassionate as if she was describing insects in a glass display case. She continued: "Statistically, it's been suggested that one in ten individuals are gay, so I just assumed that at least one of them might be gay. Don't you agree?"

Their conversation was interrupted by the soon-to-be bride and groom, who had been told to wait for their number to be called. When Mrs. Middleton noticed the slip of paper in her son's hand, she said, "Should I have called Ed?" She was referring to Ed Koch, the mayor of New York, of whom she approved because, even though the mayor was a Democrat, he was friends with William Buckley.

"We'll wait like everyone else," Marshall said softly.

The small wedding party formed a circle away from the registration desk, waiting for their number to be called. Marshall and Lily held hands, smiling. It didn't take long before they were able to enter the wedding chapel, a small windowless room with an American flag and lectern. When the officiant said, "I now pronounce you married," Mrs. Middleton was the first to applaud, then the others joined in. When the couple kissed, Jane leaned into George and said, "I brush my teeth longer than that ceremony lasted." George, who had never met Jane and only knew what his college buddy had told him—that she was brilliant and beautiful—laughed. Mr. Webb approached Mrs. Middleton, who extended her right hand to him. With both hands, Mr. Webb took her hand in his and smiled.

"I imagine your wife must have been an interesting woman to have had such independent and beautiful daughters."

"She would have been thrilled," Mr. Webb said, taken aback and a little emotional.

Following the ceremony, the group headed to Le Cirque at the

Mayfair Regent Hotel at 58 East Sixty-fifth Street. Mrs. Middleton and Marshall had known the owner, Mr. Maccioni, when he was at the Colony in the sixties, back when Marshall was a teenager who would visit the restaurant during holiday breaks from boarding school at Exeter. Every time Marshall saw Mr. Maccioni, he charmed the young immigrant by attempting to speak Italian.

Heads turned when Lily walked in. They turned again to get a glimpse of Jane. It was not unusual for brides to show up at the restaurant in gowns or white suits. But the sisters, observed together, were dazzling. It was a combination of their stature, the absence of pretense, and the openness with which they carried themselves. They exuded a warmth that was intoxicating.

Mr. Maccioni fawned over Lily appropriately. "*Quanto sei elegante!*" he said before reaching for her hand and kissing it lightly. Lily was disarmed by his chivalry but then gave it right back to him. "I couldn't be happier to spend the most important day of my life here with you." Marshall slipped his hand around her waist, resting it on her back. Had the Webbs walked into Le Cirque without the Middletons, they would have been seated in the rear of the dining room. It was that sort of place. It was like stepping into another world—a rarefied world of the elite. Circus-themed. Enchanting décor. Tented ceilings. Flower wall sconces. Monkeys painted on wall panels. Orange Limoges dinner plates with more monkeys. Glittering crystal and shiny silver.

Jane went to the restroom, and when she returned to the table, she was giddy. The others were seated and chatting. Placing her hands on her sister's shoulders and leaning in, she whispered, "I think I just peed in a stall next to Whitney Houston." Lily looked around, smiling from ear to ear. Reaching in front of her sister, Jane picked up one of Lily's forks and said, "I can see myself in the silver. I look pretty good." Old friends of the Middletons approached the table. Introductions. Handshakes. "Congratulations!" "Joy and happiness!" "Cheers to the happy couple!" Mrs. Middleton was beaming, and the newly married couple couldn't take their eyes off each other.

Once the champagne was poured, George raised his glass for the toast. He talked about Marshall's best qualities. His sense of loyalty and generosity. How taken aback he was when he learned that Marshall was engaged. Couldn't wait to meet the woman who had finally captured Marshall's heart. All of their buddies had thought he would be a lifelong bachelor, living in a hut somewhere in the Amazon counting exotic birds.

Looking at Lily, George said, "You have revealed to us a side of Marshall that has been hidden. We all knew Marshall as a loyal friend and brilliant scientist, but you have shown us, dare I say, a man consumed by passion." Then turning to the groom, George added, "Our wandering scientist has come home and has found his true love." Crystal clinked. Cheers all around. The mood was contagious. Mrs. Middleton followed George. She raised her glass and said, "Here's to the Webb family for raising a wonderful daughter. Here's to my new daughter-in-law."

Lily was moved by George and Mrs. Middleton's remarks. She wanted to make her own toast. She wanted everyone at the table, especially Marshall, Jane, and her dad, to know how happy she was. She wanted to tell them that, yes, life takes unexpected turns and there are losses, great losses, but love can be found again. Lily recalled what her father had said the night before. The sisters had been in their father's hotel room. He had taken Lily's hand and said, "When your mom knew that she probably wouldn't see this day for either of you, she said to me, 'I just want them to find the love we found.'" Mr. Webb's voice shook, forcing Jane to look away. Overwhelmed, all Lily could say was, "Oh, Daddy," as she wrapped her arms around him. She wondered if this was how happy her mother had felt when she married her father. She wanted Jane to find this sort of love. A companion. Trustworthy. Kind. But brides don't make toasts. So she sat back. Her shoulders relaxed. At ease. Soaking in the moment, committing it to memory. She turned to look at Marshall. He had his hand on his old friend's back, and they were laughing. In between Jane and her father, her new mother-in-law had captivated their attention with stories of who's who at the other tables. Jane was leaning in, listening attentively. That was a good sign. Her father smiling. "A perfect gentleman," Mrs. Middleton would say weeks after the special day.

The meal was off-menu. For the Webbs, most of the dishes were beyond the sensibilities of their middle-class palates. Early on, while dating Marshall, Lily had learned that even food was a matter of class distinction. She found this fascinating. It was a gastronomic feast: champagne by the bucket, Caspian Sea caviar, lobster with artichokes, duck legs, sea scallops with black truffles, warm skate fish salad, softshell crab, and Dover sole. The conversation was lively. With her arm around Marshall's shoulders, Lily fed him bites of her meal. Waiters kept the champagne flowing.

"Marshall tells me you are a proud Yalie," Mrs. Middleton said to Jane.

Jane had been conflicted about meeting Mrs. Middleton ever since she had learned that the woman was friendly with Phyllis Schlafly, a flaming national conservative who represented everything that Jane found deplorable and indefensible. But at dinner, Mrs. Middleton seemed harmless enough. Plus, both women by then had a good buzz on.

"I worry about Yale's turn toward conservatism," Jane said.

"I don't understand. Yale conservative?" Mrs. Middleton raised her brows.

"The spring that I graduated, in '82, there was a symposium and the initiation of an organization called the Federalist Society. Its conservative members want to go after abortion and other progressive legislation that will impact women and minorities. They're trying to remake society. The members of this little club have their eyes on the courts. All the courts. District courts, appellate courts, and the most obvious, the Supreme Court."

"I thought you studied math," Mrs. Middleton said.

"I did."

"I knew a feminist once," she said.

Jane laughed and took a sip of her champagne.

"Abby Rockefeller," Mrs. Middleton added. "David Rockefeller's daughter. She was into women's liberation."

"How could she not be?" Jane said.

"Are you lesbian?" Mrs. Middleton asked, seemingly out of the blue.

"I'm pretty sure you mean 'a lesbian.' In this case, it's a noun. The question is, 'Are you a lesbian?' Otherwise, you're using it as an adjective."

Mrs. Middleton, having switched to martinis, took a sip of her drink, which might have been her third, and after placing her glass on the table, turned to Jane and asked with a wry smile, "Well then, are you *a* lesbian?"

"Kudos to you," Jane said. She admired the woman's sauciness. And then she added, "Not full-time."

They ended the night with Grand Marnier, crème brûlée, and raspberry napoleons. A couple of days later, Marshall would return to pay the bill. Back at the hotel, Lily didn't want the night to end. She didn't want to take off her wedding dress. But she did, of course, much to Marshall's delight.

ITHACA, NEW YORK

1986–1990

It was Marshall's idea to take the photos. Lily had just come out of the shower, and instead of drying off completely, she wrapped a towel around her waist, picked up a hairbrush from the bathroom counter, and walked into the bedroom to sit down. Marshall came into the room and saw her sitting on the edge of the bed, still wrapped in a towel from the waist down. Her arms were raised over her head as she untied her hair from a bun. Her breasts fully exposed. Late afternoon rays fell across her lap and lit the wooden floors.

"You look amazing," he told her. "Let me photograph you."

When Marshall came back with his camera, Lily was wearing a long camel-colored cashmere robe he had bought her at Bergdorf Goodman for Christmas. She held the robe closed at the top, near her neck, to cover her breasts. At first, he clicked away, watching her from behind the camera.

"Take off the robe," he told her. It was almost a whisper.

Lily pulled the robe off her shoulders.

He was so taken by her beauty. She smiled, knowing that his de-sire had gotten the best of him. With a surge of confidence, she stood in front of the window and lowered her robe. Over and over, he said, "You're so beautiful."

He got closer, holding the camera in the palm of his hand out to the side. She reached around his neck, drawing him to her, their lips touching lightly.

"Come over here," he said, pulling her away from the window.

She followed him to the bed, where he turned her around. Lily placed the palms of her hands on the edge of the bed, bending slightly. His hand searched for her, first caressing her belly, and then moving between her thighs.

After, Marshall said, "Time stops when I'm with you; everything else fades away. I'm never more present than when we make love."

Lying on her side, Lily stroked his chest. She knew what he was describing, a change in one's perception. The stillness of time. She had felt it years ago with the boy. But in this moment, she focused on her husband. "How lucky am I that I found you," Lily said.

The early years of their marriage were idyllic. Their happiness as a couple was welded to their shared intellectual pursuits. Marshall had accepted a new position at Cornell University in upstate New York. Lily spent hours in the library among the stacks of periodicals, reading the latest ornithology literature, keeping copious notes. Every year, Marshall attended two or three professional conferences and Lily joined him, attending panel after panel, listening to experts in the field.

In 1988, they traveled to Pittsburgh, where they spent spring break at the aviary, home to more than five hundred birds. Conservationists were having great success breeding the endangered Guam rails, and Marshall and Lily were thrilled to see the birds, considering that the species had gone extinct in the wild a few years before.

For Lily's thirty-first birthday, Marshall surprised her with front-row seats at Shea Stadium in New York to see the Rolling Stones. They were so close to the stage that Lily could see the buttons on Mick Jagger's coat and the black leather studded belt slung around his hips. George Mellon, who had contacts with the parks commissioner, had secured the tickets. Days afterward, Lily found Marshall in the kitchen imitating Keith Richards's iconic guitar riff. "Duh-da-dah, da-dah-da-da-da . . ." Then he strutted like a rooster with his fists tucked into his ribs and his elbows oscillating. In his best Jagger accent, he belted out the lyrics, "*If you start me up . . .*" ending with "*You make a grown man cry-y-y-y-y,*" all the while jabbing his finger in the air and pointing at Lily with his lips protruding. It was the fact that he did it all with a straight face that made Lily cackle.

After they had been married for three years, they decided to start a family, and Lily went off her birth control pills. The tone of their lovemaking changed a bit—the sex was slower and more tender, less vigorous. The passion remained, it just felt more intimate. As the months passed and Lily hadn't conceived, they gradually moved back to their former patterns, when sometimes sex was short and sweet and other times urgent, exhausting. And Lily was fine with it all, but she worried about when she would get pregnant.

She managed to see Jane and her father several times a year. Lily would've liked to have seen them more, but their work schedules prevented it. She did, however, speak to Jane every few days. They had a system: Jane would call, letting the phone ring three times before hanging up. Then Lily would call her right back so that the long-distance charge appeared on Lily's telephone bill and not Jane's.

Sometimes Jane would call to tell Lily about one of her many lovers and how great—or not-so-great—the sex was. She was obsessed with the murder of a young woman from Ben Lomond who had been hitchhiking home from a party in the Santa Cruz Mountains. Lily freaked out when Jane told her that she had hitchhiked the same route several times. When he found out, Marshall sent Jane a couple grand to buy a used Saab.

Once Jane had a car, she frequently drove north to Palo Alto to hear prominent mathematicians lecture. For a time, she was dating a tech millionaire who took her to wild parties in Los Gatos, but when he asked her to go on a retreat at Esalen, she told Lily, "I love Big Sur, but I can't take that New Age introspective bullshit." So she broke up with him.

Jane was practicing tithing; she had started to give away 10 percent of her annual wages as a waitress to the poor, something she had learned from her parents. She got fired from the Crow's Nest because she threw a drink in the bartender's face after he refused to stop harassing a younger waitress. A few days later, she found another job. One night, she called Lily, excited about having attended a lecture at UC Santa Cruz by a physicist who worked on dark matter. "Do you remember the night Mom took us to the monastery gardens when we were little? The guy I heard last night has changed our understanding of the universe's fundamental composition."

What Jane didn't tell Lily was that she had taken to using speed to pull all-nighters to work on proofs after double shifts waiting tables. And that on her days off, she liked the effects of oxycodone over weed when she could find some.

…

ONE EARLY EVENING, MARSHALL came home and asked, "Would it be too much trouble to throw together a dinner party for a big donor, a few colleagues, and students next weekend?"

"Jane's coming this week," Lily said, looking up from her book.

"Well, that's perfect, she can cook."

Working in restaurants over the years, Jane had vastly improved her culinary skills since she was a teenager. Suppressing a smile, Lily remembered the chicken her sister had prepared after her abortion.

"We could have it catered."

"Whatever works best."

Marshall's reputation had attracted new donors, who liked their names attached to buildings. One in particular, Frank Martin, considered himself an amateur ornithologist. An avid participant in the annual Christmas Bird Count, he was a widower and retiree who had made his money in aviation and defense technology and was eager to help Marshall expand the laboratory facilities.

While the sisters were in the bathroom putting on makeup for the party, Lily said, "Even if this guy is boring, will you pretend you're interested?"

"I'll do my best," Jane said.

"I have no idea about his politics, so if he says anything off-the-wall, try not to react," Lily added.

"Got it."

"And no talk about the Iran—Contra affair."

"Check!"

"And nothing about the Soviet—Afghan war."

"I get it, I get it," Jane said, chuckling.

Normally, discussions about politics were not off-limits at faculty dinner parties, but given that the main objective of this evening's dinner was to secure a donation, Lily wanted to play it safe. Given how wealthy Frank Martin purported to be, Lily was guessing his and Jane's politics wouldn't match up.

For the past two days, Jane had done all the heavy lifting for the party: She had handpicked the filet mignon and vegetables, shopped for the bread and French butter, prepared a flourless chocolate cake, and had a case of some trendy Washington State merlot delivered to the house along with a blue-and-white flower arrangement. She cooked all day while Lily set the table with Wedgwood china and polished silver.

When the guests arrived, together Marshall and Lily mixed drinks, poured wine, and made introductions. Lily had a seating arrangement in mind, but academics, she had learned over the years, were sometimes oblivious to social conventions. Her guests soon picked their own spots. Gillian, Marshall's colleague, sat in a center seat. To Gillian's left was Henry Potter, Marshall's senior colleague, now in his mid-seventies, who had spent the past fifteen years collecting data and researching the decline of the Florida scrub jay; he was considered a leader in the endangered species management movement. Next to Professor Potter sat Andre, one of the nicest graduate students Lily had met over the years. He researched tropical birds in Ecuador. Marshall's colleague Bert Colburn sat across from Gillian. Bert was on the cutting edge of identifying genes associated with migrating warblers. At one end of the table was the guest of honor, Frank Martin, who looked exceptionally pleased when Jane stood behind her chair and smiled at him, indicating she would be sitting next to him. Marshall sat at the other head. Lily maneuvered around all of them with grace while Jane poured the wine. Glasses sparkled; cutlery clattered against the plates. When Andre commented on the meal, the others chimed in "Delicious" and "Best meal I've had all year."

An effort was made to keep Frank Martin at the center of the discussion. He talked about his latest adventure to Thailand, where he had been promised he would see more than four hundred different bird species in the bamboo forests, on the lakes, and in the rainforests. He told the others about his encounters with the rare Gurney's pitta.

"Spectacular neon-yellow underparts with a blue-and-black crown."

"What does it sound like?" Jane asked.

Frank pursed his lips and let out a wobbly, high-pitched *prru-uupp*. When Jane tried to copy him, he was charmed, instantly. Others lamented the demise of Thai forests due to development. With his mouth half full, Frank turned to Jane and asked, "So, what do you do?"

"I'm a waitress," Jane said.

Lily looked around at the others, who, if they were surprised by Jane's response, did their best to conceal it. She felt protective of Jane in the midst of all these well-credentialed scientists.

"Jane studied mathematics at Yale," Lily told them.

Gillian froze as if she were trying to avoid a bee buzzing around her head. She had her fork raised to her mouth and said "Really," in a tone that infuriated Lily.

"Yes, really, I can count really high," Jane said, smiling.

Andre and Frank laughed.

Gillian wouldn't let up. "You studied number theory?"

"Yes," Jane said as she took another bite of the beef.

"Now you're waiting tables?"

The room went still. Everyone was looking at Jane when they should have been looking at Gillian, Lily thought.

"David Mumford, a Fields Medal recipient, was impressed enough to tell Jane that he would work with her when she was ready," Marshall said, breaking the silence. And then looking at Jane, he added, "My sister-in-law is extraordinary."

Jane looked over at Marshall and said, "Continue."

The others laughed.

"And when she was in school, she was tutored by a key figure on the Manhattan Project with Oppenheimer," Marshall added.

It meant the world to Lily that Marshall respected her sister in all her complexities, particularly given her unconventional style and habits. Other than the fact that they were both exceptionally bright and possessed a penchant for the sciences, Marshall and Jane couldn't have been more different, Lily thought, watching them both over dinner. Marshall had beautiful manly manners. Jane, on the other hand, well, Jane was Jane: unruly, unapologetically forthright, and wildly profane.

Tonight, Lily felt comfortable among Marshall's colleagues. Logical minds. Open to uncertainties. Spending time with them, except for Gillian, who was arrogant, brought back childhood memories of her parents. Surrounded by books. Endless curiosity. A keenness for the mysteries of nature.

"Well, I'm impressed," Gillian said. Then she added, "Don't you think your mentors would have wanted you to pursue graduate work?"

"Of course," Jane said, taking a sip of wine.

Whatever buttons Gillian was trying to push, Jane wasn't responding.

"What about your tutor, the one who worked with Oppenheimer, didn't he encourage you to continue your studies?"

Jane paused for a second, took another sip of wine, and said, "He's spent most of his life in a moral crisis over his contribution to the atom bomb, so honestly, he's just glad to see me when I return home for a visit."

Gillian continued. "But why not tutor or teach?"

"Why not exactly?" Jane said diplomatically. Except she knew the real reason: She did not want a career interfering with her depression and drug use. In a different setting, she might have said that aloud to get a laugh, but she was on her best behavior tonight.

When Lily stood up to collect dinner plates, Jane followed her. The conversation at the table shifted to Bert's genetic studies on warblers. Out of earshot, in the kitchen, Lily apologized for Gillian's behavior.

"You're probably the smartest one at the table and you know that," Lily said.

"That's not what it's about for me. Never was."

Lily left the kitchen to continue clearing the table. Jane was standing with her back to the door and didn't see Lily turn around and watch Jane reach into her front pocket, put something into her mouth, and wash it down with a swig of vodka.

Lily observed her guests that night like the birds they studied; she didn't miss anything. Bert had one glass of wine, no more; Andre barely touched the beef; Henry Potter talked a bit more than Marshall would have probably wanted him to. Once in the living room, Lily couldn't help noticing that Frank, the donor, who was sitting next to Jane, patted her knee and left his hand there a little too long. Lily had met very few men who did not fall for Jane.

When Frank stood to indicate he was ready to leave, Bert stood as well.

"I'd be happy to drive you back to the hotel," Bert said.

"I'll walk, if you don't mind," Frank replied.

"Great idea. I could use a walk myself," Marshall said.

"That won't be necessary; Jane's agreed to walk me back."

When Jane and Frank walked out the front door, Lily caught a glance of her sister's eyes. She knew Jane's eyes better than her own. Whatever Jane had popped into her mouth in the kitchen had taken effect. *Her pupils can't lie,* Lily thought.

About six-thirty the next morning, Marshall and Lily were sitting down to breakfast when the front door opened. Jane joined them in the kitchen and went right for the coffee.

"Just getting back?" Marshall asked, looking up from the morning paper spread out in front of him.

"Yep!"

"Well, that's one way to score a big donation," Marshall said.

"Listen," Jane said, taking a sip of her coffee, "let's just say that after last night, the university might be naming a building after *me*."

Lily shook her head. Marshall grinned and stood up from the table. "I'll let you two have your postmortem in private." Leaning in, he kissed Lily's cheek and added, "Let me know later if I need to start looking for another job."

Jane laughed. "Trust me on this one; you'll thank me later when that check comes in."

The first thing Lily said to her sister when Marshall was out of earshot was, "He's in his seventies."

"And what's your point?"

"Why?"

"Why what? Why have consensual sex with a single, attractive man?" Jane said, smiling.

"Jesus, Jane."

Jane sipped her black coffee. "I'll tell you this, he was one generous lover."

"Stop!" Lily said, laughing.

"No, I'm telling you he was one of the best. He must've gone down on me for fifteen minutes. From now on, I'm going to have more requirements. If the guys I'm with don't know how to go down on me, then I'm not giving them a second chance."

Lily laughed again; only her sister made her laugh this much.

She wanted to ask Jane about her recent visit with Tim Jones. Years ago, she had signaled to her sister that she needed to put their high school years behind them. Jane understood and acquiesced, so much so that it was Mr. Webb who mentioned to Lily that Jane had seen Tim. Lily felt a little apprehensive bringing up his name. She just didn't know what she was going to hear or where the conversation would lead. She had waited until it was just the two of them. That way, they could avoid Marshall's possible questions.

Lily took a bite of her toast and wiped the crumbs from her mouth with the back of her hand. "Tell me about your visit with Tim Jones."

Jane looked over at her, paused, and then said, "He told me he was gay."

Lily's jaw dropped. "What about the navy? Do they know?"

Jane reached over, took a piece of her sister's toast, and said, "Nope."

"Does his father know?"

"Nope. He was so honest, said living a lie was killing him, said he had sex with a man before his wife's second pregnancy, and during the pregnancy he started having panic attacks, thinking that he might've infected his wife and unborn baby with HIV. Couldn't live with it. Said he's known he was gay since high school. He's getting a divorce."

"That takes a bit of courage," Lily said.

"A bit? Try a fucking truckload—he's a Black man, an officer in the navy, over ten years in, and he's gay."

It made Lily sad that her old friend had struggled all these years. She wondered the extent to which keeping secrets was self-preservation or self-destruction. Or both. Instead of focusing on the skeletons she had in her own closet—the ones she kept hidden from Marshall about the boy—it was easier to turn her attention to her sister's, which were starting to worry her.

"I have to ask you something," Lily said.

"Shoot."

Lily wrapped her hands around her coffee mug and asked, "Did I see you take something last night?"

"I don't know. Did you?"

"Yeah. I did. We were standing in the kitchen after dinner, and you took something out of your front pocket and put it in your mouth."

"Well, then you must've seen me take something. Does that answer your question?"

Undeterred, Lily asked, "What was it?"

"What was it?"

"Yeah, what was it?"

"It was Percocet. Two to be exact."

"Were they prescribed?"

"Give me a fucking break, Lily. I busted my butt for this party."

ITHACA, NEW YORK

1991

It was late afternoon on a Wednesday, and Lily was waiting for Marshall to return from Manhattan. She had spent the afternoon reading Andre's research on the velvet-purple coronet—a radiant bluish-green and deep-purple hummingbird of Ecuador's Pichincha province—which she had willingly agreed to look over as a favor to the graduate student. But she was preoccupied and had a hard time concentrating. Every once in a while, if she thought she heard a car, she jumped up from the sofa to look out the window. Marshall had driven down to the city to seek a second opinion from a urologist, a former classmate of his from Exeter, one of the best. He had already seen a urologist in Ithaca and had been told that his sperm count might be low. Once it was determined that Lily was capable of getting pregnant—from hormone study after hormone study—they turned their attention to Marshall. Lily sat in the living room, the chapters of Andre's dissertation on her lap. She would read a page and then reread it, retaining

little. She understood the main argument: Deforestation and fragmentation of the colorful hummingbird's habitat disrupted breeding
and nesting sites and created challenges for the tiny birds to find food.

When they first moved into the house in Ithaca, Lily had the interior
repainted from its seventies mustard and avocado colors to a warm
white. She had exercised restraint when it came to the excesses of
home décor in the late eighties. Matching floral chintz with window
treatments was simply not her style. Instead, she paired the white
walls with a cream-colored sofa and a red antique Persian rug with
geometric shapes that Marshall had inherited from his grandmother.
Lily had put red-and-blue Turkish covers on her decorative pillows
and placed blue-and-white vases around the room, filled with freshly
cut flowers. In the winter months, Marshall would bring her two
dozen white roses.

They had started collecting oil paintings, nothing extravagant.
Her favorite, one they had purchased from a local artist, hung over the
fireplace. Lily had found it at an early summer art show; it reminded
her of Turner's *Fishermen at Sea*. When she first saw it, she thought of
a line from a well-known poem: *I must go down to the seas again, to the
lonely sea and the sky*. The painting was of a dramatic stormy seascape
captured in grays, blues, and a brilliant white. Rising waves, whitecaps, a small wooden boat, and a dark sky. Marshall had teased her
about the intensity of the painting and questioned why she was drawn
to it. At the time, Lily couldn't say what compelled her so, besides its
seemingly otherworldly quality. In the end, Marshall said, "It's because you're a Rhode Island girl."

When she heard Marshall's car pull up, she met him at the front
door. He kissed her on the forehead and smiled. She sensed the news
wasn't going to be good, and she was determined not to cry. She

rubbed the back of his shoulder as he walked past her into the living room. Noticing the unbound dissertation chapters spread out on the sofa, he sat down on one of the side chairs.

"What do you think?" he said, gesturing with his chin to Andre's work.

"It's really coming along," Lily said as she gathered up the pages and placed them at one end of the sofa before sitting down.

They looked at each other. She was waiting for him to tell her the news.

"Walter said my sperm count is too low." He smiled wistfully at her until he couldn't hold her gaze any longer and lowered his head. Then, looking up and raising his eyebrows, he added, "It appears there aren't enough mechanics in the paddock. Not enough boys in the clubhouse."

"I understand," Lily said softly. Her head tilted to the side. She was worried about how this news would affect him.

Marshall chuckled at his own jokes, but when he looked at her again, Lily saw sadness in his eyes.

She knew what he was feeling. She had panicked herself when the doctors were testing her for infertility. At one point, she worried that the reason they had not conceived was the abortion she had had in high school. But she knew that was silly, that thoughts like that were born of toxic pro-life propaganda.

"Had I known this before we got married, I never would have . . ." Marshall stopped and closed his eyes.

Lily was stunned. "You never would have what?" she asked.

"Put you in this situation . . ."

"You mean, you never would have married me?"

Marshall looked at her and said, "I know you want to have children, is what I'm trying to say, and I want them, too, with you, but it might not be possible. And, yeah, had I known, I wouldn't have asked this of you. You know, to give up on your desire to have children."

By now she was sitting on the edge of the sofa. She extended her arm to hold his hand. He reached back and held hers.

"I love you," Lily said and didn't take her eyes off him.

He smiled, but the disappointment was plain. "Are you ready to try IVF?" he asked.

Lily fought back tears. "Absolutely."

As she stood, so did Marshall. She wrapped her arms around his neck, lifting her face to his to kiss him sweetly on the lips.

Early in the process, when Lily was being tested, they had talked about the possibility of IVF. They had both read a piece in *The New York Times* about a federal investigation into fertility clinics. It appeared that many clinics were not collecting medical or genetic histories from donors. On top of that, they weren't testing for HIV or other infectious diseases. The industry was unregulated. This made them uneasy. Marshall had said things like, "We'll cross that bridge when we get to it."

Well, now they were certainly at the bridge, and Lily was comforted that he was willing to cross it with her. It wasn't lost on Lily that Marshall had been thirty-three in 1978, when the first baby conceived through in vitro fertilization was born. The occasion had sparked huge debates. Lily remembered heated discussions in her biology classes at Smith, with students asking: Who owned the embryos? Will it lead to a rise in designer babies? What about accessibility and affordability? But few people were asking why infertility was always framed as a female problem. While male infertility had been recognized by scientists, it was still not widely discussed in public, due largely to the way masculinity was viewed. The lack of public discourse was because it was stigmatized. And yet, Lily never once sensed that Marshall's early reticence stemmed from shame or the fear of feeling emasculated. By now, Lily and Marshall had been married for five years, and she never, ever wanted to take him for granted.

1991

Mrs. Middleton was scheduled to arrive in Rhode Island for a two-day visit with her son and daughter-in-law. Her visit to Aquidneck Island coincided with their and Jane's annual summer visit. Lily was much less intimidated by her mother-in-law since the wedding. Jane could take Mrs. Middleton in small doses as long as Jane was stoned or had a few drinks in her. And it was better when Mrs. Middleton had a few drinks in her, too. That's why Jane had agreed to spend the afternoon with her sister's mother-in-law.

In an odd way, Lily had grown fond of her mother-in-law and looked forward to seeing her. The only problem was, what would they do? The Webbs were not members of any tennis or beach clubs, and they didn't own a sailboat that could accommodate the group. So Lily was relieved when Mrs. Middleton called to say that an old friend had invited them for lunch at Bailey's Beach, an exclusive club for families like the Astors, Vanderbilts, and other members of elite society. Mrs.

Middleton had decided that it would be an all-girls day out and that they would join Marshall and Mr. Webb later in the evening for dinner.

Lily wore white linen slacks with a black fitted top and her gold bracelet and ring. Her Wayfarers rested on her head. What Jane wore, however, caught the attention of her father.

"Is that lingerie?"

Jane looked down at her dress, which was a mid-length pale-pink slip with spaghetti straps. Mr. Webb was right; it was actually meant to be worn under a vintage dress that Jane bought at a consignment store.

"Probably," Jane said, then kissed her dad's cheek before walking out the door.

The sisters picked up Mrs. Middleton at the Viking. Passing the mansions on Bellevue Avenue, Lily's mother-in-law repeated stories about the homes' residents, many of which the girls knew from local lore. "That's Rough Point, where Doris Duke accidentally hit the gas pedal, pinning her interior decorator against the gate, killing him." And "That's where poor Sunny von Bülow's husband tried to kill her with insulin." Like everyone in Newport, the sisters had followed the trials, especially the appeal in which Claus von Bülow was acquitted.

The clubhouse was painted dove gray with canary-yellow trim. The three women were the guests of Mimi Hamilton and were seated outside on the porch overlooking the ocean.

"Our first year at school together they made us eat at the fat table," Mrs. Middleton explained. Her old friend chuckled. Seeing the look of surprise on Lily's face, Mrs. Middleton added, "There was a table for the girls who were too thin and a table for fat girls—girls like me and Mimi who had to lose twenty pounds or so."

Lily grimaced. Jane couldn't resist.

"Are you serious? They made overweight girls sit at a separate table?"

"Oh, yes," Mimi said, sipping on her martini. The two older women had gone to Miss Porter's, a finishing school for daughters from the wealthiest families.

"We became best friends instantly, the only two girls at the fat table. Bunny Topper was at the thin table," Mrs. Middleton told them.

"Where she stayed for four years!" Mimi said.

"She's still anorexic. That's what they call it now," Mrs. Middleton said, pressing her hand on the forearm of Jane, who was sitting to her right.

The sisters nodded. Lily was polite and restrained. Jane, however, acted like a social anthropologist, asking question after question. Lily was happy her sister had joined them and was grateful she remained curious enough to carry the conversation. Except for Lily, the women each had two martinis before their meals were delivered.

"What was Marshall like as a child?" Jane asked Mrs. Middleton.

"He was always different," Mimi said.

Now Lily was all ears. "What do you mean by different?" she asked.

"He had no interest in sports like tennis or clay shooting, just nature. We couldn't go anywhere without him rescuing animals," Mrs. Middleton explained. "One summer, he nursed an owl and a baby squirrel. I remember he made a bed out of fleece and fed the squirrel with a syringe. It slept in his room for weeks."

Hearing this, Jane placed her hand on her heart. A gesture that was not lost on Mrs. Middleton.

"He's a good man," Jane said, smiling at Lily.

"One of the few," Mrs. Middleton remarked and then added,

"When I am honest with myself, and that's not too often, I wish I was more like Marshall."

"What a wonderful thing to say about your son," Lily said to her mother-in-law and then thought, *I'll tell Marshall this. He deserves to know what his mother thinks of him.*

Lily caught herself wondering to what extent her own children would be like Marshall. For the past six months, they had put their hopes on IVF.

After their plates were cleared, Lily went to the ladies' room and Mimi excused herself to speak to her grandchildren. Jane turned to Mrs. Middleton and asked, "Were you disappointed that Marshall wasn't more endogamous in his choice of a life partner?"

"Endogamous?"

"To marry within."

Mrs. Middleton laughed. "Endogamous? As if we are some sort of a tribe."

"Well, we are. Aren't we? Different tribes with different customs," Jane said, smiling.

"Since we're being so direct, I was surprised, but I couldn't be happier that my son married Lily. I've never seen him as happy. How lucky that your sister was single when she and Marshall met."

Jane nodded, but this time she kept her thoughts to herself. While Jane's fondness for her brother-in-law continued to grow, particularly as she saw how good he was to her sister, she often wondered if Lily regretted marrying him instead of her first love.

"When he said he was going to the Amazon, I thought he'd be eaten alive," Mrs. Middleton said.

"Seriously?" Jane asked, making a face.

"Of course. I knew Michael Rockefeller, who was killed by the natives in New Guinea. Needless to say . . ."

By now Lily and Mimi had returned to the table. When Mimi

overheard the conversation, she interjected, "That's a dreadful story. I still think about him."

"I thought he drowned," Jane said.

Ignoring her, Mrs. Middleton said, "Look what happened to Captain Cook and Percy Fawcett."

"Cook died in Hawaii and Fawcett was in the Amazon. Not New Guinea," Jane explained.

"What's the difference?" Mimi said. "The natives ate them. They were headhunters."

Jane took a sip of water. Lily knew she was suppressing a laugh and a sarcastic remark. She was relieved that Jane didn't say something like *Are you fucking kidding me?* Lily had once told her sister, "You have no room in your life for anyone who says anything unacceptable about another group of people unless, of course, you're the one saying it."

Lily thought about how humans are always drawing lines between themselves and others: Westerners versus others, Europeans versus Native Americans, Chinese versus the Mongols. She looked around the private club. Members versus nonmembers. And then she wondered what the lines of division justified.

Halfway through dessert, Mimi drew her guests' attention to a table of four seated a few feet away.

"He is the third husband of one of the Wetmores," Mimi said, mainly to Mrs. Middleton.

The sisters had already noticed the gentleman to whom their host was referring. The man was a loud talker and spoke in a harsh tone to the waitstaff. The first time he did it, he complained about how his cocktail was prepared. The second time, his steak was overcooked.

"Does this look like medium rare to you?" he asked a young man, who looked to be about eighteen. The waiter blushed and stumbled over his words.

Jane couldn't hide her disgust, but she had a plan. She discreetly removed an earring and slipped it into her pocket. Once in the foyer of the clubhouse, as the women were saying their goodbyes, Jane announced, "I think I may have lost my earring. Just give me a second." As she turned to go back to the table, Mrs. Middleton said, "You were wearing two during lunch." Then Mrs. Middleton reached over and moved Jane's hair back so she could get a better look—thinking it might have fallen and gotten lost in her long hair.

"Let me go check around the table," Jane said.

Jane walked back outside onto the porch and approached the table of four where the rude man was sitting. She smiled seductively, capturing the man's attention. Anyone watching would have thought Jane knew the man. They locked eyes. Jane was still smiling coquettishly. When she got close enough, she tapped her finger on the table directly in front of him and said quietly in her most enchanting voice, "This isn't some Dickens novel; we don't treat people like that. Plus, one would think with all your money you could afford to buy yourself some manners."

...

WHILE DRIVING BACK TO Ithaca, Lily and Marshall had lunch at the diner they'd been stopping at since they moved to upstate New York. It was halfway between Lily's father's house and their own.

It was a place right out of the sixties: chrome countertops, red leather stools and booths, and the smell of coffee brewing. Filled with working-class men, traveling families, and senior citizens. It was a Monday, close to noon, and they both ordered grilled cheese sandwiches and chips. Marshall later ordered a piece of key lime pie for dessert, and that's when the waitress mentioned that the diner had been sold and would be closing.

Once the waitress walked away, Lily said, "We always stop here. I guess we'll have to find someplace else."

Marshall looked at her and his eyes narrowed. Then they grew wide. "That's it! It's not the breeding ground or the winter ground, it's the stopover site."

Lily knew exactly what he was talking about. Warbler migration.

They had long-running conversations about the decline of the species and whether it was due to deforestation of the wintering grounds or a problem at the breeding grounds, especially with forest fragmentation and habitat loss.

Marshall said what he had been thinking: "Might the stopover sites be the critical piece of their ecology?"

They both sat in silence thinking about how this would change the general understanding of seasonal migration, not just for warblers but all birds that travel thousands and thousands of miles.

"See what you do to me?" Marshall added, squeezing Lily's leg beneath the table.

"We feed off each other like Pierre and Marie Curie," Lily said, laughing.

Marshall lifted his coffee cup to his lips and peered at her over the rim. She reached across the table and took his other hand.

In that moment she thought, *Even without children, this is going to be a good life.*

NEW YORK, NEW YORK

1992

They had sought treatment in New York City at Weill Cornell Medicine, which had established itself as the leader in fertility treatment. The drive from Ithaca was a little more than four hours. Eight hours round trip. For each attempt, Lily's eggs had been retrieved, and a sperm sample had been collected from Marshall. After five failed attempts, the fertility specialist called them in for a consultation.

Lily and Marshall sat side by side holding hands in the doctor's private office. They exchanged glances, offering each other fragile smiles. Before getting out of the car, Lily had reached over, put her hand on his shoulder, and said, "No matter what happens, we're going to be fine." Now she listened to the sound of the clock ticking as they waited for the doctor. The clock sat on a heavy cherrywood desk. Three large framed photographs of sailboats hung on the wall. Marshall tried to make small talk. It had worked on the drive down, but now they were both a little on edge.

The doctor entered the office from a door behind his desk. He didn't waste any time. There were no viable embryos. There likely never would be.

At the end of the visit, he stood and said, "I wish I had better news."

They walked in silence to the parking garage, holding hands. When they got to the car, Marshall turned around and leaned against it. He reached for Lily, holding on to her arms. "I'm sorry," he said. "I'm so sorry."

A few days later, standing in the shower after Marshall had left for work, Lily wept. Shampoo ran down her breasts and belly. Being childless was not what she had planned for her life. Up until they started fertility testing, Lily had imagined she would stay home and take care of their children. She imagined herself as a homemaker with an emphasis on education, supplementing what her children learned in school, much like her mother had done. Reading in the afternoons with her children. Taking long walks in the woods, learning about the flora and fauna. And now she would have to imagine a different life.

She loved her long discussions with Marshall on all matters related to ornithology, including talks about his own research agenda as well as the broad material he was required to teach his students. Lily now decided to pursue a life of independent research. She would need to identify an area of focus. She had access to Cornell's libraries and archives, and she so enjoyed attending professional conferences and listening to experts. Lily thought of Caroline Herschel, the sister of renowned astronomer William Herschel. She had never attended a university, yet between 1786 and 1797, she made significant contributions to the field by discovering eight comets. And while Lily did not yearn for fame, she liked having the historical reference for inspiration. She knew she had the self-discipline required to do research and saw herself as a lifelong learner.

Lily remembered what her mother had said upon returning from her book club. "I'd give anything to read eight hours a day." Without children, that's the type of freedom Lily would have. Just like the monks at the Priory and Thomas Jefferson, whom she'd recently learned had kept a rigorous daily reading schedule from morning until night. She decided she would read along with Marshall's graduate students, following the syllabus for every class. And she would read more widely in environmental studies and climate-change science and then dip into history and astronomy.

This bought her some peace, for a while.

ITHACA, NEW YORK

JULY 1992

Outside in the backyard under a tall sycamore tree, Marshall had positioned a large wicker chair with a high back, a footstool, and an outdoor side table for Lily's books and cool drinks. That way Lily could sit under the shade and still feel the summer warmth. On a Friday afternoon in July, she watched the hummingbirds flutter about nearby, blessing the lupine and foxgloves. The family bird feeder attracted its share of cardinals, blue jays, chickadees, and finches.

When Marshall returned from running errands, he presented her with the day's mail—a Saks Fifth Avenue catalog (he said it made it easier for him to buy her gifts) and a letter from Portsmouth.

Lily looked at the letter and return address. Who had a P.O. box in Portsmouth with such feminine penmanship? Lily opened the letter. An announcement. Class reunion. Fifteen years. Green Valley Country Club. October. She looked it over for a second and then placed it on the table next to her. She had no intention of going. She closed her eyes and leaned her head back.

She spent the weekend alone. Marshall and a few of his graduate students were attending a summer conference. Sitting in her living room chair, she picked up a book she had borrowed from the university library, a copy of *Incompleteness, Nonlocality, and Realism,* which covered the past twenty years of advancements in quantum mechanics. Entanglement theory. Action at a distance. These were highly controversial subjects among physicists, she recalled from her days at Smith. At great distances, subatomic particles affect one another without being physically connected. Objects separated by space. Interconnected. Mutually constitutive. What did this mean for time? Her thoughts lacked coherency. She felt herself nodding off.

In that moment with her feet up and the book resting on her lap, an image of the boy came to her from nowhere. His broad back and slouching shoulders at the trial. Memories of him had come to her over the years, spurred by another man's profile, the forearm of a stranger. Flashes she'd turned from, canceled with a blink. But here, now, in her living room, the memories came like waves during a hurricane, one after the other: his triumphant smile as he walked off the field of his last game; the tenderness of his mouth in Escobar's cornfield; the glow of the porch light on his face and the snow in his hair that Valentine's Day.

Entangled quantum particles had sparked a light show of images.

Do my feelings for him respond like a light wave? Are we an entangled photon pair?

This thought, emerging someplace between her conscious mind and her dozing self, made her nervous. For years she had buried her feelings, any and all remnants of desire for the boy kept at bay. She wanted to be a good wife, a loyal wife, even in her thoughts. Her guilt was layered. She felt guilty for having ruined the boy's life, she felt guilty for imagining his body. She didn't want to be reminded that she might still love him.

She took a deep breath.

Once, she had asked her sister if she had heard any news about him. That was close to ten years ago. Jane had kept it short. Told her that he had left Portsmouth when he got out of prison and joined the merchant mariners—that he was somewhere in the South China Sea. She had learned this before she started dating Marshall, when she was trying to let go of the boy in earnest because that's what he wanted. To have nothing to do with her.

It was spring 1978. Lily had returned to Rhode Island to visit the boy. She turned off Route 37 in Cranston and pulled into the parking lot. She was taken aback by the sight of the prison. Bizarrely, it looked like a castle. She remained in the car, taking it all in. It was a mid-nineteenth-century, three-story granite block building. Gothic style. From where she was parked, she could see only one of the five observational towers with its armed guard. On each side of the castle-like structure were stone walls more than twenty feet high. She assumed that the prison yard was contained within these walls. About three feet beyond the curb was a high chain-link security fence topped with coiled razor wire. Beyond that fence, about six feet away, was a second identical one.

She knew about the prison's reputation. She had been fourteen when a riot had broken out and made national news. It had taken close to one hundred heavily armed state policemen to quell the riot. The inmates had taken over the south wing and set fire to the wood-working shop.

Head's uncle, who had worked as a correctional officer and was there during the uprising, had told Head, who had then told Jane, about how the prison was run by the mafia and that an ambulance had remained parked outside every day—not for the inmates but for the guards.

She was getting out of her car when she heard someone yell "Hey!"

It was Mr. Kenny, the high school football coach. His face was red; it looked like he had been running. He was out of breath.

"Hey!" he yelled again.

Turning around, Lily said, "Hi." She thought about hugging him, but his demeanor seemed a little off. She wondered if he had been drinking.

"He's having a hard day today," the coach told her.

When Lily didn't say anything, Mr. Kenny said, "Why can't you just leave him alone?"

"What? I'm coming to visit."

"Yeah, I know what you're here for, and I'm asking you, why can't you just leave him alone?"

Lily got angry. She tried to get around the coach, but he was a pretty big man and kept blocking her.

He spat on the ground and said, "He's not going to want to see you."

"Excuse me?" Lily said, forcefully and with no intention of being polite. When Mr. Kenny didn't move, she looked around the parking lot to see if she might call for help. They were alone.

Towering over her, he said, "I got to tell you, it troubles me that you can't remember anything."

"I—I don't know what happened," she snapped.

The coach was unrelenting. "Yet Cooper was so enraged that he almost killed a boy. And you stand there and tell me you don't know what happened. Are you saying that maybe David McCarren didn't force you to have sex?"

Lily was silent, her rage expanding in her chest. She wanted to get into the car and drive away.

"What sort of girl goes to parties without her boyfriend unless she's hoping to meet up with another guy?"

Lily put her hand up in front of her to block his face.

Coach Kenny was breathing heavily. "McCarren is awfully attractive. Maybe you wanted to have sex with him and used the booze as an excuse for not remembering—could that be it?"

"No, no. Absolutely not!"

"You're absolutely sure? Yet you can't remember what happened—that sounds like a contradiction. . . . If I were Cooper's father, I might've advised him to stay clear of you."

"That's an awful thing to say. You don't even know me," Lily said.

"I know enough to know that that kid is in jail instead of at training camp because of what you claim you can't remember."

Lily was stunned. She turned to get back into her car, but then she felt a rush of anger. Turning, she yelled, "Fuck you, Coach Kenny! How dare you presume to know anything about our relationship?"

His face turned redder. He took a breath and his muscles flinched; she thought for sure he was going to hit her, but that didn't stop her.

"And don't think for a minute his talents reflect your coaching." She moved closer to him.

Coach Kenny raised his hands, backed up, and made a face as if she was the one out of line, as if she had started the fight. He turned and walked away. But Lily wasn't finished.

"And what sort of name is Ken Kenny? Fucking ridiculous. And you know what?" she added. She followed him, gesturing with her arms and hands. "When your kids grow up, they're going to realize that you deprived them of one of the greatest childhood joys. What kind of father tells his kids there's no such thing as Santa Claus? Fuck you."

She got into her car and drove out of the parking lot before he had a chance to respond. Then it hit her. Her lips quivered. She lost it. She cried so hard she couldn't see the road. She passed the on-ramp to the highway and turned in to a gas station. Her shoulders hunched forward, and her hands gripped the steering wheel. She took a deep breath and wiped her face with her shirt. She managed to pull herself together and told herself that no one was going to keep her from seeing the boy. Pulling out of the gas station, she turned back toward the prison.

Lily was still visibly shaken when she presented herself to the correctional officer. He was sitting behind a desk typing, pecking away with only his index fingers. There were stacks of files and two phones beside him, one ringing. Near the officer's desk was a hall. At the end of the hall was a massive door with a window. When Lily peered down the hall and through the window, she could see metal bars and the profiles of two inmates. The only other visitor was a white woman cradling a sleeping toddler who was holding a pink stuffed bunny.

What a sad place for a child to be, Lily thought. *Such innocence.* Her heart went out to the little girl.

She waited for thirty minutes on a gray plastic chair welded to other chairs and bolted to the floor, only to be told by the officer, "He's not seeing anyone today." She suddenly understood why the chairs were bolted to the floor—she had the urge to throw one. When Lily tried to get an explanation, she was told to come back. And she did the following weekend. Again, she was told the same thing. "He's not seeing anyone today."

She wrote him letters, begging him to respond. Sometimes, she sent two in a week. Apologizing profusely. Telling him how she should have taken the babysitting job that night. Other times, she wouldn't write for a month, hoping that the passage of time would stir his desire to see her. Never an answer. The summer between her first and second years, she went to see Mr. Cooper.

Even though it was a sunny day in June, the curtains were drawn. There were rolled-up newspapers, still in protective plastic bags, on the lawn and on the concrete steps leading up to the door. Lily knocked. She waited and knocked again. She knew he was in there, probably drunk or maybe sleeping. She used the side of her fist to bang on the door.

Then she heard footsteps coming from inside. Mr. Cooper opened the front door. He was wearing boxers with no shirt.

"Why isn't he letting me visit? He doesn't even answer my letters," she blurted out.

Mr. Cooper had aged considerably since the trial. He was unshaven and his skin a little gray. He wouldn't open the door completely.

All he managed to say at first was her name.

"Please tell me what's going on," she said.

"You need to lead your own life now," Mr. Cooper said, and then he shut the door.

Finally, a few weeks before she was due back at school, the boy agreed to see her. Waiting for him on the plastic chair, she felt hopeful, a sense of relief. She loved him more than ever.

Lily was taken down the hallway and up a set of stairs to a large room with tables and benches. Other visitors were there to see their family members. Four guards were positioned around the room. But the boy barely looked at her as she approached. He had been issued sneakers and drab olive-green pants and a shirt. He was a little thin in the face. His long hair was cut short. His hands were folded on his lap. On impulse, Lily reached for him across the table. She was startled when the officer overseeing the room shouted, "Hands to yourself!"

It felt like a nightmare. When she asked if he was sleeping and eating, she got one- or two-word answers. "Yeah." "Food sucks." He was stone-faced. Expressionless. Shoulders slouched.

"Please, please just tell me what you're thinking."

He looked down and shook his head.

A sick feeling rose in her stomach. She wondered if Coach Kenny had infected his thinking.

"At least return my letters," Lily said. In desperation, her tone changed to one of anger. He registered it and raised his head and one eyebrow. Lily knew the look. It was *What the fuck?*

Softening her tone, she whispered, "Promise me you'll write."

He got up to leave. With his back to her, she started yelling, "Please come back, come back!"

He turned, but only partially, never fully facing her. Looking at the wall instead of her. She had never seen him look so defeated, so demoralized. Then he spoke to her. "Jesus Christ, how much more do you want?" The disgust in his voice felt like a punch in the gut. She understood in that instant that he blamed her. He was saying that she got herself into a situation and he had taken care of it. He had lost everything because of her. Of course he had every right to blame her, to stop loving her. He made a sacrifice that changed the course of his life. So now it was her turn. If it was what he wanted, she would have to let him go.

In the car, she was inconsolable. She hit the steering wheel repeatedly with the palms of her hands, screaming, "No, no, no!" When she started to hyperventilate, she opened the car door and vomited on the pavement.

...

HER UNSPOOLING MEMORIES OF that long ago summer were interrupted by the call of a crow. Rising out of her chair, she opened the French doors and stood on the back deck. Not far off on a wooden fence, a large black crow perched. It cawed again upon seeing Lily.

"What do you want? I see you looking at me," Lily said to the bird.

Again it cawed.

Lily was interested in the mythology of birds. She had read that the crow was a symbol of prophecy.

"You're beautiful and smart," Lily said to the bird.

Uncannily, it called out when Lily stopped talking.

"Prophetic messenger, tell me something I don't know."

It called out again, a higher pitch this time, and then again and again as if it was trying to make itself understood. In that moment, she got a little creeped out. For some reason, Lily was reminded of an old man who had walked up to her on a street in New Orleans. It was her first time in the city, where she'd joined Marshall, who was attending a conference.

"Don't go into the water," the old man had said.

"Are you talking to me?" she asked.

The old man repeated himself, word for word.

Instead of ignoring him, Lily asked, "What do you mean? What water?"

"You'll drown. Broke, broke, broke." The old man stared wide-eyed into Lily's face, shaking his head back and forth, as if Lily were a girl who had gotten her Sunday clothes muddied before church.

At the time, she had been overcome by a wave of nausea.

The old man had pointed to his head and said, "I see before the eyes even see."

Standing on the deck, Lily wondered, *Did he have the gift of prophecy like the crow? Could the old man see what was yet to come? That's silly; I would never drown.*

The phone rang, breaking the spell. It startled her. She returned inside and picked up the receiver.

"Were you sleeping?" It was Jane.

"No, I was talking to a crow and thinking about quantum mechanics."

"Save me some of whatever it is you're smoking."

"I received an invitation for my class reunion," she told her sister.

"I know, that's why I'm calling. Head called me last night."

"I'm not going," Lily said. When Jane didn't respond, she said it again. "I'm not."

"You've avoided going back for years, but you've got to be honest. You've got to own all parts of your life; you can't just bury the difficult parts."

Lily wasn't in the mood to point out the irony in her sister's comment.

Could I really go? she thought. *Would he be there? Could I face him? Would it be a chance to make amends?*

"Head said that Jimmy and Tim were planning on going but that he wasn't sure about anyone else. You should go. It'll be good for you to see old friends."

"I'll think about it," was all Lily said to her sister.

"Aren't you curious about how the guys turned out?"

Of course she was curious about her old friends, but that wasn't enough for her to step into the past.

"You just want me to go to get the dirt on Jimmy Sullivan."

"That's not true. We had such good times. So many laughs," Jane said.

"It's not like you to be so nostalgic," Lily said.

Then Jane cut right to the chase. "It might be good for you to see him."

Lily's first thought was, *I doubt he wants to see me given what he said the last time we saw each other.*

"Why don't you come, too?" she asked Jane.

"I'm not going to be one of those losers who attends other people's class reunions."

Later that night, Lily pulled down her high school yearbook from the shelf in her closet. Seniors used the yearbook to announce their interests and plans. Her page: Joni Mitchell, Smith College; the boy's page: Creedence Clearwater, University of Michigan; David McCarren's page: Bruce Springsteen, Boston College.

They were all so young and full of promise.

OCTOBER 1992

Lily could not account for her change of mind. Maybe nostalgia crept in. Maybe she was hoping Head and Jimmy and Tim would have news about the boy, about how he had made something of himself, beyond football. Maybe Jane was right—it would be good to see old friends.

When she approached the Newport Bridge, she was hit again with the memory of visiting him in prison. After the boy had pushed her away, Lily had driven home over the same bridge with the Narragansett Bay beneath her, full of white sails. *I'll never survive this,* she had thought. But she had. And now she had Marshall. She gripped the steering wheel. So much had changed. When you're young, it's hard to recognize that life holds many possibilities. There were so many ways her life could have unfolded. Or was that a story we tell ourselves when our dreams don't work out? She didn't have all the answers. What she did know for sure was that she was driving home into what felt like the past.

In all those years, even in the summers when she was home from college, she had never run into anyone. Her visits to Portsmouth were typically confined to the grounds of the Abbey, cut off from the rest of town unless she popped into the local grocery store. This had always surprised her but was also a relief.

Lily woke in her childhood bed to the sound of her father gently rapping his knuckles on the bedroom door. She sat up and smiled as he placed a hot cup of tea on her nightstand. As he bent down to kiss his daughter on the forehead, he said, "Oh, right, listen. There's something I need to tell you."

"What is it?"

"Mr. Cooper's in Newport Hospital. Liver's shot."

Lily's chest tightened. *He's here, he must be,* she thought.

...

GREEN VALLEY COUNTRY CLUB was not a huge banquet facility, but it had a large enough room with fake paneled walls, golf memorabilia, and an American flag. A group of classmates Lily knew but wasn't particularly close to had decorated the room with red, white, and blue balloons and white tablecloths with red carnation centerpieces. The colors of the Portsmouth Patriots. Empty aluminum chafing dishes sat on the buffet table alongside name tags and raffle tickets.

Lily stood in the lobby, mingling with others and waiting to check in, until the anticipation of possibly seeing the boy became too much for her, and she slipped into the ladies' room. Once in a stall, she lifted her dress, pulled down her underwear, and sat on the toilet. She didn't have to go; she was just incredibly nervous.

If he hasn't forgiven me, will he even show up tonight? And if he has, then what? Is he hoping to see me after all?

She just needed to get through the next couple of minutes.

He's either here or he's not.

Back in the main room, Lily tried her best to discreetly scan the space for the boy, hoping she would see him before he saw her. She recognized a group of guys from the football team gathered near the bar. One or two noticed her and waved. She raised her hand and smiled, still scanning the group. She thought she spotted him. He had his back turned. The lines of his shoulders and the light curl of his hair were familiar. Her heart raced. But then the shoulders turned, and she saw that she'd made a mistake. Across the room, she locked eyes with Tim Jones, who practically pushed others out of the way on his path toward her.

"Damn, you look good," Tim said, smiling from ear to ear as he reached out to embrace her. He was dressed in his khaki naval uniform. He placed his hand under her elbow and walked her across the room to the others. She ran her fingers through her hair, trying to get it just right.

And there they were, her old friends sitting at a table on the other side of the room. There was no sign of the boy.

The guys could not have been friendlier. When Head spotted her, he jumped from his seat and threw his arms around her. "God, I've missed you."

"Beautiful as ever," Jimmy Sullivan said.

Lily had to fight back the tears. She hugged them both, squeezing them tightly. Tim held out a chair for her. She sat down, and the stories started rolling. Jimmy was divorced and had become a detective in Smithfield. He proudly passed around a photo of his daughter, whose hair was as dark and curly as his. She was in the fifth grade and played ice hockey. Jimmy wore a blue polo shirt with tan dress pants, while Head was sporting a Hawaiian shirt and light-colored pants. He had never married and was a public defender in Providence. Lily wondered how much of Jimmy's and Head's career decisions had been shaped by the events of the summer of 1977.

She hadn't seen any of them since the sentencing; it wasn't just because she had been avoiding contact but that they had all moved away. It was obvious to her through the stories they told that they had all kept in touch over the years. She was relieved that David McCarren did not attend the reunion. She learned that his parents had placed him in a group home for men with traumatic brain injuries, but after a year, they had pulled him out and he was living at home. She was struck by the tragedy of it, but the guys pulled her back with their stories.

"Remember the substitute teacher we had in English for a month our senior year?" Jimmy asked.

"The one with the red hair and beautiful body," Head said. "How could we forget?"

"Well, I didn't tell you guys this, but we got together about two years ago. I met her at One Pelham East. It was probably right up there with some of the best sex I've ever had."

"Un-fucking-believable!" Head said. "How long did you end up seeing her for?"

"Couple of months. I tell ya, she might've been the one if she wasn't already married."

Everybody laughed.

Just like old times, Lily thought. *But he's not here.*

As they sat around the table, the guys took turns buying rounds of drinks. Nostalgia took over: being in French class with Paul Pacheco whistling like the wind and the French teacher thinking it was the old windows; food fights in the cafeteria between the juniors and seniors;

a language trip to Quebec City sophomore year when they smuggled two cases of beer into the hotel room, put the empties in the elevator, and pushed all the buttons so the elevator would go up and down for a while; the morning the guys from the football team picked up Mr. Carr's Volkswagen bug and moved it sideways in his parking spot so he couldn't get out; and, of course, plucking Head's calf hairs in English class while trying to keep a straight face when he squealed.

"Best years of my life," Head said. Jimmy swung his arm around Head's shoulders and kissed him on the cheek.

There were toasts and speeches followed by dinner, during which the DJ played the top songs from 1977. A little Fleetwood Mac. Some Bowie and James Taylor. Sitting there with her old friends, Lily couldn't believe how much time had passed and how their youth was all but behind them. After a meal of baked haddock, Swedish meatballs, and green beans almondine, it was Lily's turn to buy a round of drinks. Head joined her. Walking to the bar, she leaned into Head and said, "I was hoping he would be here."

"Me too," Head said. "That would have been fun. We tried to get him to come. He spent the day with his dad at the hospital. I guess he wasn't up to coming."

Lily wondered if it was because he didn't want to see her or his old teammates, whom he might have felt he'd let down. *Probably both.*

Lily ordered beers for the guys and a wine for herself. As she was reaching for her cash, Head said, "He's still in town."

Lily turned to look at Head. She couldn't say anything, but the way she searched Head's eyes said it all.

"He's at the marina. Pirates Cove."

"Should I go see him?" she asked.

"Yeah, I think you should," Head said.

"Really?"

"Yeah, go see him. It's a Bristol 36. Second dock on your left."

As Lily headed to her car, her heart raced. She didn't know if she was anxious or excited. *Has he forgiven me?* she wondered. She tried to prepare herself for the possibility that he might send her away. If he did, she would leave gracefully and not make a scene. But if his anger had mellowed, she would ask for forgiveness. Even after all these years, she needed it.

Ten minutes later, she turned into the parking lot of the marina. She opened her window and listened to the clanging of the cables against the masts coupled with the creaking sound wood makes when it rubs against pilings. She looked out. From where she was parked, she could see a few galley lights and wondered which boat was his. It was so dark out, and the water was the color of ink, except for a shimmering white light cast by the only streetlamp.

Once on the dock, she heard music. A mandolin. Following the sound, she stepped aboard the deck of a Bristol 36. There was a light breeze. When the boat swayed, she steadied herself, grabbing hold of the rail. The music stopped.

He must have known I would come, Lily thought.

The entrance to the galley was open, and she braced herself on the companionway. Leaning in, she saw him sitting there, holding the mandolin, looking up at her. He took her breath away. It was the strength of his confidence and the intensity of his gaze that made him magnetic. She climbed down the ladder, self-conscious of her hips and figure.

No longer the boy she remembered. Still handsome. Just a few lines between his eyebrows and a few crow's-feet. He was wearing a midnight-blue cotton sweater with a rolled neck and a pair of faded jeans. His hair, not as long as it was in high school, curled around his ears, down his neck, touching the top of the sweater. He was still fit and muscular the way she remembered.

He watched her carefully, trying to be cool. He studied every move she made in that small cabin—her eyes glancing around, landing on the books over his shoulder, her neck muscles bending, the tip of her middle finger pushing her hair behind her ears just as she had done when she was a girl. It was a gesture that reminded him of how her long hair used to fall in his face when she would straddle him.

Lily scanned the books to see what sort of man he had become. Who was this person with his music and literature? There were stacks behind him, obscure poets from the early twentieth century like Lola Ridge, an Irish writer and advocate for the working poor.

They looked at each other. Lily held the boy's gaze until her body ached with desire. She knew in that moment there was no turning back.

They hadn't said a word. When he couldn't take it anymore, he stood up.

"I was hoping you would come," he said.

Lily put her hand to her mouth. She couldn't speak.

A deluge of feelings came rushing back. She gripped the teak handhold to maintain her balance. Her face flushed. Tears welled in her eyes. There was no hiding it anymore—her love for him was unmatched. Standing there in the galley, she knew she was risking everything she had with Marshall.

He reached for her and placed his hand on the side of her face. She turned her head, closed her eyes, and kissed the palm of his hand.

Then looking up at him, searching his eyes, she asked, "Where have you been?"

"Waiting for you."

The smell of her neck between her earlobe and clavicle reminded him of their youth, her laughter, the bed in his basement, the rustling of cornstalks, holding her ass with her legs wrapped tightly around his thighs as he stood in the music room after the bell rang. It all came back to him. He untied her dress and let it fall to the floor.

Afterward, lying in his arms in the V-berth, she said, "I see you've been reading a lot of poetry."

"Some."

"Recite something, anything," she asked him.

Without hesitating, he recited: "*It was many and many a year ago / In a kingdom by the sea / That a maiden there lived whom you may know / By the name of Annabel Lee / And this maiden she lived with no other thought / Than to love and be loved by me.*"

Lily sighed. She remembered the poem. Senior year. Edgar Allan Poe. A young couple whose love made the heavens jealous.

Water lapped against the hull. Docks creaked and halyards clanged. The galley lights were soft, and his arms were wrapped around her. Lily thought: *He was the one who sailed around the world; I'm the one wearing the albatross. He was my sea, my ocean—the deepest part of me. What was I to him? Dense fog, ice, hurricane, every burden and possible obstacle.*

Lily sat up and pulled the blanket to her chest. As hard as it was going to be, she had to ask him about the last time they saw each other.

"Why . . ." she started to say, and then she stopped herself.

"Why what?" he asked, reaching over and stroking her calf. His eyes were so loving.

"Why didn't you want to see me?"

"That wasn't it; I wanted to see you," he told her.

Confused, she didn't believe him. *There was no way you wanted to see me.*

She remembered it all as if it were yesterday.

"Then why did you send me away? Why didn't you answer my letters?"

"I was in rough shape. Prison docs put me on some kind of medication for a while."

He seemed a little ashamed. Still, she needed to push him, to find out exactly what he recalled.

"Do you remember what you said to me?"

He was still lying on his side, facing her. He paused and then shook his head.

They were quiet for a while until he said, "I don't remember word for word, but I do remember being angry."

All these years I've replayed it, and he barely remembers, she thought.

He took a long, deep breath and said, "I was hanging on by a thread. To be honest, I don't really remember much of that first year. Whatever I said, I didn't mean it. I stayed on meds the entire time I was in prison and then took myself off, cold turkey, as soon as I got out."

"So it wasn't Coach Kenny?"

"What do you mean? What does he have to do with this?"

"I thought he convinced you it was all my fault."

"I never blamed you. Never."

While what he had said all those years back had crushed her, there was no way she was going to force him to relive those early months in prison. It didn't seem fair. Perhaps it was depression. His lost dreams and the depths of his sadness had broken him, at least at the time.

She lay back down on her side, facing him, and covered them both with the blanket. He reached over and brushed her hair away from her face. "Whatever I said, I know I pushed you away. When I finally came out of it, I wanted to call, but then I couldn't let you waste your life on a felon. I didn't know if I could get a job when I got out. How would I have taken care of you? I'm not even allowed to vote."

Lily propped herself up and rested on her elbow. "Wait, you didn't call me when you got out because you were worried about getting a job?"

"It was about being a provider. . . . There was no way a bank was going to loan me money for a house. I just didn't think I could put you through all that."

Lily was beginning to recognize that his need to live up to the expectations of what it means to be a man was the boy's greatest undoing—both in terms of how he responded on the night of the fight and his assumption about being the primary breadwinner.

It was not that Lily was taking stock of the boy's character flaws and mistakes, it was that she was recognizing a pattern, a highly gendered pattern. It made her wonder, *Where is the line between a good man and an almost good man?* She could never hold his impulses against him, though—the one who had brushed her tangled hair in the gymnasium and tenderly applied a heat compress to her belly.

"It could have been so different if you had told me all this."

She thought of Marshall. She had admitted it out loud—that she and the boy could have been together had he only talked to her, that she would have taken her chances with him instead of living her current life with her husband. It was a realization that she couldn't hide anymore, and now here they were, and she had no idea—at least not in the moment—what the future held.

"I heard you married yourself an older guy, a silver-spoon-in-hand kind of guy."

Avoiding the topic of Marshall's trust fund, Lily said, "He's a college professor."

"Did he serve in Vietnam?" the boy asked.

"No. He managed to avoid the draft."

"Ah! A fortunate son," the boy said, a little disparagingly.

Changing the subject, Lily said, "I want to know where you've been—I mean since you got out." She lay back down and rested her head on his chest.

Fifteen years or one hundred and eighty months. Even if only one thing happened each month that was worthy of telling—one event, one encounter, one mishap, one joy—then there were at least one hundred and eighty things that Lily didn't know about him, whereas fifteen years ago, she had known what time he woke and when he fell asleep and everything in between.

"Where should I start?" he asked.

He told her that he had reread *Moby-Dick* in prison. "Herman Melville saved my life." He laughed after he said this, but she could tell he meant it with utter sincerity.

"Like Ahab, my desire for revenge took everything from me," the boy said.

Lily caressed his chest with her hand. The boy's insight was not lost on her.

"I read it daily. I would read two or three pages but no more; I needed it to last for the entire duration of my sentence," the boy said. He paused and then recited a line from Melville: "*I thought I would sail about a little and see the watery part of the world.*"

There had been odd jobs until he found the merchant marines. There had been blackout nights in Thailand, short-term affairs, Thanksgiving dinners with his father, weeklong vacations with Tim Jones in Maryland, fishing trips.

He told her a story about rescuing Vietnamese refugees in 1984. He had been working in Singapore in the South China Sea.

"It was typhoon season—not the time to take chances. Waves were about ten feet that day, but that's nothing. I was on watch duty, you know, lookout. . . . I spotted a boat in the distance. When I notified my officer, he told the captain, who didn't give it a second thought. We were going to rescue those poor souls. There were about a hundred people on a boat that was barely seaworthy. They'd been out for fourteen days and had run out of water and food. When I say the boat was overcrowded, that doesn't do justice to what we saw. One woman

wouldn't let go of her daughter—the child had died a few hours before we got to them. We tried to convince the mother to put the child
down so she could climb the rope ladders. There were little kids carrying infants. They were all so weak, they could barely climb—"

"Wait," Lily said, "I need to know how the woman got up the
ladder."

The boy paused and said, "I climbed down. When I reached the
deck, I held out my arms. We looked at each other. I'll never forget
her eyes—so dark, so lost. She leaned in, and I lifted the body from
her arms. Then she climbed the ladder."

Lily didn't ask what happened to the child's body, nor did the boy
tell her.

"Less than a day later, a Category 2 typhoon came in. Those people never would have survived. Waves as high as thirty feet. They
would have drowned. I later heard stories from guys whose captains
had been aware of boats nearby, but they refused to stop. They didn't
want to be inconvenienced. I can't fucking imagine it. We ended up
taking them to a refugee camp in Indonesia. I still think about them
and wonder what happened."

Lily was silent, wrapped in his arms, her head tucked into his
chest. She wondered about the story he was telling her. She understood that he was trying to show how he had changed. That he wasn't
the same guy he had been that day near the tennis courts when he
didn't help Tim.

She got up to use the toilet. When she was done, she stood in the
galley, naked, looking around. The galley lights gave off a golden hue.
He was admiring her, taking her in. "Come lay beside me."

After they made love again, he held her face and asked, "Is it too
late for us?"

"I'm married."

"But you're here."

...

BACK AT HER FATHER'S HOUSE, Lily slept in the next morning. When she woke, close to noon, she had a pit in her stomach, like something terrible was about to happen. She felt like her quiet world of books, butterflies, and birds was imploding.

Once she pulled the covers back, she sat on the edge of her bed and took a few deep breaths. She met her father in the kitchen; he had been to Sunday Mass and had the kettle boiling for tea.

"I'm surprised the phone didn't wake you. Jane's called three times asking about the reunion," her father said.

"I thought she would, so I unplugged the phone in my room."

As she sipped her tea, she told him that the gang stayed out all night.

That was the first lie of many. She had something to eat, and then she carried a second cup of tea back to her bedroom to call her sister.

Jane picked up on the first ring. "How was it?"

Lily paused. She was sitting in bed holding the phone to her ear.

"What? Was he there?"

In barely a whisper, Lily said, "I slept with him."

Silence on the other end.

"For the love of God, say something," Lily said.

"What are you going to do?"

"Nothing. Just go back to Ithaca." Having blurted this out without thinking, she knew that that was what she had to do, return home to her husband. She reached over to her nightstand, picked up the mug of tea, and brought it to her lips. She blew on it and watched the ripples move across the surface.

"Listen, I don't think you need to tell anyone. I mean, don't tell Marshall. Don't be one of those people who think they have to come clean—the way people unburden themselves just to burden others," Jane said.

"What about honesty?"

"Fuck honesty; it's overrated," Jane said.

"Don't you have any moral codes?" Lily asked.

"Sure I do. Just not ones based on a system of shame and control."

On the drive home to upstate New York, Lily beat herself up with the old story. If she had just stayed home or taken that babysitting job and not gone to the party all those years ago, the boy would be a national star now, a professional sportsman. For all her grasp on the boy's misplaced heroism, she couldn't shake her feeling of responsibility. The feminist in her failed against the swelling tide of her own guilt. Because she went to the party without him, two men's lives had been destroyed. And now, she was bent on destroying another man, her loving husband.

Blame was not always rational.

She had been to another place where she was not meant to be—a place where her presence would change everything, this time for Marshall.

How do I act as if nothing happened? I just do. That's the price I have to pay.

It was clear that prison had not destroyed the boy, that he had battled on and made a future for himself. A future it was impossible for her to be part of. Just north of Providence, she made up her mind that she would not contact him again. Her future was with Marshall, and despite last night's transgression, she would keep her vows.

When she hit I-90, the Mass Pike, she put in a cassette that Marshall had made ahead of the reunion, a compilation of songs he had thought she would like for the long drive. It took her a while to recognize the melodic piano chords of Stevie Wonder's "All in Love Is Fair." A ballad. But instead of thinking about her husband, her heart traveled to the boy.

She saw him on the boat, pulling on the oars, smiling in the sun. She saw him on the field with the ball tucked under his arm, leaning forward, head down. She saw him driving and glancing over at her when her favorite song came on the radio.

I should have never left your side, Stevie crooned.

PART
III

MARCH 1996

Lily looked out the front window just as the mail truck pulled up. It was about 33 degrees outside. She put on her coat and slid on her boots and went to collect the mail. She noticed immediately the stamps on the top envelope. The upper-right corner was lined with colorful images—an orchid, an orangutan, and a white tiger. Stamps she had never seen before. Her heart raced as she walked back to the house. Without removing her coat and boots, Lily sat on the bench in the hallway with the mail on her lap. She closed her eyes and took stock of the years since she'd seen him.

There had been Marshall's promotion and numerous publications in scientific journals, including an article they co-wrote for *Ibis* in which they argued that climate change impacted warbler migration. Then there was her dad's heart attack following his sixty-sixth birthday, which he survived. And, of course, there were the summers in Rhode Island with Jane, sitting on the beach while her sister got stoned and contemplated the mathematical notion of infinity while staring out at the horizon.

But these events hadn't dominated her thoughts.

There were stretches of time when she was absent from her life. She read the newspaper with Marshall in the mornings, folded laundry and took long walks in the afternoons, shared meals with him in the evenings. She was present for some of it, but other times she was a shadow of herself. She wrestled with feelings of intense guilt. And the guilt competed with her desire. She obsessed over whether she could be equally in love with two people. Doesn't one always win out? Or does the love for two people ultimately diminish both? Was that the price she would have to pay?

In moments when she was deeply disappointed in herself, she considered confessing to Marshall about the night on the boat. Then he would be the one to make the decision about her future. But that's not what Lily wanted. She didn't want there to be a choice, Marshall or the boy. She wanted them both. She didn't want to imagine the rest of her life without either of them now that she held both in her heart, and in her mind.

One Tuesday morning that January, she had unfolded *The New York Times* at the breakfast table. Marshall sat across from her looking over lecture notes. The headline read, *World's Leaders Bid Farewell to Mitterrand,* and there on the front page was the official mourning photograph of the president of France: a flag-draped coffin, his sons, his wife, his mistress, and his daughter by his mistress. When she pointed out the photo to her husband, he had said, "Loads of men like that have girlfriends. The only difference is the French don't hide it."

Looking at the photo in the newspaper, Lily wondered about the origins of her guilt. *Men have mistresses. Good men. And history celebrates them. Even in death, women and men are judged by different moral codes.*

Do you know women like that?

That's what the monk had asked her mother all those years ago at her book club.

She had learned in college that the history of monogamy was linked to the origins of private property and that paternity—patriarchy, yes, but paternity and, more specifically, who rightfully inherits a man's property—was the reason why so many cultures around the world police women's sexuality. The burka. Female circumcision. Foot binding. All of these cultural practices ultimately aim to ensure that the children a woman bears are her husband's legitimate heirs. Lily was feeling guilty and fighting the guilt simultaneously. She wondered if her critique of monogamy was just a way of forgiving herself.

She thought about how long her love for the boy had lasted, how it didn't seem to fade with time. They had met a year after her mother died. Falling in love with him had saved her; perhaps it was her mother she missed, not him? Was that what had held her captive all these years? Her first love. Her mother's love. But that didn't feel quite right. It certainly wasn't the whole story.

Sleeping with the boy had made her question her identity. She didn't recognize herself. *Who cheats?* she often wondered. *Lovers. Liars. Selfish people.* She was compelled to say a common prayer over and over: "Forgive me." She lived with a quiet sense of desperation and confusion.

Now, sitting on the bench, Lily turned the letter over in her hand and placed her thumb under the flap of the envelope, sliding it up and breaking the seal.

Dear Lil,

I hope my letter does not prove to be a disruption in your life. I realize that you have decided not to be in contact with me, but I've been thinking of you and had to write.

The Pacific Ocean is massive; I can't even wrap my mind around it. Just to put things in perspective, it's 5,600 miles from Australia to Hawaii! I learned something last night from one of the other guys. Humans started making rafts 40,000 years ago. The last place humans settled was eastern Polynesia from the Cook Islands to Hawaii about 900 CE. Those ancient sailors navigated the ocean by studying how the waves hit the bow of their dugout canoes.

Wait until you hear this, Lil. I went to Laos, and I saw the most extraordinary prehistoric site. The place was beautiful—lush green fields, pine trees, and rolling mountains. But the fields were littered with jars—that were nine feet tall! That's higher than the ceiling in my basement at the house on Water Street. The jars date back to about 500 BC. A French scientist in the 1930s documented the archaeological site. There were thousands of them. Not just one or two, and not all were nine feet. Some were six feet and some as small as three feet. The locals believe that there was a race of giants that fought for a king, and they used the jars to store rice wine and alcohol, which the giants drank after battle. Sadly, among the jars, there were tens of thousands of unexploded bombs that the Americans dropped over Laos.

I've saved the best story for last. Two years ago, we sailed through the Blackett Strait where JFK's PT-109 was destroyed by a Japanese ship. We stopped by one of the Solomon Islands. I met a local, a real nice guy, who introduced me to his grandfather. Ready for this, Lil?

The old man was one of the guys who rescued JFK and his men in '43. Eroni Kumana. He and his best friend, Biuku Gasa, were coast watchers and found Kennedy on a small island. Kennedy wrote a note on the outside of a coconut and then the two local guys paddled 35 miles at night by canoe to an Australian station, avoiding Japanese patrollers. This is after Kennedy swam for four hours towing an injured crew member with the strap of the guy's life jacket between his teeth. JFK invited the two men to his inauguration, but the Solomon government sent someone else.

Talk about heroes.

I miss the overcast August mornings of New England with its blues and greens.

There's not a day that goes by when I don't think about you.

Beyond the heavens, beyond the stars . . .

With the letter open, Lily traced the first line of penmanship with her fingertip. She studied the curves of the letters and sighed. Folding it, she let it rest on her lap. She was disappointed there wasn't more. Something intimate. Something tender. After years, why write stories about strange jars and war heroes?

She waited until it was afternoon to call Jane in California.

"That's it," Lily said to her sister after reading her the letter.

"Well, it certainly says a lot about what humans are capable of, doesn't it?" Jane said.

"Yeah, but you'd think he'd write more."

"Maybe he's concerned that Marshall would find it and read it."

I didn't set out to love two men, Lily thought. She didn't say it aloud. She didn't have to. Jane knew; she always knew. But she wouldn't write back. She couldn't.

"Mom would have loved the story of how he met the guy who saved JFK," Lily said.

"Can you imagine being Kennedy out there in the Pacific? The fucking Pacific. It's massive, and he swam in open waters for hours pulling some dude by a strap clenched in his teeth. Who does that?"

"Heroes. That's who," Lily said.

Then without missing a beat, Jane said of the boy, "He was supposed to be a hero. Not a felon."

Lily thought about the similarities between heroes and saints. When life gets dark, heroes and saints manage to climb out of the darkness. They just keep climbing and climbing, and when they get up far enough, they turn back and extend their hands to others.

But what about him? Lily thought. *Some saints are heroic, but not all heroes are saintly. Do real heroes seek revenge?*

NOVEMBER 1997

Every year Lily and Marshall returned to Portsmouth for a quiet Thanksgiving with Mr. Webb. Sometimes Jane would fly in from California, and most years Father Thomas would either join them for dinner or stop by for dessert.

Typically, Lily would prepare several dishes ahead of time at her home in Ithaca so that by Thanksgiving Day, they had only the turkey and stuffing to cook. This year, the day before the holiday, she had to make a run to Clements', the local grocery store. Her father, who grew up working-class, loved canned cranberry sauce, whereas the cooks for Marshall's family always prepared fresh cranberry sauce with brown and white sugar.

Standing in the canned fruit aisle, Lily jumped when she felt a hand on her shoulder. She turned around and let out a high-pitched *ooh,* stunned to see the boy standing there. There was no mistaking her reaction. He knew she was thrilled.

She threw her arms around him. She was wearing sweatpants and an oversize Portsmouth Abbey sweatshirt that belonged to her father. She was genuinely surprised. For as many times as she had returned to Portsmouth to see her father, she had never run into him. She had just assumed he was out at sea.

"You look great," was the first thing he said to her when they separated.

She couldn't stop looking at him. She was overjoyed.

"How long are you home for?" Lily asked, looking up.

"Another week."

"How's your dad?"

"Still drinking. Cirrhosis of the liver."

They went back and forth like this, standing in the aisle, catching up on his dad, Mr. Webb, Jane, and the guys until he asked, "Can you grab breakfast?"

Of course, Lily wanted nothing more than to spend the morning or the whole day with him. He'd been on her mind and now he was standing in front of her, looking so good in his black wool peacoat and faded jeans. Unshaven and a little scruffy. But her first thought was Marshall, back at the house with her dad.

"I don't think I can." She hated telling him that. But she knew she had to.

"What about a quick cup of coffee?" he said, gesturing with his index finger to the new café the store owners had opened near the pastry counter.

Lily thought it would be easier not telling Marshall about a quick cup of coffee than not telling him about sitting down to an entire breakfast with an old friend.

A lover's lie.

"Let me just get these," Lily said, reaching for two cans of cranberry sauce.

The chairs in the café were still on top of the tables from the night before, so the boy suggested they drink their coffee in his truck. He waited for Lily at the end of the checkout line, holding their coffee cups, and then they headed out the door together to the parking lot.

"Let me put this in my car," she told him.

By now the parking lot was filling up.

"Where's your truck?" she asked, after placing the bag on the passenger seat of her car.

"Right here," he said.

Parked right next to Lily's car was a black 1997 Ford F-150 pickup.

"I bought it for Dad, but I use it when I'm home."

"What are the odds that you parked next to me?" Lily said.

"I have to confess. I saw you pull out of Corys Lane, so I followed you here."

"Why didn't you beep?"

"I wanted to surprise you."

"Well, you certainly did that." As she said this, she placed the palm of her hand on his chest.

He handed her a cup of coffee and the two of them got into his truck. Once settled, he reached over to the glove compartment, and as he did, his hand grazed Lily's knee. He opened the compartment and—after searching deep within, under the car registration and its manual—pulled out two mini bottles of Jameson Irish whiskey and offered her one. She took it and looked at it for a second.

"It's not even nine A.M.," Lily said, amused.

"It's a holiday," he said, unscrewing the cap and pouring the whiskey into his coffee.

Morning drinking is something alcoholics and college students do, Lily thought.

"Do you do this a lot?"

"Only when I'm celebrating," he said.

Looking over at him, she lifted her coffee for a toast and said, "What are we celebrating?"

"Running into each other," he said with a big smile. And then he added, "Are you going to drink that?"

"No," she said with a little giggle and passed it back to him.

She watched as he unscrewed the bottle and poured it into his cup.

"Jesus," Lily said, looking out the passenger-side window. "That poor woman has been trying to back out of her parking space, and no one will let her go." Handing her coffee to him, she got out of the truck and stood in front of a car with one hand up like a traffic cop as she waved to the older woman to back out.

When she was back inside the truck, he said, "You're a righteous woman, Lily Webb."

He did his best to keep the conversation light, talking about old times from high school just to hear her laugh. They reminisced about the time the gang stole Mr. Sylvia's life-size polyresin horse, carried it in the dark through the neighborhoods, and placed it on the fifty-yard line in the early morning hours of graduation day. Head and Jane had gotten stoned, had the giggles, and fell behind. They started running to catch up, and the next thing Jane knew, Head had let out a yelp and landed on his back. He hadn't seen a clothesline.

"Bless Head," Lily said.

By now, Lily had turned her body so she was leaning against the passenger-side door, smiling and holding her coffee cup. She let her eyes wander to the lines of the boy's shoulders and forearms. Then up to his jawline.

God, he's beautiful.

"Here's one," he said.

She was grateful for his stories—it was so much easier to talk about the past than to speak of themselves.

"When Jimmy was promoted to detective, he didn't have a decent suit or dress shoes, so Head and I took him to the Swansea Mall. First we went to Sears because Head needed jeans. We're standing at the checkout counter so Head can pay for his Levi's, and there is no clerk to be found. So we wait, and we wait. Nobody shows up, and Jimmy's getting pissed because he hates shopping, and then the phone starts ringing. Head goes behind the counter, picks up the phone, and says, 'Sears.' And all we hear from Head's end of the phone call is, 'Yep, that size is on the floor. I know for a fact because that's my size and I just got a pair.' Then the caller must have asked if Head could hold a pair and leave them up front. And we hear Head say, 'No, I can't hold them for you because I'm leaving.' The caller starts to go off on him, so Head says, 'No, I can't find someone else to hold them because I don't know anybody here.' Jimmy and I are cracking up, and Head holds the phone out so we can hear the caller getting more and more worked up. Eventually, Head says, 'I don't even work here,' and hangs up the phone."

"That was a good one," Lily said, smiling. "I miss seeing those guys."

A teenage boy appeared to the right of the truck; he wasn't wearing a coat despite the November chill. He caught the boy's attention.

"Can you see that kid's T-shirt?" he asked.

Lily looked out just as the boy crossed in front of the truck. His shirt featured the iconic image of the album cover for *Wish You Were Here*. Two men shaking hands in a studio lot. One of the men is on fire.

"You gave me that album when we were juniors."

Lily remembered. She looked over at the boy, met his gaze, and smiled.

"That Christmas you gave me a gray wool scarf, too. When I wore it, you said I looked like a poet. We went to midnight Mass, and Jane had the hiccups, and even your dad laughed."

She chuckled and said, "We were so young."

"Do you remember the words to 'Wish You Were Here'?"

"Of course, try me."

"*We're just . . .*" The boy trailed off, waiting for Lily to pick up where he left off.

She hadn't listened to the song in its entirety since high school. Every one of the dozens of times it had come on the radio in the past twenty years, she had changed the station. Not wanting to be reminded of the boy.

Now, sitting in his truck, she looked out the passenger-side window and pursed her lips. Concentrating.

He laughed and kidded her. "You don't remember."

"*Two lost souls swimming in a fishbowl year after year . . .*"

He nodded, smiling wide, and then he sang the rest of the verse.

How fitting, Lily thought. *A clarion call from the past: the loss of innocence and the price paid for the passage of time.*

His singing triggered a memory: the two of them, back when they were sixteen, poring over the lyrics on the inside of the album cover, searching for meaning and in the process finding themselves.

Smiling, the boy said, "I still have the scarf."

...

WHEN THEY HAD RUN out of things to talk about, Lily said, "I should get back."

"Did you get my letter?"

"Yes, I did."

"You never wrote back," he said.

Lily turned her body around in the seat and looked out the window. Before looking over at him, she said, "I'm married."

"As if that could ever change how I feel about you."

When she didn't respond, he said, "So is this how it's going to be? We run in to each other every five years or so?"

She wanted him to reach for her. She wanted him to hold her face like he did when they were young. She wanted him to lose control. But in the same instant, she gripped the door handle and was ready to jump out.

"Being without you is killing me," he said.

She tried hard not to cry. She bit down on her lip and looked out the window again.

I can't do this, she thought.

She took a deep breath and remained quiet. He leaned in and kissed her head. She reached for his hand, squeezed it tightly, and got out of the truck. He pulled out of the parking lot, and she watched as he drove away.

…

THEY HAD THANKSGIVING DINNER close to two P.M., just the four of them: Marshall, Mr. Webb, Father Thomas, and Lily. It was a simple traditional meal—turkey, stuffing, cranberry sauce, mashed potatoes, and green beans—compared to when Jane joined them for the holiday and made brown-butter potatoes, grilled butternut squash, and roasted vegetables with pecans.

Between dinner and dessert, Father Thomas recited "Sailing to Byzantium" by Yeats, a poem he had memorized as a student at the Priory in the 1930s. The others looked on, impressed with his recitation, applauding when he finished. Lily wondered why this poem of all poems? What did it mean to him? Did it force him to think about the condition of his soul? His desire for a spiritual journey? If so, she understood the impulse.

But it was the last line that really spoke to Lily: *Of what is past, or passing, or to come.* It made her think about the boy, her future, its uncertainty, and the guilt she felt about it all.

Was he right? Lily thought. *Is this how it's going to be?* That they would only see each other every four or five years? She felt a little panic wondering if she could go on like this.

Sitting at the dining room table, Lily recalled a story she had heard years before from Father Thomas. How he was ordered to report to the Southwest in 1945 to work on a secret project. How he and a few of his buddies from the labs at Los Alamos drove to a desert basin known as *Jornada del Muerto,* or "dead man's journey," to watch the first detonation of the atomic bomb. And how, when the bomb didn't go off on time, they thought it had failed—until suddenly the land around them, the basin and the mountains, were lit up with light, and there was fire in the sky.

Looking over at the monk, she wondered about the magnitude of his guilt. His conscience. She had learned from both Jane and her father that he had left the secular world behind after the bombs dropped and become a Benedictine monk. Had he sought forgiveness all these years?

If he had, surely so could I?

Now, standing in the kitchen helping Lily with the dishes, Marshall whispered, "He has such great social skills for a monk."

Lily hadn't been expecting the remark and laughed. She swatted her husband's butt, saying, "I didn't know you knew many monks."

"I don't, really. In fact, he's the only one I know," Marshall said.

He pulled her in for a quick kiss. Lily felt a sudden pang of regret accompanied by images of the boy: her holding on to him in the grocery store aisle and then sitting in his truck, laughing at old times. Lying by omission. Who was she protecting? Marshall or herself?

The Detroit Lions had just scored another touchdown over the Chicago Bears and they were all on their second glass of Glendronach when Father Thomas asked about Jane.

Lily had always harbored a little jealousy that Jane had commanded Father Thomas's attention when they were children, but she understood that the monk was the only one who could reach her sister. Plus, Lily had garnered Brother Mark's affection. Still, Father Thomas called Lily "the little flower," which she took as the highest compliment. He was likening her to Saint Therese of Lisieux. A mystic. A good woman who remained strong through her suffering.

Later that night, after Marshall had gone to bed and Mr. Webb was cleaning the kitchen, Lily walked Father Thomas back to the monastery. It was a clear November sky.

"Look up at the stars," he told Lily.

"There's Cepheus, and over there is Cassiopeia," Lily said, pointing first to the north sky and then to the northeastern sky.

Both knew the Greek myth well so neither needed to mention Cassiopeia's vanity or that they were the parents of Andromeda. Instead, Lily said, "The Greeks managed to keep their stories alive, didn't they?"

Standing next to her, looking up at the sky, Father Thomas said, "Never underestimate a storyteller. Storytellers are powerful. Storytellers have convinced kings, queens, and presidents to go to war."

Lily thought about the stories she told herself about herself. She understood completely.

As they approached the monastery, Father Thomas stopped, looked up at the sky again, and said, "A cold front is moving in." Then, looking at Lily, he said, "Tell Jane to come see me the next time she's home."

...

TWO DAYS LATER, THE sun was hidden behind clouds. It had snowed. Seasonably early. Marshall corrected papers at the dining room table while Mr. Webb sat in a darkened living room in his favorite reading chair.

"He carried his wife's bones in a bucket," Mr. Webb said. He closed his book, removed his glasses, and wiped the tears from his eyes.

"Come on, Dad. Let's go for a walk," Lily said.

She pulled her father's down coat closed and handed him his hat. Mr. Webb used a tissue from his pocket to wipe his nose. They walked in silence to the railroad tracks near the bay. Snow crunched beneath their feet. Trees lined both sides of the tracks, and their dark criss-crossing branches, layered with snow, formed a canopy overhead.

"When he tripped, her bones rattled in the bucket," he added, looking straight ahead while his daughter turned to study his face.

The night before, Lily's father had shared with her the subject of the new book he was reading, *The Bells of Nagasaki* by Takashi Nagai, a Japanese radiologist. Dr. Nagai was working in a hospital and had access to a shelter when the atomic bomb fell from the sky and annihilated his city. Passing skinless children and charred bodies, he found his wife's remains among the ashes of their home. The doctor's memoir was being passed around the monastery, and Father Thomas had loaned it to Lily's dad when he came over for Thanksgiving dinner. Lily's first thought was that it was brave of Father Thomas to read a book like that.

"When the bones rattled in the bucket, he asked his dead wife for forgiveness."

Lily sighed and stopped on the tracks as her father kept walking.

She understood all too well why her father would read a book about the lives of the faithful, the near saints. Her father, whose devotion to Catholicism was quiet, asked his daughter how much more faithful one can be than a man who has lost everything but still had a commitment to peace. Who saw his suffering in the context of what was good for humanity.

Lily thought of something Brother Mark had once told her: "Pain makes us attentive to others' pain. Holy pain—the redemptive dimension of suffering."

Her father had stopped about five feet ahead and turned back to his daughter, who was still standing on the railroad tracks.

"The flames of Nagasaki became the light of peace. The Paschal candle. A sacred fire. Takashi Nagai spent the rest of his life teaching forgiveness."

By now the two were standing side by side, looking out onto the bay near a clearing in the woods. In silence, they watched a cloudy mist moving over the water, like ghosts drifting out to sea.

Lily would have liked to have talked to her father about her own desire for forgiveness—for going to the keg party that night, for the night on the boat.

Maybe this is Dad's way of letting me know that I need not carry the responsibility of what happened.

She thought about what her father had told her and then asked, "What would this man—"

"Takashi Nagai," her father said, interrupting her.

"Yes, Takashi Nagai. What would he have said had he met Oppenheimer or Father Thomas or Truman, for that matter?"

What Lily was driving at was the question, What is unforgivable? Death brought on by an atomic bomb? Her involvement in destroying the boy's dreams? David's head injury? Infidelity?

"I imagine Dr. Nagai would have opened his arms in peace," her father said.

Unfathomable.

Lily thought it was just too radical. She thought about the boy and whether he had ever forgiven his mom. Then she wondered about her own life. Could she ever have a faith so deep as to view her own suffering as connected to other suffering souls?

...

FOR LILY'S BIRTHDAY THAT YEAR, Jane had given her a copy of *The Brothers Karamazov,* saying, "There's something here for you between these pages. . . ." It took Lily weeks to read it, savoring every sentence. She finished it on the Sunday following Thanksgiving. After she put it down, she went to the beach for a walk while Marshall helped her father set up his new computer.

Lily parked at Surfer's End near a massive puddingstone rock. She walked down the old wooden steps and over the seawall. There was no snow on the beach or the dunes, and she was taken with the silkiness of the gray morning sea. She walked along the beach, which even at high tide seemed wide. She watched a brown thrasher defend a winterberry shrub. She watched purple sandpipers scurrying at the shoreline as if they were running to catch the receding waves. She spotted a cormorant and a striking common eider with its contrasting white, black, and green plumage. A gull standing at the water's edge squawked. Northeast winds blew hard, and there were few people on the beach. She pulled the hood of her down coat over her head and walked on.

She thought about the book's major theological themes of freedom and faith and how the night of the fight and the night on the boat bumped up against her childhood understanding of good and bad.

When is self-forgiveness not a sign of self-righteousness? she wondered.

She stood looking out at the Atlantic. She just wanted to know how to be good.

...

"I GET WHY DAD fell in love with Father Zosima from *Brothers Karamazov*," Lily said to Jane when she called her on the phone after returning from the beach.

"Yeah, I get it, too," her sister said. "Remember how Father Zosima's dying brother asked the birds to forgive him?"

Lily sighed. That part of the book had stuck with her. *"Ask the birds for forgiveness."*

Lying on the bed, with the phone to her ear, Lily thought, *Sweet sparrow, forgive me. I have sinned.*

"Dostoevsky believed that *each of us is guilty before everyone and everything*," Jane said, quoting *Brothers Karamazov*.

"I don't know what that means," Lily responded. "I'm not guilty of the sins of Heinrich Himmler."

"Think about it this way: Asking for forgiveness from all is about God's love. When we ask for forgiveness and when we forgive, we are with God. Each of us should ask forgiveness for everything—this is what Father Zosima learns from his brother. This is what Dostoevsky is writing about. Asking for forgiveness for everything acknowledges our interconnectedness with everyone."

Switching the phone to the other ear, Lily said, "Slow down." Then added, "Do you believe that?"

Jane laughed and then said, "Who the fuck knows."

Now Lily wondered what her mother would have thought about

this conversation. Surely, she had read the book; she'd read every-thing. *What,* Lily thought, *would she make of us now?*

She thought of the long conversations they had had growing up about their moral obligations. Carol Webb had never wasted an op-portunity to talk about their purpose in life and how it related to oth-ers.

"Do you see how Caravaggio captures the works of mercy?" Mrs. Webb had asked as she and the girls looked at an image of *The Seven Works of Mercy*.

"What does the light capture?" Mrs. Webb had asked.

The girls, who were about eleven and nine at the time, had been quiet as they studied the painting. Mrs. Webb tilted her head to see her younger daughter's face, which appeared scrunched up.

"Wait a minute. What's going on over here?" young Jane asked, pointing to the lower-right of the painting. "Why is that lady breast-feeding that old man?"

Jane giggled and so did Lily.

"The man is in prison," Mrs. Webb explained. "She's using her breast milk to nourish him."

"I don't know about that," Jane said. "Gross."

Lily had thought the painting was exquisite. "He uses light to show us where to look for goodness."

Lily cradled the phone between her neck and shoulder. "Dad's reading a memoir about a Japanese doctor who survived the bomb and spent the rest of his life teaching forgiveness."

"Oh, Dad! Jesus Christ," Jane said. "He's so true to his Catholic theology."

"Did Father Thomas ever talk to you about how he felt after the bombs were dropped?"

"Just a bit. He was conflicted. People rationalize their conduct all the time. Those guys at Los Alamos thought the Japanese would never surrender. They believed that had we not dropped the bombs, the war would've lasted for months to come. Rationalization is a powerful tool," Jane said.

That goes without saying, Lily thought. She understood all about rationalizing.

Sometimes she caught herself rationalizing her desire and love for the boy, telling herself, *He deserves my love; after all, I wrecked his life.* She didn't say this to her sister. She wondered if she even had to. Jane could see right through her.

"I saw him at Clements' Wednesday morning," Lily said.

"When were you going to tell me?"

"I'm telling you now." Lily hesitated. The thought of her father picking up the other phone downstairs caused her to panic a little. She got out of bed, carrying the phone to the bedroom door, and opened it. She listened for the sound of her father's and husband's voices coming from downstairs.

"Hello? What are you doing?" Jane asked.

"Nothing," Lily whispered. "Just trying to figure out where Dad and Marshall are."

She shut the bedroom door and sat on the edge of her bed, pulling on the tangled telephone cord. Lily told Jane about sitting in the truck, the coffee, the whiskey in the glove compartment, the reminiscing, how she didn't mention it to the others.

She ended with, "I don't know what I'm going to do."

"Well, look on the bright side: You're not a sociopath."

"Where did that come from?" Lily asked.

"I don't know, just trying to make you feel better. All this talk about forgiveness. I've known you the longest; you're a good person. You've always been, and I know that you struggle with everything that happened. You blame yourself for the fight. And you've got yourself all worked up over the night of the reunion. And now the parking lot. I know you want to be a good wife. I know you have regrets. Nobody's perfect. Look at it like Dostoevsky. Perhaps guilt is rooted in one's desire to be better, to realize humanity's goodness at its highest level. Think of guilt as a transformative force—I mean, if you really want to go down that road." Jane chuckled as she said the last part.

Lily took it all in—the message and the messenger. In moments like these, she was grateful her sister knew her as well as she did. Lily would've liked to have been able to see her sister's face. Such an iconic reading of guilt; leave it to Dostoevsky. For the love of God. But did Jane take any of this seriously? Lily most certainly did. She was a bit surprised by what seemed like Jane's deep appreciation for the Russian writer's Christian morality, but she wasn't surprised in the least that her sister was drawn to his depiction of humanity's darker side. Lily had long wondered what her sister believed in besides mathematical proofs.

ITHACA, NEW YORK

JUNE 2000

It was a warm Saturday afternoon. Lily had just come into the house through the back door to use the bathroom, having been working in the yard. As she removed her gardening gloves in the kitchen, she noticed that Marshall had left the day's mail and a brown paper bag on the counter along with a note that read, *Be back in 10 minutes.* She peeked in the bag, where she found six June peaches. Her favorite. She looked forward to them every year. Years ago, she had told herself that she would only eat peaches in June, no other season.

After nearly fourteen years of marriage, Marshall was still thoughtful. Not all the time. Like many couples in long marriages, they didn't always stop to ask important questions like, *Is there anything wrong?* And like some others, their passion waxed and waned. For weeks at a time, there would be nights when the only affection for which they could muster energy was to hold hands in silence before falling asleep.

She finished in the bathroom and returned to the kitchen to grab a glass of water just as Marshall was returning home.

"Who do you know in Asia?" he asked.

Before thinking, Lily said, "Nobody." Her heart raced a bit.

"A letter arrived today," Marshall said, gesturing to the counter.

"How do you know it's from someone in Asia?" Lily asked, as she looked through the pile of mail. They were standing side by side at the counter. Marshall reached in front of her, taking a peach from the bag. She did her best to remain composed.

"Because a black-naped oriole appears on one of the stamps."

Lily spotted an envelope with colorful and unusual stamps. She swallowed. Pretended to be disinterested. "Oh, it must be from a friend from high school," she said.

Marshall turned on the faucet to wash the peach. "Just as long as it's not your old boyfriend." He was half joking, but when Lily didn't say anything, Marshall glanced at her and asked, "Is it?"

Marshall knew little about the boy, only that they dated in high school and that their relationship ended soon after she started college.

"He's probably just saying hello."

"So it *is* him? You just said you didn't know anyone in Asia."

"I wasn't thinking."

"Is this the first time he's written to you?"

Lily didn't say anything. Instead, she gathered up the pile of mail, walked into the dining room, and set it on the table. "It's no big deal," she said, sitting down at the table. The unopened envelope remained on top.

In the years they had been together, Lily had never seen Marshall jealous. He never had a reason to be. Not that he didn't notice how other men looked at his wife, but it would not occur to him to view them as a threat. It was probably a combination of his self-confidence and the bond he felt they had, their connection.

Marshall followed her into the dining room. He hadn't taken a bite of his peach yet. He was holding it in his hand. "It probably isn't. But look at it from my perspective. What if an old girlfriend wrote to me a couple of times and I never said anything to you about it? It's not what's in the letters, it's that you didn't tell me there were others."

"Just one other," Lily said.

"When?"

"Years ago."

"Have you seen him?"

"At the reunion. That was eight years ago." Lily lied.

Over the years, Lily had done her best to focus on Marshall and their relationship. She thought she had made progress, but now it was coming undone. *There are two types of lies in marriage,* Lily thought, *the ones I tell my husband and the ones I tell myself.*

Still standing, Marshall said, "I'm not going to beg you to let me read the letter."

It was not lost on Lily that this was "a moment," as they say, in her marriage. What she did next mattered. She picked up the envelope, offering it to Marshall, and said, "You can read it first."

Lily sat there hoping to God he wouldn't read it.

Marshall looked down at the letter and then back at Lily. He held her gaze and said, "You read it first, and if there's anything you think I should know, then you can share it with me."

Then he walked out of the dining room, out the back door, and into the yard. *He must have known that an ornithologist would be able to identify a bird and where it lived no matter how exotic it appeared. Did he do this on purpose?* Lily wondered. If he did, she couldn't be angry with him.

The letter would remain on the dining room table on top of the stack of mail for the rest of the afternoon and evening and all through Sunday. But that didn't mean that Lily didn't think about it. It had its own gravitational pull.

...

LATER THAT NIGHT, THEY had plans to meet some of Marshall's graduate students, new ones and a few older ones, at a bar in town. Over the years, Lily had joined Marshall for drinks with his colleagues and students dozens of times. Less so these days, when she liked staying home. Earlier, she'd thought about bowing out. Any other weekend, Marshall would have understood, but given the arrival of the letter, she thought it was best that she kept her promise to join him.

The Chanticleer, or as locals called it, "the Chanti," was a typical college bar. When Lily and Marshall walked in, "You Were Meant for Me" by Jewel was playing but barely audible. A few regulars sat at the bar, including one of Marshall's colleagues from the university. Some guys in their twenties were shooting pool. A waitress hustled, delivering drinks and taking food orders. There was a baseball game playing on one of the large TVs and a soccer game on the other.

Marshall had been quiet the rest of the afternoon and during the car ride to the bar. He wasn't the type of guy to give Lily the silent treatment. That would be manipulative. Passive aggressive. Lily understood what was going on. Marshall was sad, and she was sad for him.

When he saw his students, however, his mood changed for the better. He became animated, introducing Lily to three new students who had gathered around an empty table. After brief introductions, he held a chair for her, and she stayed seated at the table while he went up to the bar to order drinks. Lily talked to the others, getting acquainted. When she looked over her shoulder toward the bar, she saw Marshall take a shot. It wasn't that unusual. A couple of times a year, after a successful grant proposal or having had an article published in an important journal, he and his students might celebrate with a round of shots. When he walked back to the table, he was carrying two pitchers of cold beer. A waitress followed him with a tray of mugs and some pretzels.

The group was about five graduate students and the Middletons. Before long they had finished five pitchers of beer and Marshall had entertained the students with stories from his days in the Amazon, stories Lily had heard many times over the years. When he started telling the one about how he had shared an outboard motorboat with a Yanomami chief and a missionary for two weeks to travel through the jungle, Lily kept to herself while the others oohed and aahed.

By the time they left, Marshall had a good buzz on, but he wasn't drunk. Lily had never seen him wasted or fall-down drunk like Jane or Jimmy Sullivan back in the day, but his speech was slower.

Sitting in the passenger seat, Marshall said, "You didn't have much to say tonight."

"I was listening to your old stories," Lily said.

"Old? Were you bored? Is that it?"

Lily took her eyes off the road and glanced at her husband. Reaching for his thigh, she said, "What are you talking about?" What she didn't say was *I know those stories by heart.* Instead, she added, "I love those stories. And I know your students do, too."

Marshall didn't say anything for the rest of the short ride back to the house. When they arrived home, rather than going straight to bed, he poured himself a scotch on ice and told her he was going to do a little work in his study. Lily went to bed, and when she woke up the next morning, close to seven o'clock, Marshall was beside her, sleeping. He never slept in. Usually he rose before dawn, before the birds. Lily could count the number of times on one hand she had woken up next to her husband. She rolled over and went back to sleep. When she woke again, he was gone.

She found him downstairs with his back to her, standing at the French doors overlooking the deck, wearing jeans and a black T-shirt. His hands were in his pockets. He didn't turn around when she entered the room. She watched him place the palm of his hand on the windowpane, as if to stop something from coming in. She came up behind him and wrapped her arms around him. She knew he was still upset.

She was hit with the thought: *My father lost the love of his life. My mother's death was beyond his control. What about my love? Is it out of my control?*

…

ON MONDAY, AFTER MARSHALL had left for the lab, Lily sat down at the dining room table and finally read the letter.

Dear Lil,

Are you well? How are your father and Jane?

I have now spent close to twenty years living and working in and around the South China Sea. Had drinks one night with an anthropologist from the states. Apparently, he's well known. He's been traveling here since 1967, studying the Ilongot. He told me that when he first came the locals practiced headhunting but it took him years to fully understand why they did it. The Ilongots told him it was their way of managing grief—of bearing the unbearable and releasing the rage that came with it.

Do you remember Queequeg and his shrunken heads? You were so curious about the practice. With a cultural practice like headhunting, which represents such a radically different worldview, at least to us, we can try to expand our understanding of what it means to be human, and in that expansive space we find our commonalities, our sameness: We all suffer great loss.

We were young and hopeful.

So now we know the headhunter's perspective as to why he would sever another man's head; it's his grief. But our innocence at the time, all those years ago, would have protected us from truly understanding. Now here we are, older. And life has turned our hopes into old dreams and tried to crush us.

We are getting further and further away from our dreams on the bay.

I have seen oceans sparkle in the blackest of nights, bioluminescence in the Maldives, and you're the only one I want to share this with.

Dad died last year. I found this photo of us in his wallet. It's a bit faded and worn, but the truth is still there.

Full fathom five thy father lies.

Lily's initial thought was, *I don't want to think about what would have happened had Marshall read this.*

And her next thought was, *Oh, Mr. Cooper.*

When she reflected on the boy's father, she thought of a kind man. He had never gone to college. Worked his ass off. Carried the stress of a one-income household. Against the odds, he raised his son alone. An alcoholic, for sure, but never a mean drunk. Only a drunk with a broken heart.

She looked at the high school photo of the two of them. His suit was powder blue with wide lapels, his long hair falling to his shoulders.

The boy had seen a photo of Barry Krauss, who played for the University of Alabama, in a glossy magazine wearing the same color tux, and that had settled it. Lily was wearing a floral print, frilly polyester dress. She had searched for the right thing to match his suit. They looked so young.

What was the name of the theme song for our prom?

She looked at the picture, got up from the table—leaving the letter on top of the other envelopes—and walked into the living room toward the wall of books. She found the shelf where she kept her mother's art books. She pulled down H. W. Janson's *History of Art,* opened to a random page, slid the picture between the pages, and closed the book.

Had life tried to crush her? she thought. *More than once, for sure.*

When Marshall returned from work, they met in the kitchen. She had made dinner, and he helped her carry the meal and plates to the table. He couldn't miss that the letter had been opened. Marshall sat down, and before Lily joined him, she picked up the mail, sorting through it quickly, making two piles: one for bills and another for trash. It was a performance. She placed the letter, nonchalantly, in the trash pile. He was watching her. She was making a risky bet that he would not reach over and pick it up to read it. And she was so relieved when he didn't.

That night in bed, she reached for him, and he rolled over onto his back. When he got hard, Lily climbed on top of him. He felt below her belly, moving his fingers. Lily's hips moved rhythmically. Right after they both came, she whispered in his ear, "Now, does that seem like I'm bored?"

Marshall laid on his back with his arm around Lily, who was lying on her side, her head resting on his chest, tucked into his neck, with her arm around his torso. A feeling of regret set in. How could she hurt a man who had only been loving and loyal?

"I don't know what I would do without you," Marshall said.

"I'm not going anywhere. I should've told you about the letter. It doesn't matter . . . that was a long, long time ago. You're my man."

Marshall only knew about the two letters. But Lily knew the real number of transgressions—the betrayals she was keeping track of on an abacus in her mind. She didn't want to hurt Marshall, but she didn't know how or if she could stop thinking about the boy.

She wasn't living a lie. She held two truths.

...

A FEW WEEKS LATER, when Jane answered her cellphone, Lily could hear the wind in the background. "Where are you?" she asked her sister.

"At the beach."

"Who says I can't love more than one man?" Lily said. She couldn't get the comment out fast enough.

"Maybe the men you're in love with?" Jane said.

"Of all people you should understand this."

"I'm not even married," Jane said.

"Exactly! That's my point. You've been free to love whomever you choose," Lily said.

"That's not quite how it works."

"Whatever. You still managed to reject the idea of marriage."

"I never married because no one ever asked me," Jane said loudly into the phone.

Lily laughed. "That's not true, and you know it."

"Okay. So maybe there was one or two," Jane said.

"I think there's been three," Lily said.

"Ooof," Jane grunted.

"What was that about?" Lily asked.

"Washing and folding laundry, grocery shopping, having to be accountable to someone else. Dear God, shoot me," Jane said.

"My life is more than that," her sister said.

"I'm not talking about your life. I'm talking about the social institution of marriage with its gendered division of labor. You're right. Somehow, I managed to escape it all. Can you imagine it? Some boomer expecting me to cook and clean for him? Jesus Christ."

ITHACA, NEW YORK

MAY 2003

While Marshall was busy with a writing deadline, Lily attended a lecture on campus by a visiting professor, a paleo-archaeologist. She arrived at the auditorium just as the introductory remarks about the speaker were finishing up. Taking a seat in the orchestra section, Lily was struck by the attractiveness of the speaker. He looked to be about her age, an Asian American man with longish hair and thick, black-framed glasses, faded blue jeans, a white collared shirt, and a black blazer. Jane would say the type of guy who could make a menopausal woman ovulate.

Lily smiled at the thought.

Projected on the large screen behind the speaker was an image of the shaft of the Lascaux cave in the Dordogne region of southwestern France. Painted in black on the cave wall was a figure of a man with the face of a bird, standing in front of a bison. "Or was it a mask?" the speaker asked.

Lily wondered, *Is this the life my mother craved? The life of the mind. Long stretches of time to think about subjects such as the role birds play cross-culturally, across time and space.*

The stick figure appeared to have an erection. Next to the figure was a long staff, again with a bird's head. The speaker suggested that the bird-headed human figure was a shaman who had descended into the cave tens of thousands of years ago, perhaps after crawling through dark tunnels and small chambers to reach the shaft, where, while in a trance and state of ecstasy, he painted the image.

Lily listened attentively. Animal fat burned in sandstone lamps with wicks made of juniper twigs. Birdman and the bull. The Magdalenian era with its reindeer and blue foxes. Deep time. Remote time. Why the bird head? Why the mask?

The professor told his audience that the cave paintings were the earliest expressions of religion and that shamans, in their varied contexts, were the mediators between this world and others. Dark otherworldly places have always required guides like shamans. Birds, then, were required for the shaman's voyage. Lily was drawn to the mysticism that birds and shamans promised. She had read that only the wisest understood the language of birds: The Norse god Odin had his ravens, Saint Francis had his sermon to the birds, and the Sufi poet Attar created a world where the language of birds was the language of the divine.

So this is how it was, Lily imagined, *birds commingled with the origins of our collective spiritual consciousness.*

Lily thought more about divinity and birds. When she was younger, her mother told her that the dove represented the Holy Spirit. As a child, whenever she heard a dove cooing, she wondered if it was one of the divine ones speaking or just one of the old regular ones.

What was it about the mythology of birds that captivated her?

Myths were stories told for a particular lesson. To explain the unexplainable—nature's mysteries. The sacred and the profane. And above all, how to live, how to be.

What bird could serve me now?

The owl of Athena? She sees in the dark. The owl, not Athena. Well, perhaps Athena, too. Perhaps they both can see through the darkness. Her mind wandered back to the last time she and the boy made love. The way he held her as if he were drowning. Then sitting in the truck. "Being without you is killing me." That's what he had said. And that's what she heard over and over all these years later. She was learning that the harder she pushed thoughts of the boy away, the more they resisted.

She needed a sign. She needed the wisdom of Athena's owl.

What silent wisdom could be revealed? What truth in the darkness? she wondered.

...

THIS IS WHAT LILY was thinking about later that night when the phone rang while she was getting ready for bed. Marshall was still in his study downstairs.

"What's the weather in Paris going to be like a few days from now?" Jane asked without saying hello.

"It should be nice, a little rainy."

"What time is your flight?"

"We'll have to leave the house at six A.M."

"Tim Jones is on his way to see you," her sister blurted out.

"Here? In Ithaca?" Lily asked. Her pulse quickened. "Has something bad happened? Do we know—"

Jane cut her off before she could finish asking her question. "No, I asked him if everyone was all right, and he assured me that everyone was still alive . . . well, that's the sense I got. He should be there in the morning."

"Did he say why he was coming?"

"He said he wanted to talk to you first. He told me he retired from the navy last year. Anyway, he said this was between you and him. I gave him your email and phone number."

In the morning, Lily dressed in jeans and a white button-down blouse. The night before, she had taken a coffee cake that she had bought at a bake sale in town out of the freezer. On a wooden tray, she set out two plates, spoons, napkins, a creamer filled with half-and-half, a bowl of sugar, and two forks. Tim called when he was thirty minutes away. She wondered why he sounded so nervous. Lily waited at the front door, peering out the windows. What did he have to tell her that required him to drive five hours from Maryland to upstate New York? Last night, that was the only thing she could think about.

When Lily saw a white GMC truck slowing down in front of her house, she backed away. She let him knock twice before she allowed herself to answer the door. She had hidden herself behind a wall that led to the living room.

Dressed in a khaki shirt and slacks, Tim appeared taller and thicker than Lily remembered. He smelled like aftershave when she hugged him. Before she brought him into the living room, he noticed the suitcases in the hallway.

"I hope I didn't come at an inconvenient time," Tim said.

"No, of course not. We leave tomorrow for Paris. My husband has work there."

He stood until she sat on a side chair near the sofa.

"Coffee?"

"Please."

"Cream and sugar?"

"Both, thank you." Tim extended his hand and took the cup and saucer. He brought the coffee to his lips, sipped, and smiled anxiously at Lily.

Wanting to take the pressure off her old friend, Lily took it upon herself to keep the conversation moving. They covered the basics: Two kids in college. Wife remarried. Saw the guys when he could. Jimmy Sullivan was drinking too much. Head had both knees replaced. Lily, in turn, updated Tim on her life—her research with Marshall, her gardens and upcoming trip. Tim took a few bites from the sliced cake and set the plate aside.

Then it was his turn. "Lil," Tim said, looking up at her as she sat across from him in a wingback chair. He looked grim.

Is he trying to tell me he's gay? Lily wondered.

Tim cleared his throat and started again. "That night, the night of the fight . . ."

She had no idea what he was trying to say. *What about that night? There's no need to bring that up.*

"That was a long time ago," Lily said.

"David McCarren was with me that night," Tim said.

"I don't understand."

"David didn't rape you," Tim said.

Lily didn't respond. She felt her face flush.

"He was with me on the beach. We were having sex."

Lily cocked her head and leaned in as if she couldn't hear him.

Looking down at the carpeted floor, Tim said, "I didn't tell anyone for almost twenty-four years that I was with David." He looked back up at her.

Lily's nod was almost imperceptible.

"Actually, I didn't tell anyone until two years ago when I told Paul. That's my partner."

Lily sat back in her chair and smoothed out the fabric on the armrest. She felt nauseated but was trying to hide it.

"I convinced myself that it wouldn't have done any good to tell the lawyers or police, because perhaps his sentence would have been longer . . . I mean . . . given that what everyone thought had occurred didn't."

The two sat in silence until Tim spoke again. "David was a dick in high school. And what happened shouldn't have happened, but given what he said at the party, he provoked it. You know what I mean?"

Lily's head spun. She looked out one of the windows to avoid his gaze.

"Maybe David taunted him because he was trying to cover up what we had been doing on the beach. I'm not making excuses for him. It's just the only thing I can come up with after all these years."

Lily thought about what Tim was saying. She remembered the day she and David were working on the yearbook—the day he grabbed her breast. He had teased her about performing oral sex on the boy. She could recall every detail. He had put his fist to his mouth, gesturing rhythmically, pushing his tongue to the side of his cheek. And then he got so angry when she suggested he had experience giving head.

Lily was pulled back to the living room when Tim added, "I never would've gotten into the navy had it come out in high school that I was gay. I had to watch myself. Lead a double life. If anyone knew, I would have been discharged. Blue discharge. 'Undesirable habits' is what it's called."

In high school, David was hiding, too, Lily thought.

Once Tim opened up, neither one took a sip of coffee, and the rest of the cake remained untouched.

Fighting the urge to stand up, Lily asked, "Have you told. . . ."

"Yeah. About two months ago on a fishing trip."

"What did he say?"

"He asked me if I had told you yet. And then told me he was happy that I didn't have to live a lie anymore. Something like that . . ." Tim's voice trailed off.

It saddened her to think that Tim, who had always been such a kind man, had spent twenty-six years carrying this burden—as if he alone were responsible for David's unfairly sullied reputation.

The fact that the boy had thought Lily had been raped helped him make sense of how things turned out. That was Lily's reasoning. It had given him meaning.

Hadn't the rape given my life meaning, too? Lily wondered.

She tried to push the thoughts out of her mind. That's the past. But she had learned that the past was never really the past.

When she shut the front door after Tim left that morning, she locked it and turned toward the stairs that led to her bedroom. Gripping the banister, she was overcome by remorse and then deep anger.

...

WHEN SHE WOKE UP from a long nap, she called Jane.

"I was never raped," she said when her sister picked up the phone.

"What are you talking about?"

"Tim. He told me he was with David that night on the beach having sex," Lily said.

"What the fuck! Are you okay?"

"No, not really."

"Jesus Christ! Of all the people to have sex with."

"I don't think it had anything to do with Tim liking David. I think it had more to do with availability."

"What a fucking waste. And people wonder why I stay high all the time," Jane said.

"Will you do me a favor?" Lily asked.

"Anything."

"Will you tell Dad?"

...

LATER THAT NIGHT, LILY was sitting up in bed. The room was dimly lit. Marshall sat down on Lily's side of the bed and rested his hand on her leg, which was under the covers.

"Is everything all right? You seem preoccupied," he said. "Are you excited about Paris?"

Years ago, she had decided not to tell Marshall about what had happened at the party. And she didn't want to tell him now. She imagined it would only lead to more questions: *What else have you kept from me?*

Only another part of my life. And a part of my heart.

She would have to make sense of Tim's news alone.

In the middle of the night, unable to sleep, Lily got out of bed, put on her robe, and went downstairs. She opened the French doors and walked outside onto the deck, barefoot. The air was chilly and the night sky pressed down. She thought back to her college days, when, without the boy, she was forced to reconcile what she couldn't remember. During her junior year, Lily had participated in a "Take Back the Night" march and candlelight vigil, raising awareness about sexual violence. While walking back to her dorm, she had confided in one of her suite mates, a senior named Janice who was majoring in women's studies, about the night on the beach, the drunken night of the fight.

"If I'm not able to recall the details of what happened, you know, the rape, I mean, does that mitigate the impact? Am I still a victim?"

"What your mind has repressed, your body remembers," Janice had said with confidence.

Then Janice had added, "I knew a girl like you who was in a blackout. Never remembered a thing. Polaroids surfaced. Turns out it was more than one guy. Well, we don't need to rehash the details of the photographs, but she never knew any of this. She just couldn't remember. Now the girl agonizes—what else happened? Poor girl. She can't help but imagine."

Lily had wondered how the body remembers when there is no physical pain. In her darkest moments of self-loathing, she had wondered if all the sex she had had with the boy allayed any physical pain from the rape. Or, if there was no physical pain, did she actually want it in some way like Coach Kenny suggested? Had she cheated on the boy? Despite her friend's assurance and despite the feminist discourse that ran thick on campus, Lily had been torn up. She had carried a collective shame that wasn't hers to carry.

But their lives were ruined, she had thought. *Not mine.*

Now, standing on the deck, she tried to force herself to recall whatever she could about the keg party. It had been twenty-six years. Nothing came to her. She knew that when the boy had found her, she wasn't wearing underwear. Staring up at the dark sky, she wondered, *Why? What was I doing without my underwear on? If David didn't take them off, then who did?*

She took a deep breath through her nose and felt the cold air in her nostrils.

What am I grieving now? Lily asked herself. *The tragedy of it all. His wasted potential. Lost dreams. A gay and confused teenager permanently disabled.*

Was it better for all of us to believe I was raped?

PARIS, FRANCE

MAY 2003

Marshall had been invited to give an important lecture in Paris. On the flight over, Lily barely slept. They had been planning the trip for months. The first day, Marshall had back-to-back meetings. Lily was so distracted, she left the hotel without a map; with the exception of a few phrases, she didn't speak French, and it was her first time in Paris. She had no idea the size of the city; the Seine was just a river in a Joni Mitchell song.

She set out on her own to explore. She was only a good tourist in the sense that she kept turning. She walked and turned down one street or another on a whim. Occasionally she looked up at the old cream-colored limestone buildings with balconies and iron gates and studied the ornamental stone statues of mythical beasts. But most of the time, she walked, numb to the sirens and passing cars and motorcycles. At a light, an old Parisian woman yanked her back by her coat, stopping her from walking into oncoming traffic.

She went inside the Church of Saint-Sulpice, blessed herself with holy water from an enormous shell, and lit a candle at the far end of the church beneath a marble statue of the Blessed Mother. When she opened her eyes, she saw a nun to her left wearing a full habit and veil, and for no apparent reason other than curiosity, she felt compelled to follow the woman. After a few blocks, the nun walked down Rue du Bac and passed through an iron gate off the street. Lily looked to see if anyone was watching and then pushed the gate open, but the nun had disappeared. Lily walked down a long passageway to a wooden door, pushed it open, and it revealed another beautiful chapel. She approached the sanctuary where other devotees of the Blessed Mother had laid at least a dozen bouquets of flowers. Lily knelt before the altar and watched as an older nun collected the flowers. When she left, Lily was alone in the chapel; she gazed up at the marble statue of the Blessed Mother erected behind the altar.

"I need you," she whispered.

Lily's gaze moved over the statue to the folds of Mary's veil. She looked behind her. The chapel was still empty. *If I could just get closer,* she thought. She stood up and moved toward the statue, which rested on a large round piece of marble. Keeping her eyes on the face of the Blessed Mother, she walked up a step and on to the altar. She reached up on her toes and pressed her left hand on the foot of the statue near a stone-carved rose. She thought about hoisting herself up, gripping the marble, steadying herself with her right hand on the golden tabernacle, as if she were free-climbing up a rock.

Lily didn't hear the doors open.

"*Non non non,*" said an older nun. "*Je vais vous aider à descendre.*"

The nun walked Lily over to a pew and sat down beside her. The woman's face was milk white and framed by the fabric of her wimple.

"How do—" But before Lily could finish, the nun interrupted her.

"*Je ne parle pas anglais,*" the nun said.

And like a dam breaking, Lily let out a cry. "How do I let go of guilt?"

Back outside, she leaned against the building and wiped her nose on her sleeve. Around the corner, she found a café, where she sat down on a wicker chair beside two young men who were smoking and drinking wine. When the waiter approached, she pointed to the men and wine.

"*S'il vous plaît,*" she said, using what very little French she knew.

Instead of a glass, the waiter brought her a bottle of wine. She bummed a cigarette from a man and then another. In a nearby tree, a magpie rested on a branch. The nursery rhyme came to her: *One for sorrow. Two for joy.* The senselessness of the tragedy stunned her. Sitting outside the café, she thought she would suffocate. She reminded herself to breathe.

Lily finished half the wine, paid the bill, and walked on. If she had been more herself, she would have realized that she had stumbled into the Luxembourg Garden, with its flowers, painted metal chairs, and lovers. Above her, in the trees, she spotted three green parrots. *Parrots in Paris,* she thought. *Marshall will never believe me.*

She watched children sailing boats, the white sails made from fabric. Mothers pushing baby carriages suggested it was time for another drink. At forty-four, she had resigned herself now to not having children. It still hurt a little, but it wasn't as raw.

It was getting late by then, and when she left the gardens, she thought a young man with dark skin was following her. She picked up her pace as much as she could and then turned a corner and carried on. When she looked behind her, he was gone. The city of lights and love had failed her. *One more drink,* she thought.

In a corner café, she sat at a table alone and ordered a glass of wine, holding up her index finger. She drank the wine like it was water and watched as a man with a cane—who looked to be the same age as her—made his way down the street. Her mind wandered to David McCarren. She didn't know all the details, and what she did know she had pieced together from Jane. He lived with his parents. A lot slower, needed a cane to get around, and his speech was off. Couldn't live independently.

She finished her wine and was determined to get back to the hotel. But first she wanted to use the restroom. She hadn't used a toilet all day, and it suddenly felt urgent. Rushing into the stall, a realization hit her. *I must have wet myself when I was drunk that night on the beach— that's why my underwear was off. I'd taken it off myself. Seeing me like that, after what David had said, sent him over the edge.*

She sat on the toilet for a while, in the cramped stall, taking it all in. Then she took a deep breath and started out again. An old man approached her, begging for money. He was bent at the waist, wearing a blanket draped over his shoulders—tourists and locals walked past him. Still a bit distracted, she reached into her pocket and their eyes met. When he held out his hands, she gave him the rest of her cash, coins and all. It must have been a lot of money, because the old man called after her. She kept walking. She didn't know if she was walking toward the hotel or away from it. More streets, more sirens.

She sat down on a bench to catch her breath. A pigeon landed at her feet. She thought about what Marshall had told her about the carrier pigeons the French had used to send messages during the Franco–Prussian War of 1870 when Paris was besieged. The messages were so small, they were read under a microscope. Lily had her own message to send. She imagined herself gently tying a note to the leg of the gray bird on the sidewalk. *Please come find me, Jane.* When she looked up, the man she thought was following her earlier was standing in front of her.

"Get away from me," she yelled.

The man held up both his hands, his pink palms eye level to Lily. He stepped back.

"Look," he said in English as he opened his coat, exposing his clerical collar.

Lily put her hands over her mouth. "I'm so sorry."

"I did not mean to scare you," the young priest said.

"It's just that I thought you were following me."

"I *was* following you. Sister Françoise asked me to watch out for you. You seemed desperate."

Lily moved over on the bench and invited him to sit down. The young man told her he had just been ordained, and the more senior priests allowed him to say Mass only once a week when the other old priests met for dinner. He explained that he used the opportunity to take his ministry to the streets.

There was a silence between them until Lily said, "I'm sorry if I offended you."

He took out a pack of cigarettes and offered one to Lily. She took one and brought it to her lips, where he lit it.

"When were you certain of your vocation?" Lily asked.

"I'm still not certain."

"If we only had a sign our prayers were heard," Lily added.

"God's silence is excruciating," the man said.

The priest told her about his widowed mother and how for thirty years the city had reminded her that she was an unwanted immigrant.

Lily shook her head in disgust. *Why are humans always concerned with who belongs and who doesn't? Why do we always have to figure out who the other is?*

Lily took a long drag off the cigarette. She asked about the parrots she had seen.

"The parrots began to arrive in the seventies—rich Parisians had them shipped from the tropics of Africa. But like all foreigners in Paris, the more who come, the less welcome they will be. You see, the average Parisian may not understand the lives of post-colonial Algerians like my mother. As we like to say: Because the French were there—occupying Northern Africa—now we are here."

There was a coolness to the evening's air that Lily noticed. She took one last drag from the cigarette before putting it out with her shoe.

"I cheated on my husband," she announced, as if she was recalling the most banal detail of life. *I was doing the dishes when I ran out of soap.* She didn't mention the tragedy of David's permanent brain injury, the University of Michigan's withdrawal of the boy's scholarship, and his unrealized dreams and potential—it all seemed like too much.

But the stranger had already understood that Lily was troubled.

"You have to be careful with guilt. If you let it, it will set up residence in your bones."

Lily turned her head to look at the man's face, and in his eyes, she saw radical kindness.

When she didn't say anything, the priest reached over and placed his hand on her shoulder. "Guilt is both lonely and cruel."

...

AFTER THE TRIP TO PARIS, Lily needed to see her sister in person, needed Jane to help her reconcile what Tim had told her.

Jane had a large slab of stone leaning against the outside wall on the front porch of her house in Santa Cruz. It looked like a headstone from a cemetery and read, *Let no one ignorant of geometry enter.* Supposedly Plato had this engraved near the door of his academy. She told Lily that one of her lovers made it for her, a stone carver/surfer she met on the beach.

Jane lived in a small Craftsman-style bungalow she rented a couple of blocks up from the ocean and within walking distance of the restaurant where she worked. Philosophy, physics, programming, and astronomy books were stacked on tables, in corners on the floor, on the kitchen counters, and in a nonworking fireplace. Several of her math books had been published decades earlier. There was one on topology by Kelley from 1955, one on differential geometry from the sixties, and one by Gauss published in 1801, which Jane held up and said, "He wrote this when he was twenty-one." The only book Lily recognized was Hardy and Wright's *An Introduction to the Theory of Numbers,* and she only recognized it because Father Thomas had given it to Jane when she left for Yale.

Lily spotted pencils in the most random places—in the bathroom, above the sink, in between cushions, and on windowsills. There was a green velvet sofa that Jane had bought at a secondhand store, and on a side table were two photographs of their parents and one of Lily, Marshall, and Jane at the wedding. Hanging on the wall was a framed poster of a quote attributed to Paul Dirac: *Pick a flower on Earth and you move the farthest star.*

But other than the poster, there was nothing on the walls, no other decorative pieces.

Jane called proofs "her little poems." Over the years when she talked about math, it sounded like she was talking about a lover. Breathless, she would say, "So beautiful." On one occasion, years ago, after Jane had graduated from college and she and Lily were back in Portsmouth together, Lily had come up behind her while she was working on a problem at the kitchen table and tried to scare her.

"Boo!" Lily had said, grabbing her sister's shoulders.

The way Lily remembered it, Jane hadn't jumped. She had been so engrossed in the problem she was working on that she didn't even startle. Lily sat down next to her and after a few minutes said, "Show me what you're doing."

Within a minute, Jane had lost her. Looking down at the paper and then looking up at the ceiling, Jane said, "It's pretty."

Lily had simply seen lines, symbols, and numbers.

"What do you mean pretty?"

Jane looked at her and wrinkled her nose. "I don't know how to describe it except to say the problem is conceptually pretty."

Lily looked at the problem again and said, "Aren't you doing the same problems over and over just with different numbers?"

Jane laughed. "These types of problems tie together distinct fields like geometry and algebra. It's not like doing computations; rather, it requires instinct. Some problems I can't solve, but that doesn't mean I don't want to work on them."

Now, standing in Jane's dining room, Lily picked up a copy of Bernhard Riemann's *Collected Papers* from the table.

"Isn't this the guy who—"

"Yes," Jane said before Lily could finish. Jane knew her sister was going to ask if Riemann was the mathematician whose work influenced Einstein. Jane gently took the book out of her sister's hands and put it back on the table.

Against the dining room wall there was a chalkboard, the kind found in high school classrooms. It was filled with equations. Lily's first thought was *She doesn't need art on her walls, she just wants to look at this*. It was aesthetically appealing in an odd way. Her second thought was about procurement.

"Where did you get the chalkboard?"

"Don't ask. You don't want to know what I did to get that."

...

"I THINK I'M IN LOVE," Jane told Lily as they loaded groceries into the car. Jane seldom dressed up. She was wearing faded low-rise jeans, flip-flops, and a pink T-shirt that read, *Female Pleasure Is Political.* When Jane met her at the airport, Lily had wanted nothing more than to talk about Tim and what she had learned from him. But being with her sister was proving to be a good distraction. She knew that in time they would get to it.

Lily smiled and said, "Tell me everything."

Roger was a particle physicist Jane had met six weeks before Lily's visit. Driving home from the grocery store, Jane told Lily she would marry him if he weren't already married.

"He's kind of pale," Lily said while standing in Jane's kitchen shortly after Roger had arrived for dinner and was in the other room.

"Like, weird pale?" Jane asked.

"No, I just thought he'd be tan or something."

Jane had prepared enchiladas and rice and beans for dinner. Roger's favorite. While Jane opened a bottle of chardonnay, Lily searched the kitchen drawers for matches to light the candles.

"He doesn't really spend a lot of time outside," Jane explained.

At Princeton in the seventies, Roger had been a student of John Wheeler, a name Lily recognized from her undergraduate physics textbooks. At Smith, she had been the type of physics student whom other students asked for help, and while she could recall that Wheeler was known for the delayed-choice experiment, like many of her classmates, she couldn't grasp its philosophical meaning. In the late seventies and early eighties, many physicists still possessed a Cold War mentality when it came to interpreting quantum mechanics. Many adhered to the line of thinking "shut up and calculate," a phrase later coined by David Mermin. So over dinner, Lily was a little put out when she had a hard time keeping up with the conversation. Jane seemed to know all the right things to say.

"It's as if the photon knew what was going to happen; it knew what choice the experimenter was going to make," Jane said.

Roger's face lit up as Jane spoke. Initially, Lily had wanted to make a good impression on Roger, though she didn't know why given the fact that, according to Jane, he would never leave his wife and become her brother-in-law. Feeling like she had nothing to lose, she said, "I don't get it," as she watched Jane and Roger gaze at each other. Turning his attention back to Lily, Roger said, "Think of the double-slit experiment. What Wheeler's experiment demonstrates is that to measure a particle determines how the particle behaves. The researcher affects the path of the photon *after* it has passed through the screen."

Jane jumped in. "Do you get it, Lily? The researcher's measurement makes the photon go back in time and edit its own trajectory."

They were both staring at Lily waiting for her to grasp the implications.

Lily felt a little drunk and fumbled for what to say.

"In my world, cause precedes effect." She felt pretty good about the remark, but Roger didn't let up.

"After passing through the slits, the photon is on its course toward the back wall, but then the experimenter makes a choice, a delayed choice, to put a screen in front of the slit; this intervention determines how the particle acted at an *earlier* time," Roger explained.

"It's a fucking radical renunciation of cause and effect," Jane added.

Slamming his hand on the table, Roger announced, "That's exactly the language that Bohr used in a paper he published in the 1930s to refute Einstein and local realism."

Some of it was coming back to Lily. But still, she couldn't keep up.

Roger said, "Wheeler shows us that the act of measuring the photon impacts the photon's behavior after the fact."

Roger had earned his doctorate at Princeton and moved to California to take a position at UC Santa Cruz. He had joined a group of

well-credentialed physicists up north at Berkeley who called themselves the Fundamental Fysiks Group. Roger told Lily he had only
attended about a dozen meetings, for a year or so, before the group
disbanded. Unlike most physicists he had met at Princeton, the members of the group were willing to ask questions and try to interpret the
meaning of important experiments, like Wheeler's delayed choice.

Over the course of the night, Roger tried to convey some of the
more mysterious and mind-blowing interpretations that the Fundamental Fysiks Group had grappled with.

"Take Bell's theorem—it proves nonlocality. Quantum objects,
subatomic particles that once interacted, would always retain some
form of connection. Interact with a particle, and its entangled partner
would instantaneously move whether it was close or light-years away."

"But nothing travels faster than the speed of light," Lily said.

Jane was quick to respond. "Well, that's what Einstein thought,
too."

"Bell's theorem suggests that causality—the chain of cause and
effect, which is predicated on the distinction between past and present and future—is a misconception."

"Lil," Jane said, "do you get what this means for our understanding of time?"

Lily shook her head.

"A notion of absolute time loses its significance," Roger said.

Jane read the look of confusion on her sister's face. "Listen, get a
load of this: The night before Roger and I went out to dinner for the
first time, I had a dream that Roger's father played baseball. And the
next night, during dinner, Roger told me about his father and how he
played major league baseball after college. When I told Roger about
the dream I had had the night before, having known nothing about
his father, Roger said, 'Maybe this conversation, right now, right here
in this restaurant, caused you to have that dream last night.'"

"Cause and effect are indistinguishable," Roger said.

When the couple locked eyes and smiled at each other, Lily had a feeling that she was observing some form of foreplay. They were on their third bottle of wine, and Lily started to wonder if Roger, like Jane, used a lot of drugs.

Nonlocality. Future affects the past. Lily sat there, lost in her own thoughts, turning over the idea that the present could determine the past. What was time? A series of sequenced events. What if time was a lie? What if the past could appear in the future? Time is where mysteries meet mysteries.

Her thoughts wandered to the boy. *What if he were here with us now and we had a future together? And what of Marshall?* What sort of concept of time would allow for that to happen?

Eventually Lily found herself back in the conversation. "But that's the quantum world," she was finally able to say, trying to discount the implications of what Roger and Jane had said.

"But we inhabit the quantum world," Roger said. "Where is the boundary between the classical world like this table and this wineglass, and the quantum world?"

Then Roger added, "Look, I can understand it; I just can't fathom it."

Lily thought about that crazy fortune-teller who lived in Portsmouth near the high school, the one who had predicted, years ago, that she would never marry the boy. If time was not linear but instead overlaps with itself, was that how psychics could access the future? Were they tapping into a domain where there was no distinction between the past and the future? She was too embarrassed to ask Roger—too lost.

Gazing at the candlelight, Lily hadn't noticed Roger lighting a joint that he was now sharing with Jane. Registering it, she thought, *Maybe this is how they do it; they're just stoned all the time.* She wondered about physicists and their drug use, and then she focused back on the light from the candle. She had always been drawn to light, even before her college physics courses. Looking through her mother's art history books, Lily had been captivated by how the masters captured the light in oil. "See the sunlight on the globe and the shadows on the sea charts?" Lily's mother had said, pointing to Vermeer's *The Geographer*.

Jane had her numbers, and Lily had her light. A purple-and-orange sky over the Narragansett Bay, blue snow on a winter night, the way the flames from a beach fire lit up the boy's face and arms as he towered over her, or Marshall's face in the fields lit by the late-day's sun.

…

AFTER ROGER WENT HOME to his wife, Lily and Jane stayed up talking. Sitting on the couch, Lily sipped on wine. Jane sat on the other end with her knees bent up to her chest, drinking a beer.

"How are you doing with Tim's news?" Jane asked.

"I just can't get away from it."

"Get away from what?" Jane asked.

"The past. The fucking past," she said, looking at her sister. Lily had had more to drink than usual.

Jane nodded but didn't say anything.

"What a waste. It didn't have to happen. I—"

Before Lily finished, Jane interrupted her. "It happened. It was a tragic mistake. All of it. But this is life, and this is all you have. Now and the future."

"That's it? What happened to all that talk earlier? What did any of that mean? All that stuff about time." As she asked this, she waved her finger toward the dining room, invoking the night's discussion.

"Nobody knows what it means. Nobody truly understands it," Jane said. And then she added, "You've got to move on."

Lily retorted, "Easy for you to say. You're high every day."

Jane laughed. "Well, you got me there."

Lily placed her wineglass on the small table next to the couch. "I met a young priest in Paris. I'm starting to resent my faith. Feels like a heavy stone around my neck and I'm drowning in guilt. Something's gotta change. It's crushing."

She glanced over at the poster on her sister's wall. *Pick a flower on Earth and you move the farthest star.*

Ah, nonlocality. Entanglement. Particles are never independent even when separated over long distances. That's who we are. That's who we all are, Lily thought.

The sisters were quiet until Lily asked, "Does Roger feel guilty about his affair?"

"We don't talk about it."

"Do you feel guilty for sleeping with a married man?"

"No."

Lily tilted her head and looked at her sister. She believed her.

Jane stretched out her legs so that the bottom of her feet touched Lily's thigh. When she got comfortable, she said, "I left all that behind. Guilt is a form of social control that I never really bought into. I mean, social control isn't bad. If people are going to live together in large groups, there needs to be some kind of social contract. But we have to recognize that the current social rules about marriage, gender roles, and sex are all invented, they're socially produced, like every other aspect of culture. Man-made. And the current sociopolitical systems don't have women and girls' best interests in mind. Once I understood how societies worked, I just couldn't buy into it. I'm not going to be complicit in my own subordination. So I opted out."

And you certainly did that, Lily thought, *to the extent that anyone can without disappearing into the wilderness.*

From the sofa, Lily looked around her sister's living room and into the dining room at her bare necessities: the chalkboard, books, and papers.

Minus the pot and pills, Mom might have approved.

"Who said the patriarchy only works if women are complicit?" Jane asked, interrupting the silence.

Lily paused and said, "I can't remember."

Jane took a swig from her beer and said, "Did it ever occur to you that you blame yourself for what happened because that's what society requires of you?"

Lily almost spoke over her. Jane had barely finished when Lily blurted out, "Simone de Beauvoir. That's who said it."

Jane could tell Lily was pleased with herself. "Did you even hear what I said?" she asked.

"I was trying not to," she said as she reached for her wine.

ITHACA, NEW YORK

APRIL 2004

The year passed. Lily was caught up in the habits of a mature marriage—reading books in bed, talking about what's for dinner at breakfast, Saturday nights on the sofa, and occasional erectile dysfunction. What was more, she had gone to war with herself.

Sometimes she woke up breathless from anger stored in a dream. She struggled with the senselessness of the tragedy along with her sister's insight. Why did he have to shove him the second time? Why couldn't he have controlled his rage? How could such a good person do so much harm? Was her sister right? Was nursing her guilt less of a psychological response and more of a cultural response predicated on gender roles? She felt like she would never have the answers.

Almost a year to the date from when Tim paid a visit to Lily, she sat in front of her computer and saw an email from Head. She opened it.

Dear Lily,

Cheers from Rhode Island. How are you, my old friend? Life's pretty good. I'm in private practice now. Keeping busy. Playing a lot of golf. You should see the changes in the neighborhood. Lots of money moving into town. Folks tearing down the old houses only to build new ones with views of the water. We're all getting together this summer. It would be great if you could join us. Everybody's taking off the last two weeks of July. Thought you and Jane might join the old gang. Still looking for the love of my life. Miss you. Love, Head.

She closed her email account but remained seated at the desk. Over the past year, she had become more determined to free herself from her sense of responsibility over what had happened between the boy and David. She would ask herself over and over, *What did I actually do besides attend a party with my sister, have way too much to drink, and throw up in the dunes?*

Perhaps the need had been building, but she now experienced it like a sudden impulse. She needed to see the boy, to see for herself how he had made sense of Tim's news. How he had reconciled what had happened that night.

We need a long conversation about Tim and David.

She wouldn't respond to Head's email. She wouldn't even tell Jane. If asked, she would pretend she had never received it. But she was going to Portsmouth. She knew she had to see him.

When she told Marshall she planned to spend the last week of July in Rhode Island with her father, he said, "Why don't you have Jane fly out to meet you?" Marshall didn't have lingering suspicions; Lily knew that he was always thinking about ways to make her happy.

She lied. "She's got to work."

I'll do this without hurting him.

For the few months leading up to July, she managed to distance herself from her husband's potential pain. Lily thought about where she might find him. On the boat. At his father's house. What would she wear? She promised herself that they would not have sex. Just talk. A long conversation about what had happened. But when she didn't have her guard up, thoughts of being intimate crept up on her. She tried to remember the way he smelled and wondered what she would see in his face. Would she be able to resist him if he reached for her?

...

IT WAS A BLUE and white summer day in Rhode Island. Marshall was so far from her mind that morning, she forgot to text him. Lily put on a white pair of pants and a white cotton blouse. She kept her hair down. She told her father she was headed to Newport to do some shopping.

From her father's house, she made the short drive across the island to Mr. Cooper's old place. She slowed down as she approached the house, feeling nervous and a little excited. She was looking for his truck, the black one he had bought for his father. She stopped in front of the house. A white Dodge van was parked out front. It wasn't the house she remembered.

The trim had been repainted, and there was a new front door. The yard, shrubs, and flower beds were well maintained. Old birch and dogwood trees towered over the house. She pulled into the driveway and got out of her car. As she was about to walk up the front steps, a man who appeared to be in his thirties opened the door.

"May I help you?" he asked.

"I'm looking for the Coopers."

The man smiled and said, "They don't live here anymore. We bought this house."

Lily got back into her car. A longing for their youth took hold. Those days and nights spent in the Coopers' basement were so carefree. Innocence was always more striking in hindsight.

Her next thought was, *The marina—that's where I'll find him.* And then, *Would Marshall leave me if he found out?*

It took her less than five minutes to drive to the marina. She turned off the road and headed down a short but steep incline to the parking lot. She pulled into an empty space facing the water and kept the car running. From where she parked, she could see the entire marina: the formidable jetty that protected the cove, floating docks with dozens of sailboats and powerboats, wooden pilings with white pointed caps to keep the birds from roosting, and neatly tied lines. Lily couldn't help but notice the number of luxury sailboats, some with forty-five-foot hulls or longer. In the seventies, there were only a few yachts berthed here. The town had changed.

Still sitting in her car, Lily was overcome with nervousness and nausea. She turned up the air-conditioning.

"Forgive me, Marshall," she whispered.

And then she saw him on his boat just beyond a red Boston Whaler. His hair was grayer. He was wearing a blue T-shirt and khaki shorts. She watched him on the bow, down on one knee, working the lines. Then Lily saw someone else on the boat. A younger woman emerged from the cabin below and was now standing on the deck. She had long dark hair pulled up in a high ponytail. Well-toned and muscular. Mid-twenties, at the most. Lily watched as he spoke to the woman. She watched them laugh. She had thought of him as hers all these years.

She watched them for a minute and then put the car in reverse, backed up, and drove out of the lot. *What a fool I am. A selfish fool.*

Lily felt a strange sense of safety come over her, like she had dodged a bullet. Crushed but safe. She was going to go home to Marshall. And she was going to make some changes. She decided then and there to give Marshall the rest of her good years, completely. And like the last time she had been to the marina, Marshall would never find out. She was going home, where she belonged.

...

A FEW MONTHS LATER, during a lecture by a famous astronomer, Marshall nodded off. It was to be expected: Up before sunrise as long as Lily had known him, he tended to get sleepy close to six o'clock. The lecture was on the life cycle of stars, white dwarfs, dying stars begetting life-giving carbon—the building blocks of life.

Billion-year-old carbon, Lily thought. *What were the lines from that Joni Mitchell song?*

Lily was doing her best to match what the speaker said with what she knew about celestial bodies: exploding stars, the space between stars, blown by stellar winds, eventually forming new stars, new moons, new planets, birds, husbands, and old lovers. Life is born from stars.

Lily glanced over at Marshall; his chin rested on his chest. She noticed how dry his lips were, his mouth slightly open. She let her mind wander back to the marina. Emotions stirred in her. She felt a wave of jealousy toward the young woman but quickly dismissed it. The irony that she was sitting next to her husband was not lost on her. She thought of the axiom: Life turns on a dime. Could a statement be truer? One forceful shove. Ten seconds. Surely no more. Before David's head hit the rock, it was over.

As a girl she'd imagined herself married to a football star, having his children. Now here she was, the wife of a wealthy man with the privilege and time to think about things like the origins of a galaxy.

"The precursors of white dwarf stars are the primary source of carbon atoms in the Milky Way—we are stellar ashes," the speaker explained.

We are stardust / billion-year-old carbon / We are golden. That's right, Lily thought, *that's the way the song goes.*

Stars burn for millions and billions of years. "The sky is haunted by the past lives of stars. What we see in the night sky existed millions of years ago." Lily's mother had said this long ago, back in Portsmouth. Now Lily understood this completely as a woman haunted by a past love.

On the drive home, Lily was caught up in thoughts about songbirds and starlight and how birds migrate using star patterns.

Unlocking the front door, Lily said to Marshall, who was standing behind her, "The lecture got me thinking about how ICARUS scientists should track the migration of songbirds."

This was Marshall's love language. He would have had sex with Lily right there on the front porch if he hadn't woken up with the birds—and been sixty years old.

He put his hand on Lily's shoulder and said, "You're the love of my life, Lily Remington."

"And you're mine," she said, pushing the door to their house open, knowing that it was the truth and also that it was a lot more complicated.

ITHACA, NEW YORK

SEPTEMBER 2005

A year later on a warm September night just after dinner, Marshall decided to take a walk along some trails near the university while Lily tended to her garden. Like most people, she preferred gardening in the early mornings and evenings to avoid the sun. She was on her knees in the dirt but looked up when Marshall came out the back door with his boots in his hands. He sat on one of the deck chairs and carefully bent down to fix his laces.

"Won't be long," he said as he left through the side gate. He was on foot, headed to one of the nearby trails.

Lily turned back to her flowers; her gaze followed fall's buzzing. She watched as a bumblebee the size of a large cotton ball worked diligently in one of her dahlias—its tiny black legs gathering and gathering and covering itself with pollen. *It looks like a cheese puff,* Lily thought. Tree crickets and katydids called out along with a few American robins. She took off her gardening gloves and wiped her forehead.

It was then she noticed that Marshall's binoculars were on the deck. He must have forgotten them. That would be a first.

A couple of hours later, Lily became concerned. Marshall was never gone this long. She took the car to the trailhead. They had walked these trails for close to two decades. Not every day, but at least a few times a month. She knew that parts of the trails where the elm roots bulged out of the earth could be menacing. As the day's light diminished, the appearance of the trees and trails grew richer. She couldn't bring herself to call out Marshall's name for fear of embarrassing him. When did he figure out that he had forgotten his binoculars?

During the day, Lily could recognize the bark of hickories, the twigs of basswood, the leaves of oaks. Now as the dark settled, the woods closed in on her and the sounds emerged: a spring peeper somewhere in the distance, the buzzing and chirping of cicadas and crickets, a few high pitches. What was this acute uneasiness? Even if Marshall had stepped off the trail, he was an ace at finding his way out. He had hiked in the Amazon, followed birds to the Rockies and to roadless parts of Maine. This was his backyard for Christ's sake.

A decade ago, they had flown to Florence to hike a part of the Via Francigena, an ancient trail from Canterbury to Rome. There among the tallest sycamores and pines, the air was divine. Marshall had called it "God's very breath." Now, feeling concerned about his whereabouts, Lily closed her eyes and recalled the morning mist and sunlight, the same sun that warmed the traveling pilgrims. It was serene, sacred even. But on this particular September night, she felt betrayed by the trees; the small, thin branches looked like crooked fingers.

Lily focused on the hazards Marshall might have encountered: felled trees, moss-covered stones, steep ditches. She thought of his inevitable frailty—the decaying branches under her feet became his bones, an image she pushed away almost as soon as it arrived. It was then she heard a strange sound. She stood still, trying to figure out from which direction the sound was coming. It sounded like an old man, a whiskey voice, yelling "No, no, no," over and over.

"Marshall," she called out. Again, louder. "Marshall!"

Whatever was making the sound was silenced; it was listening, too.

When she had walked about forty-five minutes, she knew she needed to turn around and head to the university for help. Back in the car, she thought it would kill him if one of his graduate students found him curled up in a ball in a ravine hurt or, worse, lost.

Driving through town, she spotted him sitting on a bench, alone, looking down at his hands, which were folded on his lap. After she pulled the car into an open spot and turned off the ignition, she watched him for a second. What was he doing here by himself without his binoculars?

Then she remembered something that had happened a week before. It had been late in the day, and she had taken a nap in the nude. After getting out of bed, she had pulled on an oversize black sweater but no underwear. She wandered into her study and was taken by the reflection of light on the walls. Afterward, walking around the kitchen, she had caught Marshall's attention. He kissed her and rubbed her bare ass. It had been so sweet and sexy. He stepped outside, and when he returned, he asked her the name of a bird at the feeder. Looking through the window, she said, "It's a white-throated sparrow." He looked at her and nodded. "What an effect you have on me. It must be that outfit you're wearing."

But she had been surprised by the question. White-throated sparrows were as familiar to Marshall as his own shoes.

Now, Lily got out of the car and shut the door. When Marshall saw her, a look of relief spread across his face.

"Lily." He sounded tired.

When the relief dissipated, she saw sadness in his eyes. She didn't want to frighten him. Instead, she sat down next to him and said, "What a great idea. Let's have a little rest on the bench." He reached over and took her hand in his.

She never did ask Marshall where he had been, nor did she ask what might have made that unusual sound in the woods. Years later, she learned it was the cry of a bobcat. The day after Lily found Marshall on the bench in town, she called Jane early in the morning. Jane had been sober for one year and picked up on the first ring. She had moved home to Portsmouth to care for their aging father.

"Do you know where Dad keeps the facecloth he uses for his butt?" Jane asked. Soon after she quit using and went to AA, she admitted to her sister that she had started taking more pills to get the same effect. Years betray an addict—the longer one uses, the more one needs. "I understand the calculus of opioids," Jane had told her.

"Where?"

"On the counter, next to the sink, not on the floor, not in a little Tupperware container, on the fucking counter."

"How do you know it's the one he uses for his butt?"

"Because it's blue. *Blue* starts with *b* and so does *butt*. That's how I got him to remember it. We have a white facecloth for the face and blue for the butt. Did I really get sober for this?"

Lily smiled into the phone.

"Thank you for taking care of him."

"When am I going to see you?" Jane asked.

"There's something wrong with Marshall."

"Is he getting his facecloths mixed up, too?"

By the end of the month, the neurologist had told them it was early-onset Alzheimer's. Marshall was only sixty-one.

PORTSMOUTH, RHODE ISLAND

NOVEMBER 2007

It was unmistakably one of Marshall's best birdcalls, a Swainson's thrush. Lily heard it before rounding the corner from the front desk at the nursing home, and there it was again, coming from the common room. A high-pitched, thin note—so high-pitched it was piercing. And there was Marshall, sitting in a wheelchair in the center of the room, staring out and into—for all Lily knew—a mixed dense forest of evergreen trees, spruces, pines, and larches. Stopping in the middle of the hallway to watch him, she hoped he saw a cool stream and was somewhere in the Rocky Mountains. He made the call again and again until one of the older nurses snapped at him. "That's enough, Mr. Middleton." She hadn't noticed Lily standing there, and when she did, she didn't apologize. "He gets the other residents worked up. The other day, he had three of them whistling, cackling, and clucking like chickens."

It had been two years since Marshall was diagnosed, and the disease had stolen his dignity; he belched and couldn't remember to wipe his chin. The doctor had instructed Lily not to leave him unattended. His intellect had been his compass, and now he had forgotten how to hold a book. During this time when Lily cared for Marshall at home in Ithaca, he had required help in the bathroom, getting dressed, and eating. He had spent hours opening doors and closing them. One afternoon, he had moved twelve dining room plates to the floor. Marshall's mornings were spent searching for nameless objects. One snowy night, Lily found him outside, wearing his gray bathrobe, blowing in the wind, his arms out to both sides. He looked like a gull in a hurricane. Two days later, when Lily had come out of the shower, she smelled gas from the stove. It was then she decided she had to move Marshall into a nursing home.

It had been two months since Lily had come back to Rhode Island. She went to the nursing home twice a day: early in the morning and right before evening supper. As depressing as the visits were, she held hope that somehow he might sense her presence. But more than this, she needed to make sure he was cared for throughout the day.

There was nothing for her in upstate New York. After caring for Marshall, she had been ready to move back to Portsmouth, to the place of her childhood and family roots. She wanted a new home and a new garden near the water. She wanted to attend Mass with the monks and watch the winter sunsets on Narragansett Bay. Jane had promised her sober dinner parties and even the possibility of joining the book club at the Abbey—the original club her mother had participated in all those years ago. She knew she risked running into the boy in town, but it was a chance she would take in return for her sister's companionship.

Now, driving back from the nursing home, Lily thought about the last time she and Marshall had made love. It had been in Ithaca, and, coincidentally, the same weekend his mother died. If she had known it was going to be the last time, she would have made it last. He had been having one of his better days, and that afternoon, he had been particularly affectionate. He had come up from behind Lily while she was standing in front of the bookshelf, moved her hair aside, and gently kissed her neck. Reaching around, he had fondled her breasts, pulling hard on her nipples as if it was the first time he had played with them. His desire remained urgent. Later, when she was lying on her back and he was on his side, propped up on his elbow, watching her, he'd said her name and only her name, as if he was double-checking. The tone was unmistakable. She knew what he had been asking, *Is that you, Lily?*

Lily had reached for him and held him with love, sadness, and a deep sense of gratitude. She hadn't had to search for those feelings—they had been there all along.

The following day, he lost control of his bladder. The neurologist explained that this was a sign that his disease was progressing.

...

IT HAD STOPPED RAINING, but Lily felt as if she were walking through a cloud. A warm front was moving in, and she could barely make out Prudence Island across the bay. She had made her way to a wooden bench near the train tracks, which ran parallel to the shoreline. She was paying a visit to her father's grave; he was one of only a few lay teachers buried among the monks in a small cemetery surrounded by old pine trees on the school grounds. Mr. Webb had died of a massive heart attack six weeks after his seventy-fourth birthday, about three months after Marshall's diagnosis. One of his colleagues had found him on a footpath lined with pines.

Sitting down on the bench, Lily took out her reading glasses to check her phone; she couldn't read anything these days without them.

She and Jane had plans to work out: They were holding each other accountable and taking responsibility for each other's health and aging bodies. They could do that. They were sisters.

When the foghorn sounded, Lily was reminded of the boy, who had once told her that when he was too old to play ball, they would move to Prudence Island and he would man the lighthouse. He had wanted to keep a garden with chickens so they could eat omelets for breakfast made from fresh eggs. In August, after they'd made love on the beach, they would pick blueberries and make blueberry buckle. She was pretty sure the lighthouse was automated—at least that's what Father Thomas had told her—so there would be no need for a lighthouse keeper, but she hadn't told him that at the time.

What was the line from that Van Morrison song? Lily wondered. *When that foghorn blows, I will be coming home.*

Since that night at Jane's in Santa Cruz, Lily had tried to keep up on the major advancements in quantum mechanics. She had learned that atomic clocks actually demonstrate that time moves more slowly by the sea than in the mountains. Lily imagined that living on an island with the boy would have bought them more time—whether this difference would have been perceived was not the point. It was the poetics of the matter. But since the day at the marina three years ago, she had resigned herself to the fact that his heart had let her go. She was preparing herself, mentally and emotionally, for the day she bumped into him in town with that woman, or perhaps another.

...

DAYS LATER, LILY PULLED the handle on the copper-plated doors of the chapel, and while she had never taken Latin as a student, she knew from her childhood that the scriptural text sculpted in relief on the doors was from Ephesians 2:19: *No longer strangers and sojourners but fellow citizens with the saints.* The narrow vertical panels of stained glass high above the altar, which made up three walls of the chapel, had always caught her attention, even as a child. No matter how many times she had sat in the chapel, she never took its beauty for granted— its octagonal shape, its walls built from local fieldstone and California redwood. People came from all over the world to see its architecture, and here it was, a street away.

She entered one of the back rows of pews, knelt, and hoped to pray. Behind the altar, several monks in black robes sat with their heads bowed. There weren't as many monks living at the monastery as there had been when she was little. The Monday morning Mass was being celebrated by the abbot, a man Lily had known most of her life, who in his younger years had tended to all the gardens on the grounds and taught Faulkner's novels for the sole purpose of having students correct the writer's grammar.

It was during the Eucharistic prayer that her mind began wandering back to the conversation she had had with her father on the railroad tracks about the Japanese doctor and forgiveness. Thoughts on the role of forgiveness fused with thoughts on light. Fixated on the suspended crucifix sculpture made from hundreds and hundreds of silver and gold wires, Lily wondered about the oldest light in the universe. *Primordial stars. The place in between stars was where all life forms. Stardust: carbon, nitrogen, silicon, gold, silver—elements of the divine.* What Lily had come to believe was that the light of life was always interconnected, all particles and waves, all forms of life, all of us—with our human capacity for frailty and imperfection—come from the same light. *We are all culpable. And we all deserve forgiveness. And if we are all connected, then we must forgive all. The teleology of forgiveness is to bring us closer to the light. But radical forgiveness is like the notion that time is an illusion, equally unfathomable and unimaginable.*

Lost in her own thoughts, Lily left the chapel and headed home.

It was a warm November morning—"Indian summer," the weather-man had said. It was only 7:50 A.M. The school was co-ed now. Boys in blazers and ties and girls in their skirts and sweaters crossed her path, heading to classes. A lone monk headed for the entrance to the monastery, where students were not allowed. Lily passed the construction site for the future Webb Hall, a new science center that would be named after her father. Marshall had funded the project. She walked along a dirt path that cut through some pine trees leading to the road where she and Jane lived.

Her intention for that morning was to review some donation acknowledgment letters sent over by Marshall's accountant. She sat down in front of the computer, only to find a new email.

Dear Lil,

I hope this email finds you well.

I've been sailing with sea nomads in the Strait of Malacca at the southern tip of the Malay Peninsula. They are known as the Orang Suku Laut—people of the sea. There are over three thousand islands. Known for monsoonal storms and reefs of rugged rock, the seas are notoriously treacherous. Nomads navigate waters even in the middle of the night by the moon and the stars. They are born in their boats, and they die in their boats. Like long canoes with tented thatched roofs, their boats are their only dwellings. They fish with spears and baskets. The Malay are afraid of the Orang Suku Laut and their use of witchcraft and warned me repeatedly that their magic would be used to enslave me. They believe spirits are everywhere. I've seen children as young as five and six out on boats, alone, standing on the bow, navigating the waterways and the mangrove coast with long wooden paddles.

That's where I first saw them.

I saw a girl, she couldn't have been more than five, fishing alone. I was in a nearby boat maybe twenty feet away, when the girl fell into the water. I dove in after her. It caused quite a scene. Others paddled toward us, perhaps they thought I intended to kidnap her. She dove under the water to avoid me. I quickly figured out that the girl didn't need saving. It took me some time to explain this to the others. In the end, her father invited me to stay with them.

I met an old woman among the sea nomads who practiced witchcraft. She was convinced that you had put a spell on me years ago as a young boy and that's why I never married. She offered me all sorts of antidotes, spells that she promised would free me. I told her I would take nothing, ever. That I would remain bewitched by you until the day I die.

I've got some news. I'm coming home for good, Lil.

Lily closed her email account and pushed her chair away from the desk. She stared at the blank screen. Why now? Had he learned of Marshall's condition? What about his girlfriend? It had been a number of years. She wondered if they were still together. The woman she had seen on the boat was so beautiful. Had there been others like her? She could understand him dating someone in her thirties, but someone in her twenties? Jane dated younger men and women. But how much younger? Was it any of her business?

And I chose Marshall, Lily thought.

She felt anxious. One day Marshall was well and the next he was sick. One day the boy asked if they still had a chance together and the next he had found himself a girlfriend. Over the years, time had played tricks on Lily. Sometimes it was compressed, and other times she had gotten lost in its length.

She was afraid to wonder if she and the boy had a future. She had convinced herself that the future can't be trusted. Sitting there at her computer, she found herself out of breath.

She would respond to his email, just not immediately. It would be the first time she wrote back. She needed to gather her thoughts.

...

WHEN LILY SAT DOWN in the nursing home at a table next to Marshall, he didn't appear to notice her. He was dressed in one of her favorite shirts, a gray linen, paired with blue jeans. Compared to the other residents, Marshall looked fit. One poor soul was in his robe, which was untied, showing the stains on his white undershirt. *Where are his loved ones?* Lily wondered. The staff at the nursing home were leading what they called a "failure free" activity, one where the result is always right.

"It reduces agitation and anxiety," the social worker had explained to Lily at one of the new-residents' meetings.

On this occasion, residents had two activities to choose from—threading dry pasta with yarn or sorting inexpensive hardware, like nuts, washers, and bolts. Marshall had a small stainless-steel wing nut in his hand, and he was trying to figure out which plastic basket he should place it in.

"They must think I work here," he said to her. "Why else would they have me doing this goddamn job?"

Before returning home, Lily sat in front of a stone grotto dedicated to the Blessed Mother on the edge of the monastery grounds. It had been inspired by the one in Lourdes. Lily bowed her head in quiet contemplation; she had always been drawn to the Blessed Mother.

Praying to Mary came easy, but she had been looking for God since she was a child.

Some days she had specific petitions: Marshall's general care at the nursing home, Jane's ongoing sobriety, the health of one of the elderly monks she had known since childhood. On this morning, after her visit with Marshall, she simply repeated fragments of a prayer over and over: "Holy Mary, Mother of God."

Sitting on the stone bench, she thought about his email. The years had made her less impulsive. More careful. Was there a chance for them? Of course she still loved her husband, but caring for him for the past two years had taken its toll. She had done all the care herself before the nursing home. Even though she would not admit it, she was still exhausted. Losing Marshall, thought by thought, felt like the longest years of her life. His mind put up a good fight. But he eventually disappeared.

So much of her life had changed in the past two months. She would respond to the boy, but she needed just a little more time.

Rising from the stone bench in front of the grotto, she turned to leave and was pleased to see her sister's car parked on the road. Jane was waiting to drive her home.

"Were you saying a prayer for world peace?" she asked as Lily got into the passenger seat.

"No, I was praying for your saggy ass."

"What? Is my ass starting to sag?" Jane looked visibly worried.

"No, I'm just getting back at you for making fun of me."

"I'm not making fun of you."

"Yes, you are. You're making fun of me for praying," Lily said.

Jane turned the car around and headed off campus. She took a right at the entrance to the school and headed back down the hill to their house, closer to the water.

"I think it's kind of sweet."

"Now you're being condescending."

"You're right, but listen, when my ass does start to sag, will you pray for it?"

Now it was Lily's turn. "How long has it been since you've had a spiritual thought, a prayer, a sense of humility? Anything remotely related to your Catholic upbringing?"

Jane thought for a second.

"Well, there was this one time when I was at the dentist having a crown put on and I had asked for nitrous oxide. Five minutes into the procedure, I wanted more, so I fake-squirmed a little and grabbed the arms of the dental chair, and sure enough, the dentist turned up the gas. I remember inhaling it through my nose as if my life depended on it. And then I had a revelation: I kept hearing the same phrase in my head: *He gave his only son, he gave his only son.*"

Lily laughed. It was the first time she had laughed this hard since Marshall's diagnosis. Jane pulled into their driveway and turned off the car.

Unfastening her seatbelt and turning to face her sister, Jane said, "Wait, just because I had a mystical experience at the dentist's office doesn't mean it's not legit."

"You were high on nitrous oxide!" Lily insisted.

"Taking drugs and spiritual revelations are not mutually exclusive. I mean, for a few seconds, I really understood it. He gave his only son. Can you imagine giving up your child for the unwashed masses? Or even the washed masses?"

Lily shook her head and smiled. She thought Jane had been a little grumpy recently, but she could still be funny.

Her sister's phone rang. Her sponsor from AA. Jane looked at her phone and then muted the ring.

"I thought you were supposed to always pick up when she called."

"She's been a pain in my ass," Jane said.

"When was the last time you went to a meeting?" Lily asked.

Her sister turned and gave her a dirty look. "I'm going to one to-night," she snapped. And then she added, "The meetings around here are filled with Catholics going on and on about things they feel guilty about that were beyond their control. It drives me fucking nuts."

With that, Jane got out of the car and walked inside. Lily won-dered if the last remark was a dig at her. She could tell Jane was in a bad mood and decided she would tell her sister about the email later in the day.

Am I going to reply? Lily thought. *What is it that I want to say?*

...

SOON AFTER MARSHALL WAS diagnosed with Alzheimer's, during the initial stage of the disease, he and Lily had made a list of how his wealth would be dispersed. He made his sister-in-law promise that she would travel with Lily—Rome, Croatia, northern Scotland. Jane added Svalbard, in the Arctic, to which Marshall said, "Absolutely. A must." A major donation would be given to the Cornell Lab of Orni-thology. Marshall set aside funds for various land trusts in Rhode Is-land and New York, which would be used to purchase land for preservation, keeping it open space. He trusted his wife to distribute funds to agencies of her choosing, too. So Lily selected Planned Par-enthood and a nonprofit for survivors of sexual assault.

Marshall had designated a local bird sanctuary on the island to receive a major gift. That's where Lily spent the latter part of her day and early evening, meeting with the trustees, so Jane told her she would check in on Marshall after her AA meeting.

"How was he?" Lily asked, back home later that evening.

"He was good, but I have a story for you," Jane said, smiling wide. Her mood had definitely improved.

Lily had heard dozens of her sister's stories from AA. Like the one about the guy who had met the pope and had no recollection of it but carried a photo as evidence, and the cop who was addicted to Oxy. And while it was supposed to be anonymous, when the sisters were out in public together and Jane saw someone from her program, she would whisper secrets like, "That's the CEO from Mitchell's who used to run guns." At the end of one particular AA meeting held at the Elks Lodge on Tuesday nights, Jane refused to hold hands and say the Our Father with a guy she called "Fall River Eddie," who shot his wife and her "colored lover." "I don't care if he served his time," Jane had said. "I'm not holding his racist fucking hand."

"Wait till you hear this one," Jane said, opening the refrigerator in the kitchen.

"Okay, but just tell me one thing about Marshall."

"He's fine. Didn't say much. There was another guy there feeding his mom, one of the kitty cat ladies."

There was a group of women at the nursing home with severe dementia whom the sisters called "kitty cat ladies" because they kept stuffed animals on their laps and at times tried to feed them. The fabric around the mouths of the stuffed animals was usually stained in orange purée. Like Marshall, the women sat in limousine-style wheelchairs. For mealtimes, they were wheeled into the dining room, where the staff fed them like babies.

"The guy feeding his mom noticed that one of the women was eating paper, so he starts yelling, 'Lucy, stop eating the paper! You're gonna choke and die.' And I'm like, 'Keep eating the paper, Lucy, it's your only way out of here.'"

Lily laughed but then said, "That's so sad."

"I ran into Jimmy Sullivan at AA," Jane blurted out.

"No way!" Lily's mouth dropped. "How does he look?"

"Not bad, but he's been through hell. Two stints in rehab. His liver is shot, and he was addicted to Oxy."

Toward the end of Jane's drug use, she had crushed Oxy and snorted it, but they didn't need to bring that up tonight.

"Oh my God. That's awful."

"He's put together one year," Jane said. And then she added, "He kept telling me how great I looked."

"Did you tell him to get in line?"

Jane smiled at her sister knowingly.

Then Lily asked, "Is he married?"

"Nope."

"Does he see his daughter? She was around nine years old at the time of the reunion."

"Oh yeah. She works at the marina cleaning boats. She has her shit together."

"She cleans boats?" Lily's mind raced. But Jane was distracted looking for something in the kitchen cabinets and didn't register her sister's reaction.

"She's beautiful. Dark hair. He showed me a bunch of photos, one with her and the guys on a dock at the marina. It was wild. Everybody looks so old except for her. She's gorgeous. Dates women. He's totally cool with it."

"I saw her," Lily said, leaning up against the counter.

"What?" Now Jane was stunned.

"I know what she looks like. She's beautiful, just like you said."

"When? I don't understand. Why didn't you tell me?"

"I saw her at the marina, cleaning his boat. I just didn't know it was Jimmy's daughter."

"What the fuck? I still don't get it."

"About a year before Marshall got sick, I got an email from Head.

I never told you about it. I never wrote Head back. But he was writing to tell me that the guys were getting together that July. Do you remember when I came to visit Dad, a few months before you moved back home?"

"Yeah," Jane said. She was still in shock and hung on every word her sister said.

"I drove to the marina to see him. I wanted to talk to him about what I had learned from Tim. But when I got to the docks, I spotted her on the boat. I thought she was a new girlfriend."

"A much younger girlfriend," Jane said.

"Yep. That's what I thought, too. It helped me move on a little, I think. Seeing him with her."

"Did you ever tell Marshall?"

"Nope."

Her sister had a look of disbelief on her face.

"One day, a letter arrived at the house and Marshall asked me who had sent it. I ended up explaining that it was only the second letter I had ever received from him. Marshall was really upset that I had never told him about the first letter."

"When did that happen?"

"A while back."

"Why didn't you tell me?" Jane looked hurt and still confused.

"Do you tell me everything?" Lily asked.

Jane made a funny face—pushing her lips to one side, as if she was hiding something—and then said, "You're right."

Normally, Lily would have persisted, insisting that her sister tell her whatever it was she was hiding or keeping secret. Instead, she had her own news to share.

"You ready for this?" Lily said. "He just emailed this morning. He's coming home."

"Wow, Lil," Jane said. "What are you going to do?"

"I have no idea."

Lily was more than relieved that the boy hadn't turned into one of those middle-aged guys who only date women in their twenties. Looking back, she was grateful she had misunderstood who the younger woman was. It had made it easier over the past couple of years for her to believe that choosing Marshall was the right decision.

…

THE NEXT DAY, JANE passed Lily driving down East Main Road. It ran north and south on the island near the Sakonnet River. Lily beeped the horn, but Jane didn't notice her. Jane pulled off into a motel complex that had eight small cabins right off the road. For a second, Lily thought her sister was pulling over to see her. Lily had missed the turn into the motel, and by the time she came back around, headed north, she saw that her sister had gotten out of her car and was knocking on the door of one of the cabins. Lily was surprised. There was no way Jane would have known someone who lived in one of the small units. The hotel was for transients, folks on the edge of being homeless, ex-cons. The only thing Lily could think was that Jane was meeting someone from AA—a newcomer or a lover, someone she wouldn't bring to the house. Someone down and out.

Lily had promised Jane that she would make dinner for them. By the time she returned home with steaks and vegetables, Jane's car was in the driveway. Lily carried the bags of groceries in and placed them on the counter. When she called out, Jane didn't answer. Lily assumed she was with one of her students on the boarding school campus. Jane tutored students in math at the local high school and the Abbey. Shortly after Lily returned home, the doorbell rang. It was one of the students her sister had been tutoring. Jane had not shown up for the session. It was only then that Lily thought to check the bedroom.

And there was Jane lying on her bed, her skin pale, with a strange noise coming from her throat. Lily shouted for the student to call 911. Jane was still breathing, but Lily knew she was dying. Faint pulse. Blue lips.

Her brain was sending signals: *Slow down now, she's got us, slow down.*

Lily leaned over the bed and shook Jane's body. No response. She yelled for the student to "stand in the fucking road!" "Wave them down!" No delays.

Lily didn't leave her sister's side. At first, she was gentle and loving. She wasn't sure if her sister could hear her, but she said over and over, "Stay with me." And then her fear turned to rage. She clenched her teeth. "You better stay right here, Jane."

Lily didn't know how much time she had. The fire department was less than a mile away. Then she heard the sirens.

The EMT leaned over Jane's body, stuck a nozzle up her nose, and shot a mist of Narcan into her nostril. Lily was standing in the driveway as she watched the EMTs strap Jane to the stretcher and load her into the ambulance.

...

IT WAS A COUPLE of weeks past the peak season for harvesting cranberries, but Lily could still see patches of the bright-red berries on the side of the road on her way to Cape Cod. Several weeks ago, the scene would have been spectacular—autumn trees of gold and burnt orange surrounding wetlands, cranberries growing on low-lying vines in beds of freshwater, peat, and sand. Lily pulled to the side of the road and watched as two farmers wearing chest-high green waders dragged rakes over the berries in the distance.

She was on her way to visit Jane, who had checked in to a drug rehabilitation center on Cape Cod. Lily insisted on this particular facility, and since Jane was in no condition to resist, Lily made the arrangements and paid for Jane's treatment.

It was the first time Lily had seen her sister in more than fifteen days since dropping her off. The visitors' room had floor-to-ceiling windows overlooking the Atlantic Ocean and a stone fireplace that was cozily lit. Jane walked in wearing gray sweatpants, slippers, and a Pearl Jam T-shirt from the early nineties with a torn neckline.

"How's room service?" Lily asked.

Jane faked a smile and sat down on the couch next to her sister.

"What happened? You were doing so well."

Jane rolled her eyes.

"Weren't you?"

"I guess this needed to happen."

"Why now? After three years."

"I don't know. I stopped going to meetings every day. It just snuck up on me." Jane watched the fire as she said this, avoiding eye contact with her sister.

"How do you know the pills weren't cut with something?" Lily asked.

Jane laughed. "Whoa, slow down. Did you say *cut with something*?"

"Don't make fun of me! Two weeks ago, you almost died on me." Lily started to cry.

"It's just that I've never heard you talk like that . . . *cut with something*?" Jane said with a hint of sarcasm.

Lily shot back, "I lost a mother, too, and the love of my life, and you don't see me gobbling up pills and drinking night after night."

"Well, aren't you something? Do you want a medal?" Jane's tone was searing. "Do you want an award for a life of monogamy and moderation? Is that what you want? Well, technically, not absolute monogamy. There was that one night."

Lily gathered up her purse and stood up to leave.

Jane reached for her sister and pulled her back down to the couch. "I'm sorry, that was mean and uncalled for. Ask me anything. I'll tell you everything."

Lily wiped her nose with the side of her index finger. "How long had you been using?"

"A month. Just a month. I got about six OxyContin from my hairdresser," Jane explained.

"You bought painkillers from your hairdresser?"

"Well, technically, no. She gave me some, and in return I gave her an extra-big tip."

"She could get in trouble."

"She dumpster dives," Jane said, crossing her legs and leaning back into the sofa.

"She what?"

"They all search for leftover McDonald's food in the dumpster."

"They do?" Lily was confused.

"Yes, I heard them talking about it one day at the salon," Jane said.

"So what does that mean?" Lily asked her sister.

Before Jane could answer, a burly man with a beard carrying firewood entered the sitting room and Lily stopped talking.

"I'll be out of your way in just a second," he said.

He laid the logs on the fire, which crackled as the flames jumped up.

As soon as he left the room, Lily lowered her voice and said, "Just because she dives for old food in a dumpster doesn't mean it's okay to turn her into a drug dealer. Jesus."

"Jimmy was never really clean. I could tell he was high when I saw him at AA."

Lily was confused and waited for her sister to say more.

"The pills I took, back at the house, were from Jimmy."

"What? I'll fucking kill him."

"He's sick and suffering, too."

"Fuck that AA shit. Sick and suffering. I'll make him suffer."

Lily was on the verge of tears again. Jane hated seeing her sister like this. She pulled her knees up to her chest and wrapped her arms around her legs, watching the fire. The sisters were quiet for a moment.

"Are you okay?" Jane asked, looking at her sister.

"Yeah," Lily said. "As long as you're okay."

The sisters looked at each other. Jane reached out her hand. Lily grasped it and held it tightly in the air for a few seconds. When they let go, they both looked back at the fire, watching it in silence, until Jane said, "Endurance of darkness is preparation for great light."

Surprised, Lily looked at her sister and asked, "Where did you get that from?"

"John of the Cross."

Lily chuckled. "Since when are you reading sixteenth-century Spanish mystics?"

"I just pulled it out of my ass."

"Could you be more irreverent?" Lily asked, smiling.

"Probably," Jane said, adding, "Who overdoses in their forties? I'm so embarrassed."

"Aren't you just grateful to be alive?" Lily asked.

"Yeah, but come on, teenagers overdose, not perimenopausal women."

"Well, Judy Garland might've been perimenopausal, does that count?"

"When I'm high, I feel so alive. And I love everyone, even the lady at Dunkin' Donuts who touches her nose and then makes my coffee. I even find a place where I can forgive fucking Fall River Eddie. But then, you know, there's always that risk when you use too much and disconnect. I'll never find what I'm looking for in those pills."

"I'm not sure about that," Lily said.

Jane was taken aback by her sister's comment. "What's that supposed to mean?"

Lily ignored her. Jane had been looking for a way out all her life. Years ago, before Jane got sober, Lily sometimes wondered whether she was being selfish to pray that Jane wouldn't OD. Lily didn't want to bury her sister, but what was worse? Living with the grief that comes from burying a sister or wanting to die first and having a beloved sister bear the grief? Maybe they could die together, the way those elderly sisters she had read about in the newspaper did. One snowy night, returning from dinner. The old sisters were both in their nineties. One had slipped on the ice, and the other, trying to help her up, had fallen, too. They lay there on the icy driveway as the cold covered them and shut their eyes together.

PORTSMOUTH, RHODE ISLAND

DECEMBER 2007

In all the years that had passed since the trial, twenty-nine to be exact, Lily had not seen David McCarren. Since she'd moved back to Portsmouth, the thought of seeing him occurred to her on a regular basis. It wasn't as if she wanted to; in fact, she dreaded the idea that one day she would. And then it happened.

It was the week before Christmas. Houses on each side of the street were trimmed with strands of lights; wreaths adorned doors, illuminated by bright spotlights; a Salvation Army volunteer manned the red kettle, ringing the bell at the local grocery store.

She almost didn't recognize David. He had lost most of his hair—there were just gray threads now in an unfortunate comb-over—and had a potbelly.

David was at the checkout counter just a few feet in front of her emptying his pockets. He was short of money. It appeared that the woman at the register knew him.

"Let's put this back," the clerk suggested, picking up a bag of Oreos.

Shaking his head, David took the Oreos from her and placed them in one of the brown paper bags.

"What about this?" the woman said as she held up a box of Cap'n Crunch cereal.

David shook his head again and searched his pants pockets for a second time. Shame, like a sickness coming on suddenly, made Lily feel weak and dizzy. She took out a twenty from her purse, reached past the teenager who stood between them, and handed the cash to the clerk. When David recognized her, his face lit up.

"Lily, is that you? You're so . . . so . . ." He was searching for a word. "Pretty," he said.

He waited for the teenager to move aside and then hugged her. She surprised herself when she realized that she wasn't ready for the hug to end. With her arms still around David, she thought, *It shouldn't have turned out like this.*

When she figured out that he had walked to the store, she offered to drive him home.

"On one condition," he said, smiling. "We stop at Dunkin' Donuts."

On the ride through town, Lily kept glancing over at him. It seemed clear that he didn't hate her or hold her responsible for his life. There he was, a middle-aged man who could have been a successful lawyer like his dad, married with beautiful college-age children, a fancy car, and a house on the water. But instead, his day's excitement and challenge was going to be buying cookies and cereal and walking home, carrying them in brown paper bags.

It was clear he was a regular at Dunkin' Donuts and knew practically everyone, from the ladies behind the counter to the three old men at one of the tables whose hands he shook as if he were the town mayor. The built, aggressive, entitled class president with wavy shoulder-length hair and a strong jawline was gone. This middle-aged disabled man was not the boy she knew in high school.

And all of that was a mask to hide his struggles with his sexuality. It's just so sad, Lily thought.

"My mother only lets me get one," David said, eyeing his two double-chocolate doughnuts in the white to-go bag. They had picked a table away from the men. "That way the other guys won't try to talk to us," he said as they sat down.

Lily was taken aback when David mentioned that the boy had moved back to Portsmouth for good. She hadn't written him back. She had had every intention to, but things had spun out of control after Jane's OD. What would she tell him? She was still mourning the loss of her life with Marshall. During the years she spent caring for him alone, every day felt like she was swimming against a riptide. She was barely coming up for air.

There was no malice or anger in David's voice when he talked. Lily, still feeling anxious, wondered if David even knew or remembered the circumstances of his condition. He talked about the boy as if they were friends.

"How do you know he's back?" Lily asked. She was confused and assumed David was, too.

"He's my best friend," David said. "He came to visit every time he was home to see Mr. Cooper."

Lily wasn't sure if he was making things up. Why would the boy visit David of all people? She needed to get to the bottom of this.

"He never forgets my birthday. One year we went to see the Patriots play at Gillette Stadium. Best day of my . . ." David struggled to find the word *life.*

He told Lily that over the years he had received birthday cards and postcards from Singapore, South Africa, and China. David talked about the cards as if they were lottery prizes. A long strand of hair, which Lily imagined his mother had combed over, was terribly out of place, making the scar that ran along the top back part of his head clearly visible.

Lily was stunned, to say the least. She had so many questions she wanted to ask. When did the friendship begin? Did the boy ever mention Lily? Had he come to make amends all those years ago? She wanted the details of their unlikely friendship. She wasn't sure if David was capable of answering her questions accurately.

Lily tried to imagine young David and Tim having sex on the beach.

Does he even remember?

She watched as David licked the chocolate frosting off his finger.

"Where else have you gone together?" Lily asked.

"Second Beach, Frosty Freez, Red Sox games. Good times," he said as he finished the second doughnut and wiped his hands on his pants.

Lily walked David to the front door of his parents' house, and Mrs. McCarren opened the door. David went inside with his grocery bags, and Lily could hear *Judge Judy* on the television. Mrs. McCarren looked surprised to see Lily. Not angry, just surprised.

"I'm sure David told you about the Cooper boy. He started coming around after he was released. Who would've guessed it? He's David's only friend."

"Yes, he did mention it." It was all Lily could say. What Lily wanted to say was, *Your son did not rape me. It was all a mistake. A tragedy.* But she kept silent.

"He bought the old Ferreira house near the Mount Hope Bridge," Mrs. McCarren said.

Sitting in her car, Lily took a deep breath. It dawned on her that the boy had started visiting years before he knew of David's innocence. *So this is what redemption looks like,* Lily thought. This is what her father was trying to explain that day on the railroad tracks: The boy had linked his own suffering with David's, and through their friendship, he had helped David live a fuller life.

Lily turned the car on, reached over her shoulder, and pulled on the seatbelt, clicking it into place. She turned the heat up and looked in the rearview mirror. Would she allow herself to start over while Marshall was still alive? This is what had been on her mind for the past few weeks. And now, the boy was home for good.

...

THE CAPTAIN OF THE local police department knocked on Lily and Jane's front door at 8:30 A.M. the day before Christmas Eve.

"May I come in?" he asked, removing his cap.

Lily's initial thought was that something must have happened at the Abbey. Vandalism, maybe, and they either wanted to notify her or ask if she'd seen anything. As she hugged her bathrobe against the cold air and the stranger, she opened the front door a bit wider and stepped back. The morning winter chill followed him in. She watched as the police captain looked around the living room; his gaze rested on a photo of Jane and her father standing in front of a giant redwood tree, taken some time in the nineties in Santa Cruz.

"Are you alone?" the captain asked.

"Yes, what can I do for you?"

Lily looked at the captain. He was fit and had a kind face. *Not quick to anger,* she thought.

"Are you related to Jane Webb?" he asked.

"What's happened?" Lily said. She had gone from zero to sixty in a matter of seconds.

When the captain explained that Jane had been found in a bathroom at a 7-Eleven in New Bedford—dead of an apparent overdose—Lily folded at the waist. Before her knees reached the floor, he stepped over and grabbed her. With one arm around her back and the other gripping her forearm, he guided Lily to the couch. She was silent for a moment and then let out a wail. Her body rocked as she sobbed.

She wanted the details, but every time the captain spoke, Lily cried harder.

Lily had been given a prescription for Lorazepam when Marshall was diagnosed to help manage her anxiety around his illness. She went into the bathroom, blew her nose, and opened the medicine cabinet. She searched for the bottle and found it behind the Band-Aids. She had about twenty left. She put one in her mouth, turned the faucet on, and swallowed the pill with water from her cupped hand. When she came back into the living room, she looked like a frightened animal.

"We were supposed to die together," she said. "In the ice."

The captain didn't say anything; he just listened. Over the years, he had learned it was best not to say too much. It didn't matter that he didn't understand what she was talking about.

"Was she alone?" Lily asked.

"No, she was with a man. Someone from the rehab facility. They left last night together, checked themselves out. He was the one who identified her. All I know is that he is a thirty-six-year-old male from New Bedford," the captain explained.

Again, it was hard for Lily to catch her breath. "So was he with her in the bathroom?" Lily asked.

The captain was uncertain of this but said "yes" anyway. It was not his nature to misrepresent the facts, but her grief was too intense. He lied, thinking it would comfort her.

"Is there someone you can call?" he asked.

Instantly, she thought of the boy.

She called Father Thomas at the monastery. The captain left when the monk arrived.

Father Thomas, well into his eighties now, was wearing his snow boots, black robes, and a black winter coat. He sat on the couch next to Lily.

"The world kills the good ones," Father Thomas said.

Lily wept.

"There's only one thing we can do at times like this."

Lily took a deep breath. *Yes,* she thought, *we'll pray to the Mother of God, pray for Jane's soul—that she finds the peace she's been looking for all her life.* But Father Thomas got up from the couch and walked into the kitchen. Lily was confused. She could hear the cabinets open and shut and glasses clinking. When he came back into the living room, he was carrying two glass tumblers. He set them on the table, reached into his robes, and removed a silver flask, then filled the glasses with whiskey.

"I thought we were going to pray," Lily said, taking the glass of whiskey the monk was offering.

"We can do that, too. But we'll drink this first," he said.

When they had both finished their drinks, Father Thomas clasped his hands and bowed his head. He opened his mouth and let the medieval monastic prayer soak up the room's sadness.

"Hail Mary, full of grace . . ."

By the time they had said the prayer a few dozen times, Lily felt less desperate. The sedative and whiskey had dampened her hysteria.

Later that morning, she called the local funeral home. It was a family business, and the current director had been a student of her father's. They would take care of all the arrangements involved in transporting the body from New Bedford to Portsmouth. She made a few more calls, to Jane's friends from AA and the parents of some of her students. She thought of telling Marshall, but the last time Jane had visited him, he had no recollection of who she was. Jane had been showing him a video about the science of migration. After Jane left, Marshall asked, "Who was the nice lady?"

Lily thought of Marshall in his wheelchair, leaning over with one arm stretched out to the side, his hand opened as if he were trying to grasp hold of something—a memory, a way out, an acrobatics ring—anything that might free him from the hell that had become his mind.

That night, Lily had a dream in which a girl came to her. The child had long hair, the color of Jane's when she was little. Wearing all white, the girl reached up with her chubby hand to touch Lily's cheek. When the child pulled her hand away, she withdrew a veil from Lily's face. Lily woke, sobbing.

Later in the early morning hours, before the birds started singing, in between sleeping and waking, she thought she heard her mother calling. She woke to the faint scent of gardenia and jasmine.

...

THE NEXT MORNING, HER first thought was, *I have to see her.* It was snowing lightly. She used her mitten to brush away the dusting of snow on the windshield. Even though she had taken another sedative, she had hardly slept. She called the O'Farrell Funeral Home and asked if she could stop by. Before leaving the house, she selected a cream-colored, long-sleeve woolen dress with a scoop neckline for Jane to be buried in.

Lily sat in her car in the driveway. When she turned the key in the ignition and the car started, an old Christmas carol was playing on the radio, and it brought her back to her childhood: their mother curling Lily's damp hair in the bathroom with foam rollers as Jane sat on the edge of the bathtub waiting her turn; evening naps; being woken up at eleven to dress for midnight Mass; dozens of Benedictine monks in long black robes behind the altar singing Gregorian chants; the monks' deep voices reverberating in the chapel; the smell of incense; their mom and dad kneeling in silent prayer; running to the dining hall for hot chocolate and cookies; snow falling; walking back to the house, huddled together in the winter night, braced against the chill; leaving sugar cookies and milk for Santa; being tucked into bed and listening to the sounds of their father ringing bells in the other room, masquerading as Santa. And then to a memory that was harder to recall, when Lily was in second grade and played Mary in the Nativity pageant, while Jane played a little lamb. And then, of course, the memory of when Jane was seven and wanted to be gravity for Halloween. Their mother thought she should go as Hypatia instead, mainly because making the costume would be a whole lot easier. That was the year Lily dressed as Saint Catherine of Siena: a fearless mystic.

Lily turned up the heat in the car and thought about one of the last things Jane had said to her. *Endurance of darkness is preparation for great light.*

That elusive concept brought her to another mystery—back to the night of stargazing, long ago, in the monastery gardens with her mother and sister. Father Thomas had been teaching them what little scientists knew at the time about dark matter and its gravitational effects.

Jane knew firsthand of the invisible forces that acted upon her, Lily thought.

But Lily, well, she was just beginning to understand how those forces might have acted on herself.

...

JOHN O'FARRELL WAS AT the front door of the funeral home when Lily pulled up. He escorted her to the room where Jane's body lay on a stainless-steel dressing table.

As Lily took a step toward the body, her knees buckled. The funeral director steadied her. When she reached her sister, she placed the palms of her hands flat on the table and bent at the waist. The grief was physically too much to bear. She stood, gripping the side of the table.

"You promised me. You promised me," Lily whispered.

Tears and snot ran down her face. Sobs climbed out of her chest, taking her breath away. Sounds from her throat filled the space between Lily and the body. Guttural. And then she slapped her sister's face. Jane's head rolled slightly. Rigor mortis offered resistance. Immediately, Lily regretted it. She reached out and cradled Jane's head with her arms so that their faces touched.

"I'm sorry. I'm so sorry." Her tears soaked her sister's cool cheek.

When she let Jane go, she stood with her head bowed. Breathing heavy.

In that moment, Lily thought of the ancient frescoes her mom had shown her when she was a child. Had she the strength, she would have raised her hands over her head and prayed for her sister. Jane would have tolerated that—her own sister begging for mercy for her soul. But she couldn't lift her hands off the steel table.

She turned and reached for the coat sleeve of the funeral director. "You'll watch over her, right?"

"Yes, I'll be here."

"I just don't want her to be alone."

"I understand."

PORTSMOUTH, RHODE ISLAND

DECEMBER 2007

"Jane is dead. Overdose."

The news hit him like a strong wave slapping the side of a boat; he steadied himself for Lily's sake. She looked at him with a pained face that made her look old and tired.

"I didn't expect it to happen so fast," she said.

"What? What didn't you expect to happen so fast?"

"Life."

He was standing at the front door of the house he had bought near the bridge, just where Mrs. McCarren had said. Lily put her hand in her coat pocket and fingered the lid of the prescription bottle. The ocean would be so cold this time of year. Hypothermia. She could time it so that if she took the Lorazepam, all of them at once, drove down to the beach after she was done here, and walked into the water, the hypothermia and sedatives would take her in no time.

He put his hands on Lily's shoulders. "This time we're going to do it together."

Do what together? What is he talking about?

"Grieve, Lily—we will do it together."

She was standing still with her hands in her pockets, looking up at him. He stepped away from the entrance, and Lily walked into the house, not taking in the rooms or the furniture; grief was shutting down her senses. She started sobbing and said, "I should have been more vigilant. I should have seen the signs. I think she hinted at it. I should've pushed her. I should've made her tell me what she had been hiding from me. I told her that I saw you with a girl . . . but it turned out to be Jimmy Sullivan's daughter. He gave her pills. I know he did . . ." She was breathless.

He couldn't sort through what Lily was telling him. She was spitting pieces of the story out faster than he could follow. He said, "Demons have been chasing Jane since she was a girl."

"No! No demons. I don't buy it. Jane was a good girl. The best. I should have known. I should have made her tell me. I could have prevented this! Just like the night of the fight."

Despite the understanding that Lily had come to over the past few years, she felt the same old avalanche of guilt barrel toward her.

"You think you made all this happen? Jane? Me? I was the one who pushed David."

"I don't even remember it; I just remember the red flashing lights."

He lowered his head to avoid her gaze, then took a deep breath and said, "But even if what didn't happen did, it would not have been your fault. I should've handled things differently. I shouldn't have lost control."

He was doing his best to get through to her, to reach her.

"You've lived your whole life thinking that your decisions or actions destroyed other people's lives? What about their own volition? Their own strengths and weaknesses? If you were the CEO of Exxon and turned a blind eye to an oil spill or if you were a leader of a country committed to wiping out a segment of the population, well, maybe I could see your point . . . but we're not those people. We're just us. Ordinary people, living life."

Grief had become so overwhelming in that moment that it numbed her to his words; she didn't know what to make of what he said. On some level, she heard him.

"How do I live when everything is lost?"

"Not everything, Lil. Not everything."

Throughout her life, Lily had been confronted with the laws of love and logic, understanding intuitively that the difference between the two was that love allowed for the impossible.

She had been caught in life's duality—in its apparent contradictions—of love and loss, of faith and science, and, most of all, of darkness and light.

She stopped crying and caught her breath.

Time supposedly marched forward; the future held all possibilities. Why couldn't the future hold the past? Standing there in front of the boy, Lily understood that the past would keep its promise. They were meant to be. It was just a matter of time. She deserved to be with him, but she had come to believe that she might never find her way back to him. He must have recognized the look in her eyes because he said, "I've always belonged to you."

Oh, how his face held light, Lily thought.

ACKNOWLEDGMENTS

I am deeply grateful to many individuals, and I would like to acknowledge them here.

I am indebted to the scholarship that inspired my perspective, drawing on diverse disciplines, including the works of Jacques Derrida and Paul Ricoeur on forgiveness; Charles Taylor on Catholicism; Cynthia Chou on the Orang Suku Laut of Riau, Indonesia; Richard L. Hutto on stopover sites for migrating birds; Karen Jo Torjesen on female orans in early Christianity; Jennifer Ackerman on birds; Lisa Randall on dark matter; Carlo Rovelli on physics; Thomas Edwards, Jr. on ospreys; and Renato Rosaldo on the anthropology of grief and headhunting.

I heard the story of the fourteen holy helpers from a guide at the Basilica of the Fourteen Holy Helpers in southern Germany.

The National Audubon Society is a natural treasure. I relied on the abundance of material they make available online.

Becca Hansborough and staff at the National Aviary were helpful with material on conservation and endangered bird species.

Blake Billings wrote a wonderful essay on Dom Leo van Winkle, the real-life figure from whom Father Thomas was drawn.

Father Damian Kearney also wrote a profile on Father van Winkle, which contains parts of a letter that van Winkle wrote to Father Hugh in 1945, describing the night he and his colleagues watched the testing of the first atomic bomb in New Mexico.

David Kaiser's history of physics in the United States was immensely helpful. Adam Becker's discussion on Bohr and Einstein's debate, as well as his descriptions of John Wheeler's experiment and Bell's theorem, were incredibly informative. I take all responsibility if I have misinterpreted Kaiser's or Becker's insights.

In 1987, Roy King, a psychiatrist and mathematician in the department of psychiatry at Stanford University, hired me to be his research assistant. Within a few days, he pulled me aside and said, "Something's wrong." He had figured out in a short period of time that I had a learning disability and arranged to have me tested. There were some early indications. In the fourth grade, I was brought to a reading room for testing. Throughout high school, I was never enrolled in college prep courses. Instead, I took vocational courses, where I made lamps that never worked. I maintained a C- average in my classes. I barely got into college. Most college students are put on probation after their first or second year if they don't do well. My scores were so low, I was accepted into college on probation. Roy King helped me understand that dyslexia, a neurobiological condition which impacts my ability to read and process information, is not exclusively about cognitive limitations. Thank you, Roy.

Over the years, I shared many long conversations with the late Father Paschal, who was once a Benedictine monk at Portsmouth Abbey. On the footpaths around campus and in the dining hall, we talked about faith's mysteries, Dostoyevsky, and Galileo. Rest in peace, my friend.

During my twenty-five years of teaching at Salve Regina University, I had the privilege of working under the leadership of the university's former president Sister Therese Antone and Barbara Kathe, former vice president for academic affairs, whose vision and commitment to social justice help shaped Salve into the institution it is today. It was a place where I met many of my dearest friends. When I first interviewed with Barbara, a former Carmelite nun, she asked, "How do you feel about Foucault?" Instantly, I knew we were going to be friends. And when my research on sex toys made the front page of *The New York Times,* in the true spirit of academic freedom, Sister Therese graciously announced it at a full faculty meeting. I will treasure my years at Salve.

My cousin Jenifer Curtis Foley, a source of light and love, and her husband, Joe Foley—both of whom we lost far too young—helped me with my research. Joe was a librarian at the university where I worked for decades. Joe and his staff, especially Beth Blycker Koll and Adam Salisbury, went out of their way, month after month, year after year, finding relevant books and articles for me. Thank you.

Jim Chace did his best to teach me about ornithology. If there are any mistakes, then they are mine, not his.

To the members of the Portsmouth Abbey Faculty Book Club, especially Father Damian Kearney, Tom Kennedy, David McCarthy, Dan McDonough, Mary Jean McDonough, and Cliff Hobbins, I will never again be part of a club with such brilliant, thoughtful readers—what a privilege it was.

Dan McDonough, former headmaster of Portsmouth Abbey, did his very best to help me understand the mathematical mind.

Many family members and friends offered advice and support on a variety of matters related to the story. I want to thank Angelica Adams, Holly Adamy, Mark Adamy, Stacey Alzaibak, Lisa Beardwood, Garrett Behan, Mary Behan, Mike Behan, Nancy McCann Blodgett, Michael Bonin, Dakota Bossard, Colleen Byrne, Matt Campbell, Pascal Cerchi, Leila Chambers, Roman Chevassu, Maia Chrupcala, Robert Coleburn, Lauren Curtis, Martina Curtis, Donna Decost, Daniel Duryea, Sharon Dyer, Tom Estrella, Maddy Fahey, Elizabeth Fitzgibbon, Andrew Frankel, Candy Frankel, Matt Frankel, Jim Garman, Michelle Garman, Trish Haney, Jeroen van den Hurk, Harry Kahane, Nathaniel Kitchel, Arlene Kyle, Jennifer Labao, John Leary, Bill Leeman, Susan Letourneau, Eric Lubiner, Jill Lubiner, Steve Ludwig, Zulekha Ludwig, Maggie Lynch-Warren, Gene McCabe, Susan Mello, Alain Mongeon, Dan Murray, Mike Murray, Debbie Shorey Nellis, Claire O'Connor, Susan O'Connor, Rita Pacheco, Pam Philip, Deb Pine, Chad Raymond, Heather Rockwell, Norman Rusin, Katie Sarapas, Louisa Schein, Tanya Sergey, Trish Sheehan, Kurran Singh, Madeline Turano, Andrea Wasylow, Paige West, Nancy Wyatt, Dimi Zelden, Kale Zelden, and Fred Zilian.

To the members of the Redwood Library Writer's Circle, including Didi Lorillard, Mary Clare O'Grady, Paul Szapary, and Angela van der Lippe, thank you for your feedback and encouragement.

Fred Errington and Deborah Gewertz, two well-respected American anthropologists, were my intellectual mentors for decades. Fred was the first professor who ever truly inspired me. Rest in peace, dear one.

My close friends Art Frankel, Josh McCall, Jen McLanaghan, and Matt Ramsey were always there to offer encouragement, advice, and irreverent humor. Thank you.

Kevin O'Connor worked as a merchant mariner in the South China Sea. He lent me his stories and his seaman's sensibility, which I hope made the novel more interesting. In 1984, Kevin and his crew were responsible for saving the lives of more than one hundred Vietnamese refugees.

To all the Janes in my life and to those I have yet to meet—we will persevere.

Marya Withers gave me a copy of *Lessons in Chemistry,* directing me to my incredible literary agent. I will always believe that moment was divine. On top of this, at least twice a year, Marya pulls me out of my bizarrely rigid routine and takes me on vacations with her and her wife, Erin.

For more than forty years, Jane Bensel has been there to push the fear away and to show me how to move forward with courage.

Dawn Hale introduced me to the artist's way of life, showing me how to cultivate an aesthetic sensibility and how to live through art.

I met Tseten Dolma (aka Stella Curtis Frankel) in Tibet years ago. She eventually came to live with me and my family. The level of compassion she displays is unmatched. Her laughter kept me afloat while I was writing this story.

Erin McCormick listened endlessly as I talked about characters, scenes, and plotlines. I borrow from Toni Morrison's *Beloved* to capture how much I need her. "She is a friend of my mind. She gather me, man. The pieces I am, she gather them and give them back to me in all the right order."

Marion Wichmann of Ullstein Press was the very first editor to acquire my novel, thank you.

To the editors at Europa Konyvkiado, Einaudi Editore, and Editura Humanitas, thank you for believing in my potential.

Many thanks to Sophie Baker at Curtis Brown, who offered encouragement and worked hard on my behalf in the international market. Thank you to Mia Read Jones at Bloomsbury Press, Madison Hernick at United Talent Agency, Elsa Richardson Bach at Penguin Random House, and Julia Plant (Jenna Bush Hager's assistant). Thank you to Diana D'Abruzzo and Loren Noveck, whose copyediting was exceptional.

My brilliant editors, Alexis Kirschbaum at Bloomsbury Press and Hilary Teeman at Penguin Random House, are unbelievably astute, intuitive, graceful, and patient. The story came about as the result of Alexis and Hilary's vision. They saw something before I could, and for that, I will always be grateful. They made it easy for me to trust them, which allowed me to try harder as a storyteller.

Gráinne Fox at United Talent Agency has the type of discernment and emotional intelligence that I can only dream of having. She championed my manuscript, introducing it to US publishers, eventually selling it at auction and then guiding me through several intense moments during the publishing journey and for that I am forever grateful.

To the authentic and joyful Jenna Bush Hager, thank you for believing in me. Many maintain that reading fiction has a multitude of psychological benefits including increasing empathy. Anthropologists view empathy as foundational to human societies. It allows us to see past our prejudices and fears. It allows us to see our interconnectedness. It allows us to love more completely, more humanly. Given Jenna's tireless commitment to improving the public's reading habits, she's changing lives and changing our world for the better. I could not be prouder to be associated with her new imprint, Thousand Voices.

To my grandparents and great-grandparents, the ones who came to the island and stayed, thank you. I carry your legacy.

In July 1989, my father, Thomas Curtis, was diagnosed with a glioblastoma. Months before he died, he called me "his writer." This was well before I knew I wanted to become one. I'm not sure if this was a premonition or a benediction, but it has both haunted and inspired me simultaneously. Both my father and my mother, Eulalia Curtis, taught me the importance of friendships—the kind that are profound and long-lasting. Along with a loving upbringing, this was one of the greatest gifts they shared with me.

To my sisters, Ellen Estrella, Tish Behan, and Jeanne Murray, for putting out all the fires and keeping me upright.

Harry, my beloved companion, will never read this because he's a dog. But because he has brought me so much joy, he deserves recognition.

By the time I entered my sixties, I believed that I had met everyone whose lives would touch mine in a meaningful manner—and then I met Felicity Blunt and Flo Sandelson at Curtis Brown, my extraordinary literary agent and her wonderful assistant. The first time I spoke to Felicity, I made a comment that a first-time novelist probably shouldn't make if she is trying to impress an agent. "I don't know anything about writing," I said. Her response generated one of those rare life-affirming moments that echoed my dad's voice. "Oh, you can write," she responded. And with that remark, she opened the door, and I walked through it. Meeting Felicity and Flo has altered the course of my life, and I can never thank them enough.

In 1985, I met my husband, Steve Butler, at a restaurant in New Hampshire. I was preparing to go into the Peace Corps, but love had a way of changing my plans. We moved to Santa Cruz and started our life together—the life we've shared for the past forty years. I've been telling my female undergraduates for decades that the most important career decision they'll ever make revolves around whom they choose to marry. Steve has been incredibly supportive and by my side for every career move I've ever made. In 2003, when our twins were four years old, we moved to Nevis, a small island in the Caribbean where I conducted anthropological fieldwork. Steve remained behind in the States to keep working his butt off to support us and keep a roof over our heads. In my fifties, when I started experimenting with fiction, Steve would return home from a busy day at the clinic where he had seen dozens and dozens of patients and when I would ask if I could read aloud what I had written that day, he was always willing, always supportive, night after night, scene after scene. None of this would have been possible without him.

To our twin daughters, Emma and Zoe Butler, who make me want to be a better person. I try to emulate the kindness and respect that they consistently show others.

Finally, to the birds, stars, waves, colors, trees, and songs—thank you for always finding me.